SCOTT BELL

JUDGE SHIVERS

Judge Shivers
Red Adept Publishing, LLC
104 Bugenfield Court
Garner, NC 27529
https://RedAdeptPublishing.com/

---

1. http://StreetlightGraphics.com

Chapter One: Mall Walking Dead

I clocked a measured pace across wet asphalt. Not slow, not fast. My boot heels tick-tocked in four-four time, a solitary march at a funereal tempo. I tried composing a ditty to go with it, something like

I'm off to kill the wizard, a beardless wizard with flaws
Because, because, because, because, because
The horrible things he does.

The song didn't work for the mood or the tempo. I needed something dark and broody, not skippy and frolicky. I have been told it is in bad taste to be frivolous about the ways to kill somebody, no matter how much they need killing, and the zen of my mission focus denied me a single frolic or skip.

It was time to be grim. As in reaper.

Cold rain spattered drizzly wetness on and off. Trash stuck to the wet pavement, stirred by the rain-swollen breeze.

From a few blocks eastward, stadium lights bloomed yellow fog over rooftops, and an announcer's voice echoed, "Marcus Attleboro for a two-yard gain. Williams on the stop." High school football night in suburban Ohio pricked my heart with a sensation something like nostalgia as memories flickered of a different life in a distant place. I recalled scuffed helmets gleaming under the bright lights, the clack of plastic pads, the smell of sweat and grass and popcorn and Gatorade.

To the west, yellow luminescence painted the underbelly of black clouds. Lights from the distant Columbus. Or was it Cincinnati? Cleveland?

An aircraft ascended into the night sky, red flashers marking its passage into the low-hanging clouds. The rumble of its passing faded.

I paused at the fence and peered through the dripping links. The building inside the enclosure was once a shopping mall, now defunct, a derelict assembly of blocky sections with papered-over glass doors. A ghost image of old lettering on the buff-colored wall read Dillard's.

For an evil wizard steeped in power and the cosmos at his fingertips, this guy's lair needed a makeover. *Queer Eye for the Mage Guy.* But come to think of it, it was Ohio. How many mist-shrouded towers or brooding castles could there be? A Magical had to make do with the lairs available, and one named Dustin? Seriously? Surprised he wasn't holed up in a Chuck E. Cheese.

Six days after driving in from Montana, there I was. In Columbus, definitely Columbus, delivering a FedEx package of whoop-ass on Dustin Birnbaum, "Crazy Conjurer, Misfit Magus, Curse of Columbus."

I had tailed him here, to this mall, a couple of days in a row. It wasn't hard—the guy traveled via skateboard. *Skateboard. Seriously, what's next? Dragons on bicycles? Vampires on pogo sticks?*

"A freakazoid up to some strange shit," Jurgens had said.

By itself, being a freakazoid up to any kind of shit would not warrant execution under the laws of the Codex Magica. Only if a Judge investigated and found just cause that said strange behavior harmed innocent civilians or called undue attention to the use of magic—and yes, that last bit is ambiguous as hell, ain't it?—and said judge became convinced beyond a reasonable doubt (or a close approximation of reasonable doubt), then said freakazoid could be designated thereafter as persona nonbreathing and rendered *habeas corpus* and *meatus deadius.* Amen and pass the ammo.

And as it turned out, this freakazoid really *was* up to some strange shit, shit strange as pastel turds. Twisted enough to earn an unfavorable judgment and scary enough to warrant a death sentence, even after applying my relatively high bar. Now all I had to do was stalk Birnbaum into his ugly-excuse-for-an-evil-wizard lair and zap him before the young knothead could up and commit even more crazy shit, thereby endangering innocent Columbians. Columbusites?

The chain-link fence wasn't much of a deterrent, as proven by the tagger decorations coloring the mall in spray-painted immortality: AQ, TAZ13, some Jackson Pollock scribbles as indecipherable as a doctor's handwriting. I could scout around a couple of miles of fence and find how the taggers got in or climb it, juggling a backpack and stabbing the toes of my cowboy boots in the gaps. But why bother? Having magic meant doing cool stuff in a mysterious and mystical way.

With a concentrated effort, I tapped my magic and focused on the fence, removing the heat from a section of links about head-high and shoulder-wide—*all* the heat. Frost formed with a crackle, and the links iced over, frozen at the atomic level. A swift kick of a size-ten boot, and the metal shattered in a cascade of glittering shards. Voila! A gate!

I stepped through the gap, careful not to snag my black shearling coat. A breath of chill air brushed my cheeks, and a flurry of snow swirled around my legs. Every fourth parking lot light was on, so I walked through long pools of darkness cut by fuzzy globes of misty light.

At the Dillard's entrance, I tapped magic again and slagged the locking bolt on the exterior vestibule door. Ditto the interior door.

And I was in.

"Follow the yellow brick road," I sang, sotto voce. "Kill a magical toad."

Chapter Two: Freakazoid

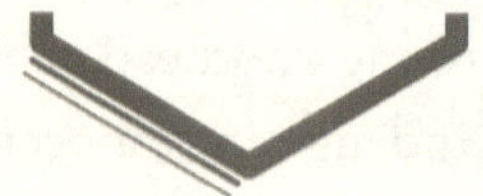

I lounged with Jurgens on the deck of the Jurgens' ranch. Majestic purple mountains defined the horizon. Amber grain waved in the foreground. I wanted to take a picture... or salute.

Administrator Jurgens handed me a thick file folder. "This one's a freakazoid. Up to some strange shit."

For an Admin, Jurgens was pretty cool. Six-two, broken nose. Spent some time in the Marines before he found his amulet and discovered magic. Most Admins spoke in commandments rather than sentences and pretended their farts smelled like cherry blossoms. Jurgens at least acted human, more often than not.

I took the file and tapped magic to force a light stream of air across my face, pushing away the burned-skunk smell of Jurgens's cigar.

"A freakazoid?"

"Has a fetish for horror movies big enough to crush Tokyo." Jurgens snorted and spat a bit of tobacco off his bottom lip. "The guy has done some shit, though, I'll tell you. Managed to figure out an energy-time connection. Can you believe that? Twentysomethingyear-old video gamer finds his stone, and within a year has done what no Magical has done in... well, in forever."

"Wow," I said with all the enthusiasm of a teenager handed a mop. "His name Zuckerberg by chance?"

Jurgens grimaced and nodded toward the file. "The guy's pretty young."

"So?"

After a long pause, Jurgens said, "Well? You have any problems with it?"

"No." I bit a scrap of dead skin from the corner of my thumbnail. Spat it out. "What difference does it make, how old he is?"

"That's the Calico Shivers I know and love. Grim as stage-four cancer and twice as relentless." Jurgens grinned around the cigar clamped in his teeth and added some scotch to his crystal tumbler. There was no ice. Jurgens was known to inflict bodily harm on people asking to pollute his Macallan Rare Cask with ice.

Jurgens turned serious. "How's your sister doing?"

I opened the case file. "Dustin Birnbaum?"

"I would help if I could. You know that, right?" The Admin watched me for a few long heartbeats. Cigar smoke curled around his narrowed eyes. He sighed and leaned back in his chair. "Dustin Birnbaum has gone rogue."

"Needs to work on his villain name." I skimmed through the summary sheet and tripped over a land mine buried in the dry prose. *Subject has mastered the art of time travel and has retrieved from the future items of gross danger to the general public. Subject has used these items in a manner which violates the Magical Code as it relates to doing no harm to the general public.* "Time travel? Now, I know you're shitting me."

"Nope. That's what I meant when I said he'd figured out the space-time continuum. Try to keep up."

I cocked an eyebrow. "Can we be a little less forthcoming? Or does too much information violate the Codex Magica?"

"Some things even Admins don't want to write in a report. Too crazy."

Jurgens's four-year-old Dalmatian trotted over and planted his chin on my thigh. *Play? Play?* His tail flapped against the patio table, rattling the glasses.

I concentrated on the dog's brown eyes. "Huck, go find your ball."

The dog bounded away and dove into the tall grass, a dog on a mission. He reminded me of me.

"Dr. Doolittle," Jurgens said. "Amazes the fuck outta me every time I see you talk to an animal."

"My superpower." I twitched a shoulder in a mini-shrug. Talking about my ability to communicate with animals inevitably led to the revelation that I preferred talking with four-legged critters more than I did most humans. A girl I dated briefly said I was emotionally distant. *Well, dear, I kill wicked people for a living. Go figure.*

I followed Huck's progress as his black-spotted tail swished above the grass like a floppy periscope. Then more words came out of my mouth: "I've done it since I was six. My mother claimed it was because I'm one-quarter Comanche, and my dad said it was because I'm a quarter Chinese. But it's not 'talking' the way you and I speak to each other, Jurgens. Animals don't talk in words. More like mental pictures. Vague impressions, most often. Pictures, smells, feelings. Pretty easy to tell what a dog's thinking. Not so easy to tell them what you want."

"What about cats?"

"Cats pretend they never heard you in the first place."

"Still. Pretty cool. Remind me: what's your other quarters? Quarter Comanche, quarter Chinese...?"

"Black and Irish." I yawned and closed the file. "What's the crazy shit he's up to?"

Jurgens sipped his scotch before replying. His craggy eyes squinted into the sun as it settled into the Beartooth Mountains. "The boy is making monsters."

Huck had recovered his once-yellow tennis ball and dropped it at my feet. *Play?* I picked up the dog-slobbery ball, flecked with bits of grass, and heaved it across the yard. Huck bounded away, tongue trailing from one corner of his mouth. "Monsters, huh? I call bull-shit."

Jurgens held up a finger. "Just a sec."

The sun sank behind the Beartooth Mountains, and we paused in admiration. The sky melted into a canvas streaked with red and gold strokes, brushed by thin, high clouds, contrasted by a purple landscape that faded to black. I toasted the scene with the two fingers of scotch in my glass and tossed it off in one gulp.

"God, you're a heathen," Jurgens groused. "Savor it, don't slug it."

I pulled a face. "Eh. Got any Wild Turkey?"

Jurgens made a puking-his-guts-out face. "What do you know about DNA?"

"Is that a metal band?"

"At some point in our future," Jurgens said, "it appears we'll have the technology to gene splice just about anything. Make pets or people or people-pet combinations. Design 'em on a computer, grow 'em in vats. Our informant says little Dustin Birnbaum has retrieved a set of these Tinkertoys, and he's creating anything his imagination can devise. And based on the reports, Dustin is one truly disturbed fuck, so his imagination is skewed to the perverted and puerile."

"Big words for a Marine."

"I'll spell them for you." Jurgens blew a ragged smoke ring then tossed out a comment that sent electric tingles over my skin. "Another thing this new tech can do... it can grow replacement organs for you. Lungs, kidneys, hearts... livers."

My heart stutter-stepped as his words settled into me and the implications became clear.

"So." Mouth suddenly dry, I snagged the bottle of Macallan and tipped a splash into my glass. "Monsters, then."

"Monsters."

Huck trotted up and plopped his slobbery ball in my lap, leaving a wet, gooey spot on my jeans. Ick. His liquid-brown eyes begged for attention, and my heart unfroze a couple of degrees.

Play? Play?

I threw the ball into the grass, and Huck scrambled away again, all happy paws and flapping tongue.

"Okay, I'll bite, said the vampire." I wiped my fingers and picked up my highball glass. "How does this mad scientist make monsters from future tech using DNA?"

"We're not sure. The local wizard who was sending us reports went dark before she could give us much in the way of details. She caught on to the problem when the news in Columbus started going nuts over a rash of disappearances. At first it was homeless and hookers and transients, so no one noticed. Then housewives and mail carriers and, you know, regular citizens started disappearing, and things got real."

"You think your local wizard got zapped by this guy?"

Jurgens shrugged and pulled a face. "Do the math. Even for an Army puke, it should be easy enough."

"Army Ranger, jarhead. Anybody seen these monsters?"

"Some wild reports by hysterical citizens. Nothing we can say for certain."

"Such as?" I asked after Jurgens appeared unwilling to say more.

"Ahh..." He shifted in his seat, pulled at his nose, cleared his throat... and in all other ways acted like a man who smelled a fart at a dinner party but didn't want to be the first to call phew. "Something that looked kind of like a werewolf, maybe. Some other people saw some weird things, too, like maybe... what're those things from *Lord of the Rings*? Ugly bastards that make up the bad-guy army?"

"Orcs?"

"Yeah, Orcs."

I envisioned a movie poster—*Coming soon from director Peter Jackson... Orcs Attack Ohio!*—then let it flicker out and knocked back another dose of Macallan. It really was quite tasty. "You know what this needs?" I held up the glass in the fading light. "A splash of Pepsi."

"I hate you."

"Most people do, once they get to know me."

The Dillard's store had been stripped to bare walls. Not so much as a single rack remained inside the cavernous space, leaving behind a dark and gloomy horror movie set from a film I had seen before: a bunch of teenagers break into a deserted mall to drink beer and have sex. Next, a monster drags one off into the darkness, and the hormone-rattled teenagers do world-class stupid, antisurvival-oriented things, thereby reinforcing the stereotype that all teenagers are idiots. I rarely watched slasher flicks—enough of that in my real life, thank you very much—but when I did, I rooted for the monster.

The far side of the place was invisible—nothing in front of me but a solid wall of black. Creating light by burning magic was contraindicated, as the smart guys would say. Using up my store of magical energy early would leave me short when it came time to snuff out Birnbaum's menorah. I had drained a fair amount of magic so far, which was what I got for being too lazy to climb over a fence.

"Hello, darkness, my old friend," I sang under my breath. "I'm here to stalk in you again."

From my backpack, I pulled a two-foot-long D-cell flashlight, a magic wand all by itself, made by Maglite, of anodized aluminum and heavy enough to knock the snot out of King Kong. The beam stabbed the gloomy guts of the store, revealing rows of support columns and cables dangling from open ceiling tiles.

I crept along, murdering Simon & Garfunkel in a subvocal singsong. Making up song lyrics was something I did when my nervous energy needed a place to discharge safely. "I'm a killer softly seeking... a bad little wizard creeping... something, something, forgotten lyrics... Umm. 'Neath the beam of my Maglamp... I shiver from the cold and damp..."

Ugh. Needs work.

I'm more of a player than a composer, anyway.

I had memorized a layout of the mall from an obsolete website. Dillard's anchored one end, with Sears on the other. Between the two, a long central corridor was lined with shops. In the middle, the corridor doglegged to the left then right again. Two other department stores anchored each end of the dogleg. A food court filled the central section, complete with tables and a fountain.

A roll-down gate, glittering silver in the beam of my flashlight, blocked the Dillard's exit into the mall. I switched off the light as I approached then pushed at the gate to get a feel for it—heavy with thick links of steel. Freezing the metal like I did to the outside fence would not have been a great solution. The tinkle of metal shards on the tile floor would have been too loud.

The last thing Jurgens had said before I drove away: "Watch yourself on this one. The Mage who reported Birnbaum's activity has dropped out of sight. No contact in two weeks, so the kid has probably nixed one wizard already."

When approaching a Magical with imminent bodily harm as your goal, second punch is first dead. From that point on, a silent approach was best.

Channeling magic into heat configured as a narrow beam required intense control, not my specialty. I was more diesel rig than sports car, more broadsword than rapier. Fine control of magic took oodles more concentrated effort for me than it did for others, but I could manage it when motivated.

A line glowed red along a thin vertical strip from the bottom of the gate, as though being struck by a laser beam in a spy film. I called it my James Bond death ray. I brought it up, turned it left, went sideways for two feet, then down. Molten metal splattered the floor, hissing and smoking. The top corner of the cut section sagged, and I caught the middle with one hand before the whole chunk of flexible mesh fell. I continued the cut to the bottom then eased the section to the ground. It rattled and clinked, but not as much as would a million shards of broken metallic links.

By the time I'd finished cutting an opening, sweat soaked my armpits and dripped from the tip of my nose. My magical charge was low, maybe down to a half or less of what I wanted in the tank to go up against a fully functional nut job like Birnbaum.

Time for a break.

I moved away from the hot metal stink of the smoking gate and put my back against a support pillar. I rested my butt on the cold floor and set my backpack between my feet. In case it proved to be a long night, I'd brought snacks, PowerBars and bottled water—nutrition for wizards everywhere.

I was unwrapping a protein bar when something wicked from the darkness my way came.

Chapter Three: Lots and Lots of Legs

Legs. *Lots and lots of legs.* That was my first impression of the thing scuttling from the shadows. About the size of a full-grown mastiff with a bigger mouth and more teeth. Lots and lots of teeth. A shark-mouthed spider. Big, hairy, scary, and needing to die in a ball of nuclear fire.

In the bit of physics class I had not slept through, I learned that energy cannot be created or destroyed—it can only be changed from one form to another. So sayeth Uncle Albert, so sayeth we all, though I doubted Einstein included magical energy in his calculations.

The energy of magic was like any other: heat, light, kinetic, electricity, and so on. Magic could neither be created nor destroyed, but it could be converted from its current state to a different form of energy through application of an amulet-holder's will. The amount, type, and power of that new state of energy depended upon many factors, not the least of which was the ability of the person doing the magicking. Some users were better with making the wind blow, some with using heat to burn their toast, and some could play with light better than the closing fireworks show at Epcot.

And some were good with electricity.

I was good with electricity. Very good.

When the multilegged shark-spider pitter-pattered from the shadows, I didn't think. I reacted. I tapped magic as naturally as sucking soda through a straw. With an application of will, I stripped a massive quantity of electrons from the atoms making up the building's infrastructure—the concrete supports, the ceiling grid, even the dust on the floor.

And I sent these free electrons to live inside Ugly Spider Thing. The thing free electrons most want to do is hook up with chicks of the opposite orientation in their atom towns.

Mr. Positive, meet Miss Negative.

Lightning arced from multiple sources and coalesced at the beast in a series of actinic flashes.

Displaced air boomed loudly enough to rattle distant windows. My hair stood on end, and my skin crawled with static. Purple blooms filled my vision. I blinked until I could see again, levered myself off the floor, and went to look at what I'd zapped. The lump of meat with its eight crispy drumsticks lay in a smoking heap about two scuttles away from my boot, having achieved a state of matter known as "charcoal briquette."

I poked a finger in one ear and jiggled it around, as if that would stop the ringing. "So much for quiet. *Oof!*"

A great mass slammed me from behind like I was a tackling dummy at a pro football tryout.

The tremendous weight of the thing drove me down. My palms smacked the floor, and I collapsed into a push-up position. The creature latched its teeth into my trapezius. My thick sheepskin coat kept the monster's fangs from piercing my skin, but the pressure was tremendous, like a Vulcan neck pinch by a hydraulic vise. A fang dug through the leather and scored a fiery streak across my clavicle. The beast's loud snarling rattled in my ears, and its seriously stinky breath made me gag.

I tapped magic for a simple blast of kinetic energy and blew the thing off my back, taking a chunk of my goddamn best coat and my Grateful Dead 1988 Oakland concert T-shirt with it. A meaty thud from a dozen feet away marked where the creature hit the ground.

It howled. Claws scrabbled for purchase.

"Screw this." I rolled upright and cast a blanket of magic-induced light.

The creature paused and threw up an arm to cover its eyes. My jaw fell open—literally, like a cartoon. My eyes may have telescoped out of my face.

Fur covered the thing from the tips of its pointy ears to its claws. Seven feet tall, the damn thing sported humongous arms tipped with razor-edged talons and a muzzle with overgrown, spit-dripping canine fangs.

Human eyes glared from the furry face, which I found really fucking freaky.

"A werewolf? Are you kidding me with this shit? An honest-to-God *werewolf*?"

The werewolf snarled then sprang forward, halving the distance in one bound.

I tapped my magical amulet for another kinetic blast, but it turned out to be more of a kinetic burp. The tank was empty.

"Uh-oh." My last blip of power struck the werewolf in the face with a weak uppercut. The thing shrugged off the hit with a grunt.

Zippo on the magic, Sunshine. Now what? Hey, wait up, Fuzzy. I need an hour to recharge.

Jurgens once asked me, "You know what they call a Judge who blows all his magic before the end of a fight? Biodegradable."

The werewolf pounced. I blocked its gaping mouth with a forearm and hissed in pain when its steam-powered jaws clamped down. It bore me backward, and my back slammed against the floor. The full weight of the lycanthrope's body came down on my left arm. The creature scrabbled for purchase, ripping at my belly with its rear feet. It released my arm and snapped, going for my neck. I shoved both hands under the thing's jaws and grabbed it by the throat.

I grunted and bench-pressed Wolfman Jack up and off me. Mostly.

The creature twisted and thrashed, all fury and fangs and ripping claws and serious fucking attitude. Letting go meant getting my face eaten off, but preserving the status quo was not a long-term option. My arms already quivered with strain. I wouldn't be benching this thing for long.

I had one more move to make. If I could get my right hand free, I could reach my other magic wand, a Wilson CQB .45 in a hip holster on my right side. No silver bullets, but then this was no Lon Chaney werewolf. Unless I was much mistaken, this particular wooly wonder was grown in a petri dish by a deranged wizard with more imagination than sense. I would bet my life that eight Glaser +P frangible rounds would seriously ruin its day.

I *was* betting my life.

Problem was, the gun was under my shirt, which was under my coat. Getting to it would take time.

Not getting to it would mean getting chewed up. The werewolf was hellishly strong. I held the thing's throat in a no-shit death grip, yet my fingers kept slipping a bit at a time. The creature buffeted me with claws, ripping long rents in my coat sleeves. It growled and twisted and spat. Its back claws had torn open my coat and were digging at my midsection, scratching my belly through the thin cloth.

"This is like putting a cat in a bathtub." *Do it now or die.*

I sucked in a breath and shoved. An Olympic weightlifter grunt exploded from my chest. It made all of six inches extra space. I shoved my knees into the creature's belly to gain an extra second.

My right hand swept down and stabbed like a blade into my coat as my left lost the battle with the werewolf's throat. It slipped free. I snugged my left arm over my throat and scrabbled for the Wilson's grip. Jaws ripped at my elbow. Stinky, hot breath panted into my face from an inch away. Wetness dripped in my eyes. Blood or sweat? I couldn't say.

The pistol came free. I thumbed off the safety, jammed the gun up next to my blocking elbow, and fired a double-tap through the base of its jaw. The heat from the muzzle blast crisped the hair on my arm. Glasers were designed not to overpenetrate but to disintegrate on impact, releasing the full force of the bullet into the target's soft tissue. However, at point-blank range, the sheer force of the high-powered rounds blew out the top of the wolf-thing's head. Blood and monster brains fountained up, and red rain spattered my face. *Yuck.*

The werewolf quivered and jerked for a long, tense moment then sagged, loose and limp.

I pushed the carcass aside and sucked wind for a while.

My ears were ringing again.

After a nice little breather, I managed to sit up and swap magazines on the .45, locked and holstered it, then brushed dirt and werewolf off my very tattered coat. My original Grateful Dead T-shirt had taken a pounding as well. I lifted it to get a look at my hide. Welts striped my chest and belly from the monster's rear claws. Blood seeped from some of the scratches, and more trickled from the fang holes in my collarbone.

I glared at the furry corpse, and my nostrils flared. "Bad doggie."

The light had faded along with the last of my magical energy.

And so much for the element of surprise. Unless Birnbaum was deaf or jamming some tunes with his earbuds plugged in deep, there was no way he could have missed the thunderclap or the bark of my .45. On the plus side, one wolf-mutant and one crispy thing-with-many-legs were dead. Two of Birnbaum's creations were down. How many could there be?

What was the monster bag limit in Ohio?

Answer: unlimited.

After dealing with Dusty, I needed to track down and kill every single beast concocted in the rogue Magical's secret laboratory, from the ugliest to the nastiest. I couldn't leave even one of Birnbaum's creations to run around loose, slaying horny teenage campers and people too stupid to stay out of the basement when the lights go out.

They all had to die.

Between rough war and rogue wizards, I had run out of fingers to count the people I'd zapped—well, wizards, but wizards were people too, at least kind of. Anyway, killing monsters for a change would be easy.

"Except when I have to put down Cate," I said aloud. "That one's gonna hurt."

One day before the Mall of Doom, I'd watched Birnbaum's house from my rental car. I waited until the Magical had skateboarded away with his earbuds plugged in, wearing two shirts—an unbuttoned flannel plaid over a yellow T-shirt, saggy black jeans, black PF Flyers, and a hoodie with the hood up, arm holes empty and hanging down his back like a cape—the very model of a modern major wizard.

The Birnbaum house, a seventeen-hundred-square-foot Cape Cod, filled a corner lot in a neighborhood of once-proud homes built for the thousands of veterans coming back from WWII at the start of the baby boom—a place to raise a family with happy dogs dancing underfoot. Smoke from backyard grills might drift on the breeze as a gang of kids played baseball in the front yard, using rocks or handy tree stumps for bases. The start of the baby boom. I could imagine signs saying "Norman Rockwell lived here."

Sixty years later, the baby boom had petered out, grown up, gone away, and shed the old neighborhoods like a snake discards its skin. For Sale signs grew from the weeds. Cars overflowed the cracked driveways and spilled into the street to line both curbs with walls of vehicles. Hip-hop thumped from a nearby house, and a pair of loose dogs peed their way down the block. An old woman dressed like a Russian babushka pulled a squeaky cart along the uneven sidewalk. It was the kind of neighborhood even syphilis would shun.

I waited until the old woman with the cart was a block away before I eased out of my car and strolled up Birnbaum's driveway. I skirted a dust-covered Volvo—did the kid prefer skateboards, or did he not have a license?—and slipped along the side of the house. A chain-link fence with an unlocked gate surrounded an overgrown backyard. The gate squalled when I lifted the tongue and pushed it open. I didn't pause or look around. Over the years, I'd found that if I acted like I owned the place and had every right to enter, people were less likely to call the cops. I could have used a light-bending trick to remain unobserved, but it seemed a waste of power. In that neighborhood, calling the police on a prowler was not high on the list of possible reactions, anyway.

Jurgens's comment about Dustin Birnbaum living with his mom had been inaccurate. The case file revealed that Mother Birnbaum had moved to Jacksonville, Florida, leaving young Dustin in the family home. I had no clue why little Dusty had stayed behind. A Magical had numerous legal and not-so-legal ways to create wealth. A tiny little bump of a roulette ball here and there wouldn't raise the eyebrows of the Admins, nor would helping a racehorse with a little extra push. A Magical could rack up a decent nest egg in no time at all by keeping it small and unobtrusive and harming no one. When asked if I had ever done such things, my default response was "No comment."

"He can time travel and pick the winning lottery number whenever he wants, but he doesn't bother?" Jurgens had sounded as perplexed as I felt when I called to report in. "Maybe it's that whole millennial lack-of-ambition thing."

"Maybe. Although more Gen Z than millennial."

"Well," Jurgens said, "quit fucking around and go find out."

In Birnbaum's backyard, I found a handy bedroom window at waist height—grimy glass with metal slat blinds and a cheap thumb latch. The bedroom appeared unused, with no bed, no furniture, just cardboard moving boxes piled higgledy-piggledy throughout the room. With a little magical manipulation of the latch and a careful lifting of the blinds, I rolled over the sill and into the house.

And froze.

A clacking, clinking noise came from somewhere in the house. Dishes, it sounded like. In two days of surveillance, I had seen no indication that Birnbaum had a companion. Had Mom come back from Florida? I cat-footed through the bedroom—carpeted, thankfully—and peered through the door crack.

The clatter of plates and the rush of running water grew louder.

I tapped magic and used the power to bend the light around me, leaving me invisible to the naked eye—or even an eye wearing a nice cocktail dress. I crept down the central hall, noting closed doors right and left. Family pictures of various sizes and shapes hung in haphazard distribution along the walls. They all had a Herman-Munster-level layer of dust covering the frames, but I recognized Dustin in several of the shots, from toddler to teenager. The other people were unknown.

I found the dining room and followed the noise to what turned out to be the kitchen. It was the exact opposite of the rest of the house: open, airy, clean, and bright. The kitchen could have been occupied by June Cleaver or Claire Huxtable. Flowery wallpaper, speckled white Formica countertops. Glass-fronted cabinets showed off china and canned goods stacked in neat rows. Pine-Sol and Pledge scented the air.

A woman in stockings, high heels, and nothing else loaded the dishwasher. Shimmery, wavy blond hair fell to her waist. And she had pointed ears.

Probably not June Cleaver. I dropped my invisibility. "Hello?"

The elven woman didn't jump at my greeting but turned with a bright smile. "Hello. How may I assist you?"

I blinked. The woman bore a disturbing resemblance—*Oh, hell no.* "I've seen you in a movie," I said. "*Lord of the Rings*, right? You played Gala-something?"

"Galadriel. I am Galadriel Seven." The woman's chipper voice sounded as though she couldn't be happier. "I live to serve the master."

"And who's your master?"

"Dustin," she cooed.

"Did Dustin make you—I mean, create you?"

The elf cocked her head to the side. "Dustin created everyone—all the Galadriels who came before me and many other wonderful creatures."

"And what do you do for Dustin?" The high heels and stockings were a clue, but I had to ask.

She flashed a bright smile. "Whatever he wants."

"Such as doing dishes. Why not dusting? No, strike that. What else does Dustin require of you?"

"Well, most often he wants sex. He likes to take me in the—"

"Stop!" I held up a hand and sighed. "Are you free to choose what you want?"

Galadriel's expression remained fixed in a *Stepford Wives* smile, her head cocked. "I don't understand the question."

"Can you leave the house?"

"Oh no, I must never leave the house."

"How many other Galadriels have there been?"

"I am the seventh."

Duh. You should have guessed that one, Shivers. "Any idea what happened to Galadriel One through Six?"

The woman with Cate Blanchett's face blinked, though her bright smile never faltered. "They were returned."

"Returned?"

"Returned." She nodded as if I should have known what that meant. *Silly Mr. Shivers, don't you know anything?*

I didn't know much, but I was pretty sure a sextet of naked Galadriels wasn't living out a comfy retirement in Florida, playing mahjong and bocce ball with Mama Birnbaum. "Returned" sounded more... final, as in returned to the pot or a great tankard of raw DNA in Birnbaum's lab.

"Can you refuse to... ah... serve Dustin?"

"No, I live to serve the master."

"I see. Thank you for your time, miss."

I left the house the way I came, circled around to the street, then walked to where I'd stashed the rental. I got in and called Jurgens on his prepaid cell. "This guy needs to go," I said when the Administrator answered.

"Glad you concur," Jurgens said in his sarcastic dialect.

"Dustin Birnbaum is a sick, twisted puppy."

"You found a monster?"

"Worse. He's defiled the only woman I'll ever truly love."

"Miss Piggy?"

"Cate Blanchett."

Chapter Four: I Hold No Rancor

I rubbed my face and stared at the melted hole in the mesh gate separating the store from the mall. Beyond that jagged opening lay darkness and possibly a fate worse than death—dismemberment, torture, and reality TV—although that was a redundancy.

If I continued, I would be low on magic, a little ragged from werewolf claws, and down to twenty-seven rounds of Glaser, three flash-bangs, and four fragmentation grenades. In my pack, I carried one flashlight, three PowerBars, and a liter of water.

I hummed a few bars of The Clash. "Should I stay, or should I go?"

A prudent and wise wizard would have retreated to regroup, recharge, reload... reinforce. I knew a couple of other Judges in the United States, like Terry down in Florida and May Lee out in California. Either one would have jumped on a plane in a heartbeat to get a shot at this wacko and his stable of homegrown horrors.

On the other hand, if I retreated, Birnbaum might pack up his toys and disappear. And if his Build-a-Creature kit disappeared, where would that leave Alizandra?

I tapped the first speed-dial number on my phone.

"Hello?"

"Hey, kiddo."

"Hey, Calico." Her voice sounded weaker than normal, scratchy as an old vinyl LP played by a dusty needle.

"How goes the fight?"

"We tried a new antibiotic today…"

"And?"

"And guess what? I threw up like Mount Vesuvius."

"Allergic, huh?"

"Just like the others." A weak laugh. "But hey, good news. I'm up to number six hundred fifty-two on the liver list. All I need is for a couple of planeloads of donors to crash, and I've got it made."

My throat tightened, and I fought to keep my tone light. "I'm near an airport. I'll see what I can do."

"'Kay," Alizandra murmured so quietly I could barely hear her. "Sleepy."

"Get some rest, kiddo. I'll call you tomorrow."

"'Kay. Bye."

I sighed and put away my phone. I needed Birnbaum's lab, and I needed it intact, so no nuking the site from orbit. What song went with suicidal charges into certain death? "Eye of the Tiger"? No, too easy. "Run through the Jungle"? *Better.*

I groaned and tossed aside my ruined coat then resettled my weapons harness over my shoulders, my supply of grenades dangling like Christmas ornaments. I needed Birnbaum's liver-growing technology, and for damned sure, I was going to get it. Tonight. I couldn't turn away before I recovered the technology that might save my sister's life. At least I could scout the lay of the land and see what the mall had to offer by way of diverting shopping experiences. "Come on, Johnny, let's go see what's inside the dark and dangerous cavern with warning signs painted in blood on the walls," said every dumb teenager in every exploitive slasher flick ever made, and there I was, doing the same damn thing.

I ducked through the ragged hole and entered the Mall of Doom.

"'Sympathy for the Devil.' Rolling Stones," I decided then sang under my breath, "Please allow me to shoot myself…"

A dim glow filtered down from regularly spaced skylights, shedding enough light to avoid large obstacles. I stuck to the middle of the concourse, avoiding the gaping holes of abandoned stores. Some were gated, some open. All were pits of blackness that could have been hiding anything from an M1 Abrams to a *testudo* of Roman legionnaires, a werewolf, a vampire, or a humanoid-fly hybrid, like from that movie with Jeff Goldblum. Scared the bejesus out of me when I was a kid, that movie.

How many Glasers does it take to kill a Jeff-Fly?

I pulled the Wilson, thumbed off the safety, and kept a finger against the trigger guard, cupping my grip with my left hand. *Look at you, Mr. Badass, ready for anything.*

That was good, as three orcs spilled from a Payless shoe store, roaring their battle cry and charging with pikes extended. Yes, pikes. Long poles with pointy ends.

I lined up and shot them, left to right, with a double-tap each, six rounds in two seconds or less, creating a percussive drumroll of solid noise and bright flares of light. Black blood sprayed, and Birnbaum's *Lord of the Rings*–fetish creatures flipped, spun, and died.

"Look at you guys," I said, "bringing a pike to a gunfight." I blinked away the purple afterimages of muzzle flare then dropped and swapped magazines.

I plucked out my flashlight and panned it around, not trusting my spotty vision in the dusty mall corridor, with its gutted kiosks and blank storefronts. Nothing moved. One of the dead orcs juddered with random nerve impulses that slowed and stopped as I watched. I stepped closer and confirmed my first impression: grotesquely twisted faces, bat ears, and long, snaggly teeth marked them as *LOTR* orcs.

"Just my luck," I said aloud. "Birnbaum is a Tolkien fanboy. Call him Saruman the Necromangler."

"No," said a voice from the darkness. "Gandalf the Grey, at least."

I spun and fired before the last syllable ended, spotting Birnbaum in the beam of my flash an instant before my finger pressed the ridged trigger. The bullet stopped in midair, dropped to the floor, and rolled away.

Well, shit. Didn't see that coming, did you?

Dustin Birnbaum laughed. "Seriously? You planned to *shoot* me?"

I dove for the floor, emptying the Wilson's magazine on the way down, and scrabbled for the cover of an empty, boxlike kiosk in the center of the mall corridor. Yanking loose a flash-bang, I tossed it overhand then ducked and covered, eyes squinted shut.

When neither flash nor bang happened, I growled some salty curses, swapped magazines, and toggled the slide release.

Birnbaum's chortle faded as the young Magical retreated into the mall. "This should be fun. I think I'll leave you with my Rancor."

"Rancor?" I risked a glance over the top of the kiosk. Empty corridor. No Birnbaum. *The fuck is a Rancor?* I pinched my cell phone out of my back pocket and tapped a speed-dial number.

Jurgens answered on the third ring. "What now, Shivers?"

"Update: Birnbaum knows I'm here. I'm in a firefight with orcs, werewolves, and spider-things."

"Oh my."

"Yep. Magic gone, ammo low."

"Run, Forrest, run."

"You ever heard of a Rancor?"

"Un-ass that mall, Shivers. Savvy?"

"Roger that." I thumbed off the phone as a metal roll-up gate rattled from deeper in the mall, too far away to get a fix on its location. A howl of distilled hate, laced with malice, split the air. The roar of something big, mean, and hungry echoed off the empty storefronts, distant but coming closer. Footsteps vibrated the floor, raising dust.

Whatever a Rancor was, it was big and in a hurry. I probed the dark with my flashlight.

"What the..."

The size of the thing! My flesh sleeted over with needles of freezing sweat. Walking on its hind feet, the Rancor's shoulders nearly touched the ceiling. Its ugly, misshapen head sagged forward between two outrageously long arms that bulged with muscles and ended in four-fingered claws—long, yellow, razor-sharp claws, by the look of them. Piggy eyes glared from beneath hooded brows, and drool fell from a mouth full of teeth. It looked vaguely familiar, like something from *Star Wars.* Luke Skywalker... Jabba the Hutt's pit—

First Lord of the Rings, *and now this?*

"You need to get a life, kid!" I yelled at Birnbaum.

I braced my .45 on the kiosk, lined up the three-dot night sights on the Rancor's nose, and fired seven aimed shots at extreme range for a pistol. Skin popped on the monster's eyebrow, lip, and snout as I made hits. The other shots missed or hit without me seeing the strike.

The Rancor reared back, arms extended, palms up, and howled at the ceiling in one continuous roar.

Well, that certainly pissed you off. Even over the ringing in my ears, I winced at the volume of sound. "Try this!" I heaved a fragmentation grenade, which bounced off the tile, took a sideways hop, and skittered to the Rancor's left.

I ducked.

The grenade banged, and the Rancor screamed again.

I popped up for another look, steadying the flashlight on the kiosk wall. Black blood oozed from a dozen cuts in the beast's hide. It shambled forward at an awkward trot, apparently unaffected by a near-miss grenade or a nose full of frangible .45 ACPs. It was closing fast, as angry as a nest of pissed-on wasps.

The Rancor hit the kiosk with a swinging claw, shattering the wood and sending chunks flying. A hot bellow sprayed me with slobbery spit. I froze, momentarily stunned—and a little amazed—at the ferocity and power of Birnbaum's creation. *How many Cates does it take to make a Rancor?*

Run, idiot!

I scrambled in the slick coating of dust on the tile floor, and my boots churned like Wile E. Coyote under the shadow of a falling rock, too slow and too late. Pincerlike claws grabbed me around the middle and hauled me off my feet. I twisted in the creature's grip, trying to see over my shoulder. The Rancor wasn't big enough to swallow me in one bite, but it looked like it wanted to try. The beast glared with yellow piggy eyes. Long ropes of drool hung from its chops. The monster held me in both hands, and its mouth fell open wider than seemed physically possible.

It screamed again.

"Hey, dude, look! Sorry about the grenade!" My right arm was pinned against my side. Also pinned under wicked-sharp claws were my two remaining frags.

The .45 spun a lazy circle on the floor, knocked clear when the Rancor grabbed me. *Flash-bang, it is.* I ripped one free of my harness, used the tip of one of the creature's claws to pull the pin, then snapped a left-handed shuttle pass at the Rancor's gaping maw.

The grenade bounced off a fang and fell away.

"Fuck!" I clapped my free hand to my ear and clenched my eyes shut.

A miniature sun exploded at the monster's feet. Even with my eyes screwed down tight and one ear covered, the concussion went beyond loud into the realm of pain without end, amen. The Rancor stumbled and twisted its face away. It didn't let go of me. On the contrary, it squeezed me like a wet towel. Then it shook me. Hard. A Calico Shivers martini. My head bobbled. The walls spun around in crazy circles. My insides flip-flopped, and I bit my tongue. Between the screaming monster, the gunshots, and the flash-bang grenade, the ringing threatened to blow open my skull like a red, meaty flower. If the symphony of trumpets shrieking in my ears would stop for—one—goddamned—*second!*—I could maybe figure out a plan.

At this point, squeezed to death might be a blessing. Eaten by the Rancor, close second.

Ah.

The Rancor had repositioned its grip, freeing a fragmentation grenade. I clawed it loose only to have it bounce out of my hand when the beast shook me again. The frag jolted into space. I grabbed it, one-handed, and slapped it up. The grenade bounced off my chest, caromed off my chin, then danced along the Rancor's claw. I experienced many long moments of ass-clenching terror before I trapped the baseball-sized bomb against my chest and hugged it tight, like a tiny, knobby little baby. *Thank you, Exploding Jesus.*

The walls were moving again—no, the Rancor was lifting me to chomp off my head.

I snagged the grenade's pin on the same claw tip as before then held the spoon down with two fingers to keep the ignition timer from starting.

No missing this time. Wait for it. Wait for it.

The Rancor's maw opened wide. Jagged, yellow teeth dripped with sticky saliva. A pink gullet invited me in for a quick bite.

I held the grenade and waited until I could count the cavities in the Rancor's teeth before releasing the spoon.

One Mississippi. Two Mississippi.

I jammed the grenade deep into the soggy wetness of the beast's mouth and yanked my hand back. The thing swallowed convulsively. Its ugly mug took on an expression that was almost confused.

Thud! The grenade went off deep in the Rancor's belly, and red, pulpy goo splattered my face. *Note to self: wear a face mask next time you go monster hunting. First the werewolf, and now this. I think I got some in my mouth. Ugh.*

The monster belched, and more of its insides spewed out. The claws relaxed, and I twisted free then dropped. When I hit the ground, something *pronged* in my ankle, shooting a bolt of icy-hot pain up my calf. I rolled, sensing more than seeing that the Rancor was coming down, whether I was ready or not.

The thing landed in its own guts with a *whump*, spraying gore everywhere.

The Wilson CQB rested next to my ear. I retrieved it with a shaky hand, popped in my last magazine, released the slide, then holstered it without getting up, all mechanical, automatic actions I performed without thought.

In my right ear, a high-pitched whine blocked all external sound. My flashlight had rolled away—I remembered it flaring out when I dropped it. So, yeah, it was dark again. The rich, pungent spoiled-meat odor of Rancor guts filled the air. Many, many parts of my body hurt. In the before time of my life—before magic—I had been dragged a hundred meters over rocky terrain by a runaway camel—long story—and that hurt only half as much.

I pushed off the floor, established an upright position, then winced. "Owwie."

My right ankle complained long and hard about taking my weight, but stubbornness won over pain. It would hold up for the time being. I stuck a finger in my ear and jiggled it, which did nothing for the ringing. I carried a bottle of ibuprofen in my coat pocket... but that was back in Dillard's. Of course.

I glared into the deep gloom into which Birnbaum had disappeared. If ever a Magical needed to be put down, it was this kid. What would happen if any of these things got loose on the suburbs of Columbus? Or some juvenile delinquents broke into the mall for some light vandalism? One of the signature symptoms of a Magical gone bad was a complete lack of regard for regular humans, and Birnbaum's lack could rank Olympic medal consideration.

I sniffed in a deep breath, held it, then let it whoosh out. *Count to ten, Calico.*

Birnbaum was ready for me, knew I was coming for him. The kid had to have had nearly a full charge of magic and perhaps more exotic critters to turn out like a bunch of mutant farm dogs let loose on a door-to-door salesman.

I touched my amulet. Weak. Quarter charge or a smidge over. Seven shots and two grenades, one each type. Though if I ever used a flash-bang again, it would be on a target a great distance away, preferably while I stood behind a steel door. Jurgens was right. It was time to un-ass the building.

I saluted the darkness with an extended middle finger—maybe childish, maybe valiant defiance. I hated quitting, but getting myself killed would do Alizandra no good. Alive, I still had a chance. She still had a chance. Then there was my father's voice in my head: "Second place is first loser." All these years later, it still needled me, that saying. *Quitter, quitter, chicken-shitter.*

"Well, Dad, stuff happens." Ha. I could just imagine mouthing off like that back in the day. I trudged back the way I came.

Invisible bands of force wrapped themselves around me and stopped me cold.

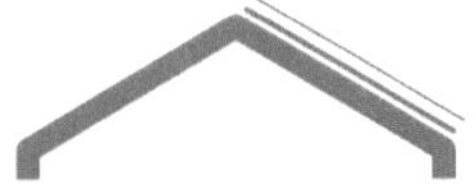

Chapter Five: Magician Burrito

Converting magical energy directly to kinetic energy with enough control to manipulate objects without crushing them required a level of finesse I could rarely achieve. I could blast through doors or crush anything from beer cans to cars with an exertion of pure force. On a smaller scale, I could even punch people with a fist-sized ball of kinetic energy, which came in handy, for example, when a guy in a huge pickup parked in a handicapped spot and needed to have a small-but-painful reminder of why that was bad form. Of course, I never did that in real life. I would never.

What I could *not* do was wrap up a person and drag them backward through an unlit, abandoned mall, using just enough force to hold them tight and not squeeze them into a two-dimensional object. And doing it without line-of-sight, too... that was a good trick. *How is Birnbaum managing that? Sonar?*

For being a crazy fuck, Dustin Birnbaum could do some magic. Too bad he would be dead soon. *Bold thought for a floating wizard burrito.*

Wrapped up like a baby in a blanket, I slid through a set of black floor-to-ceiling drapes and squinted in the suddenly bright light. The bands of force released me, and I staggered from the short drop to the floor. My ankle barked a complaint. I slumped to one knee, over-acting the injury, blinked, then looked around.

The food court had been transformed. Row after row of bubbling glass tanks lined one wall, fed by hoses and linked to electronic boxes with glittering panels of indicators and digital readouts. Forms floated inside about half the tanks—nope, not forms. Bodies. Some were human, but some not quite. The cadavers in the tanks appeared to be disintegrating in a flesh-turning-to-liquid kind of way. Mysterious fluids gurgled through spaghettilike swarms of tubing and flowed into the tanks. Other tubes carried gunk away and into an abandoned Orange Julius shop. *Where does it go after that? Down the drain and into the city water supply? Into a slushie machine? Bleh. And yuck.*

Cabling ran across the floor, connecting the instruments to a stacked bank of black boxes, which I presumed were servers. Green diodes flickered on racked machines as they clicked and hummed in happy service. Another rack contained rows of batteries, all connected to heavier cabling, which was duct-taped to a support column and trailed up past the construction lights, disappearing at the atrium skylight. An electrical source, I supposed, potentially solar, that fed the batteries their diet of electricity.

Putting two and two together, adding psycho and carrying the pucker, I came up with dead human tissue being used to construct living monsters. I hitched my chin at the setup. "This is how you get Skynet."

"Terminator reference. Nice." Birnbaum's disembodied voice came from the shadows beyond the far bank of portable light stands. "And no, this is not when I start monologuing and give you time to kill me."

My amulet had recharged enough. I had one good shot of magic available. Problem was, I couldn't get a fix on Birnbaum's position. I would be firing blind.

I worked on my pitiful poor-me body language, kneeling on the sparkling tiles of the nutso Frankenstein's laboratory—literally, no shit, Frankenstein. One of the floating bodies under construction resembled Boris Karloff in the original Big-F makeup. "Why am I here, then? Why not just snuff me and be done?"

"You're a little more dangerous than the average subject."

The human bodies in the tanks ranged from the very young to the very old, male and female, of all races and sizes—diversity in death. "Subjects? Way to euphemism, dipshit."

He giggled like a teenage girl. "I have a different plan for you, Mr. Judge."

"So is this the part where you try and convert me?"

"No. No, I'm not. This is way more fun. I'm sending you a long time away." The voice's location shifted from the abandoned Burger King to a Sako Japanese Cuisine restaurant. "Now, shut up. I have to concentrate."

"That would not be in my bessttt inntttteerrrreeessst—"

The light shifted to bloody red. My heartbeat slowed. I felt the thump-thump as it wound down, like a playing card flapping in a slowing bicycle spoke. A drop of sweat from my forehead oozed through the air before plopping on the tile and squashing outward like gelatin. My body elongated into a piece of saltwater taffy, and my vision turned murky and wet. Then... silence.

Calico John Shivers disappeared. At least, the meat creature that was once him—me, us—expanded to exist but not live. There was no me. There was no self. There was only the universe.

I knew but did not think. I sensed everything.

A roach crawled, deep in the darkness along the baseboard of a fast-food restaurant, its musky scent overpowering at close range. Its insect feet clattered on the floor. Behind the wall, hundreds more writhed, shifted, and skittered. Along with them were rats and silverfish and termites and spiders beyond counting. Though I—we, him, her... pronouns had become meaningless—could count them, if that is what we desired, for we experienced them all.

Gnats drifted in the air, each a distinct, individual bug. We knew their shapes and markings as individuals. We could name them if we so chose.

We expanded again and knew the air, the floor, the walls, the water in the tanks, all as a sea of atoms, some densely packed, nearly rigid, and some loose and disorganized, bounding free and colliding, giving off heat and kinetic energy.

We saw the connection of everything. Matter, energy, and time were all interlocked, interdependent, though both of those words fell infinitely short of reality. Everything was the same, yet different. Inextricably bound. In constant flux. A perfect, balanced, self-correcting mechanism that defined the cosmos.

For the first time in a very, very long time, Calico John Shivers wondered about the existence of God. Any god. In this place, in the present, we had all the time in the universe to think about it. *Is this God, this machine? Or did a sentient being create this from the unformed stuff of the universe?* We pondered this question for... well... time had no meaning, so we didn't know how long we pondered it.

I saw and understood how Dustin Birnbaum interacted with the machine, how he converted magical energy to bend time. He created bubbles, little snippets of mass and energy that could move in time. The bubble containing Calico John Shivers had all but separated from the time we knew. Only a thin tunnel remained, and that shrank visibly as we turned our attention to it. It resembled a balloon in a lava lamp, lifting away from the base, soon to break. I fought to regain my connection to my selves. *Focus on I, not us.* It felt confining, like squeezing a watermelon into a Mason jar and clamping on the lid.

I tapped magical energy—it was abundant and with no restrictions or limits—and reached out. My control, as always, lacked precision. Like a toddler reaching for a birthday cake, I grabbed the molten elasticity that was the Cottonwood Mall of Somewhere, Ohio, and pulled hard. *Pulled hard.*

I poured energy into the tunnel between my existence and where I once existed, reaching back, trying to drag our—*no, my*—bubble down—though "down" was a sense more than a direction of the place, time, and energy of my former existence. Birnbaum fought back. My grip on the present slipped. Like the child pulled back from an imaginary birthday cake, I was more determined than ever to have it. My willpower found Birnbaum's and latched on. I pulled harder, dragging myself back toward my time and place. I pictured myself in a tug-of-war with Birnbaum, using magical energy instead of rope.

A chunk of Cottonwood Mall separated from time, and we—I—became a bubble riding on a bubble. I envisioned pulling myself, hand over hand, along the rope of energy connecting me to Birnbaum. I felt the younger Magical's grip slipping. Felt his fear. Felt him diverting some energy to anchor himself to the ground.

That's right, kid. I'm coming to end you.

Stop, you idiot! You don't know what you're doing.

One more mighty pull, and I would have had him. Control wasn't my thing, but brute force, I could do. I gathered energy the way I would ordinarily draw breath, vacuuming all the power I could hold inside my Mason jar existence.

No! Don't!

I freshened my grip and heaved.

Something snapped.

Light. Incandescent light surrounded me, like existence inside a nuclear explosion.

My consciousness shrank, collapsing into a marble inside my jar. "Shrank" hardly conveyed the speed with which I plummeted from knowing and sensing creation into the limited and dull shell of my own meat and bone and blood. I went from full screen to a dot, just like an old tube TV picture. And like an old TV, the dot winked out then faded to black.

Chapter Six: Wherethefuckistan

Three days later

For three days after waking up somewhere far away from a mall in Ohio, I had blundered through a wilderness of high desert mountains, a place of high-flying buzzards, low-crawling snakes, thorned bushes, and horned toads. Everything seemed to either bite, cut, or irritate, and sometimes all three. Hot and dry in daylight, cold and dry at night, with no people, no cell signal, no cars, trains, or planes—not even contrails in the sky. I could have been in the twenty-first century or the Paleolithic Era.

Oh, I was not happy. I was so far from happy, I would have needed to take the Starship Enterprise at warp nine across three galaxies to get to the planet of Mildly Content, in the universe of Cautiously Optimistic. There wasn't a song sad enough to reflect how unhappy I was. Well, maybe "He Stopped Loving Her Today." I hated that song.

My memory of the time prior to regaining consciousness was spotty. I recalled entering the mall, fighting the werewolf and the orcs, and some of the battle with the Rancor. After that, all I had were random images that made no sense, a dream that crumbled even as I tried pulling up the memories.

So there I was, through the looking glass, in a land of rocks, sand, lizard shit.

And very damn little magic. *What the hell have I done now?*

In all my travels, never had I seen a place so devoid of magic. By the end of each day, my amulet had charged enough to light a campfire, but that was about it. I avoided freezing by rotating like a chicken on a spit, turning first one side then the other to the fire. More than once, I cursed my decision to toss away my sheepskin coat because of a few rips, tears, and a bit of werewolf slobber.

I found myself touching my amulet a dozen times an hour, like a man waiting for a date who checks his watch. I had to take it off and put it in my pocket.

I maintained hydration by following trickling streams until they dried up then navigating to the next-most-likely water source by examining terrain and vegetation, scouting the flight of bees, and studying tracks. Deer were everywhere, along with raccoons, rabbits, squirrels, opossums, and birds beyond counting. When an animal was close enough for communication, I queried them directly about water or invited them to dinner with a .45 bullet—rabbits killed by frangible rounds were no good. I supplemented my food and water by roasting the spines off prickly pear cactus and eating the fruit.

Physically, I had endured much worse during the mountain-training phase of Ranger school, and if I was being honest with myself, this latest jaunt was a shady walk in a manicured park compared to Camp Merrill. I had to face some cold, hard facts, though. I'd gone soft in the last six years of relying on magic rather than muscle. Why climb a fence if I could freeze a hole through it? Why lift a heavy case if I could simply will it to go up? With magic almost unavailable, my body paid the price for years of neglect. My ankle had swollen to the point where I couldn't get my boot off, and I suspected I'd blown at least one eardrum with the flash-bang at the mall. The smaller scratches and achy muscles, I ignored. If pain was weakness leaving the body, I should have been the strongest man alive.

And mentally... yeah. That. I stayed about one minute shy of running in circles and gibbering at the moon only by twisting my focus knob way, way down. Eat food. Drink water. Hike. Sleep. Perform bodily functions as necessary. Beyond that, running the speculation track was doing nothing but wearing me out. I needed my brain to disengage from higher thinking. I needed to be more like an animal. I could do that.

The terrain had varied from high-desert mountains to valleys of thick forests. On my third day of dumbed-down existence, I had been following a natural trail downhill when I realized what I had been seeing for the last however so many minutes—shod horse tracks, as in, horses shod with horseshoes. It would make the first sign of civilization I had seen since waking up in the mountains. My higher brain cells woke up. *Maybe you should follow the tracks.*

Thank you, Albert Einstein. Come up with that on your own?

The horse tracks led me downward, through a growth of the ugliest evergreens I had ever seen, twisty trees with needles instead of leaves, and then deeper into a forest of other skinny, white-barked trees. Yes, I slept through botany, even more than I did through physics.

In a clearing at the base of a jutting rock, I found a camp. And in the camp, there was a horse, bedroll, canteen, saddle with bags, and the remains of a very violently dead human male.

This can't be good, said my higher brain, providing more evidence of my fucking genius at work. I squatted on the overhanging spur of rock and studied the campsite.

The dead man wore an overcoat of blue-bottle flies and nothing else. Something or someone had flayed the skin from his torso, leaving nothing but an ugly, raw, black-and-red carcass that had been burned to char in some parts. Long sections of the man's thighs were missing, and by the odd way his body dipped at the waist, I suspected chunks of his butt were gone as well.

I wondered whether one of Dustin's creations had followed me there—wherever *there* was—or if animals had been at the dead body, tearing away neat strips of meat. A charcoal ring marked where a fire had burned. The dead man's left foot rested next to the circle, blackened and blistered from heel to toe.

A Colt Peacemaker revolver lay in the dirt, too far away for me to see if it held live rounds or not.

Tied to an elm on the far side of the camp, the horse cropped at the few sparse bits of greenery remaining within his reach. I fixed the ragged, hairy buckskin gelding with a concentrated gaze. "What's your name?"

Four-legged creatures spoke to me in a combination of pictures, scents, and sounds rather than words. Practice and guesswork allowed me to interpret the results into concepts that I mentally filtered into English, all in the blink of an eye. It was a talent I'd possessed from the age of six, at least, which was when Mom caught me telling the family dog, Gunner, to sneak a box of Frosted Flakes out of the kitchen cabinet.

An animal's emotions came through stronger than images, and the horse projected a sense of despair and self-loathing so strong that a field of summer daisies would have wilted and died if exposed to his level of melancholy.

I translated his response as *Who cares?*

"What killed your previous rider? This guy here?"

Who cares?

"Is it still around?"

The horse volleyed a mental shrug.

"All the horses in the world, and I get Eeyore." A nagging thought surfaced and demanded attention. Everything in the camp had the look and feel of the Old West. The Colt, the Western saddle, the scattered cooking utensils... There was no modern camping gear at all.

I've got a bad feeling about this.

Shut up, higher brain. You're not helping. I focused on the horse. "You wouldn't happen to know what year this is?"

Who cares?

Wherever I was, I wasn't spoiled for choices. Walking away from transportation, clothing, and camping gear would have been more stupid than... well, than venturing into a camp where a man was ripped to shreds and cooked over an open fire.

I scrambled down off my rock and entered the camp. First, the canteen. It had been some hours since my last water, and that hadn't been much more than a mud puddle. I sniffed the contents before swigging a mouthful. What I wouldn't have given for some purification tabs. It would be a miracle if I avoided a gut full of bugs, leading to dysentery, tapeworms, and creatures shoving out of my abdomen over the breakfast table.

Saddlebags were next. Inside, I found three heavy law books and, to my delight, a long, black frock of sturdy wool. The inscription on the books read Judge T. L. Moorcock.

"You're shitting me." I tilted my head. "A fellow judge. Different jurisdiction, though. What's the T. L. stand for? Too long?" Below the inscription in one book was a date. Even though I half expected it, the news slugged me hard, and my blood turned to ice. "Eighteen eighty." I took a deep breath. "Oh, this sucks. What the hell do I do now?"

The horse lifted his weary head and regarded me with sad eyes.

Who cares?

Chapter Seven: Misery Loves Company

I had not ridden a horse in years. I made a mental note to never do it again. I would shoot myself first.

Pain radiated from my hips to my calves, and I wobbled when I walked. It didn't help that my trusty steed, whom I'd dubbed Misery, had the gait of a drunken New Orleans hooker on the Monday after a Super Bowl game in the Dome. The horse had two speeds, slow and stop, and two moods, morose and suicidal. I had given up trying to squeeze more speed out of the gelding, opting instead to try and relax and enjoy the countryside.

I had food, water, camp supplies, and a vintage Colt Peacemaker with a six-inch barrel. Four fat .45 Long Colt rounds rested in the revolver's cylinder, along with two empty shells. At least Moorcock had gotten off a couple of shots before being killed. With only those four rounds and the five left in my Wilson CQB, I felt woefully under-ammo'd. When bad things arrived, I liked to get enough rounds downrange that the bad things died, departed, or were so weighted down with lead that they couldn't move. Nine cartridges weren't enough for peace of mind.

The countryside remained quiet, and whatever or whoever killed Moorcock stayed away. Half-seen things, either deer or armadillos or baby Rancors, taunted me by disappearing when I looked, leaving nothing but a feeling of being watched. I twisted in the saddle to check my back trail several times an hour. Nothing appeared, though I did pop my spine more than once, so there was that.

The terrain, flora, and fauna put me in mind of the desert Southwest. Nevada, Arizona, maybe, but evidence supported California, as one of Moorcock's law books was a California Penal Code, 1872 edition. Without that, I might have guessed one of the 'Stans, like, say, Afghanistan, Pakistan, or Sandinyourass-istan. When I almost urinated on a diamondback rattlesnake that morning, I ruled out the Middle East. Plenty of snakes there, but no diamondbacks.

I tried very hard not to think of my kid sister, huddled alone under blankets in a hospital bed, tubes and wires snaking into and over her body. She was far away both geographically and temporally unless I could get back.

After midday on the fifth day of my new life in the No-Name Mountains, I passed a hand-lettered sign that read Geyser Falls, 2 miles.

"Geyser Falls? Sounds like an oxymoron." My voice rasped like a dry file on rusty steel. A layer of dust lined my throat, no matter how much water I sucked down. "Geyser or falls but not both."

My horse refrained from comment. Perhaps "oxymoron" didn't translate well.

As the trail slithered out of the mountains, a panorama of a wide valley opened. I pulled up and studied the distant town, which I presumed to be the oxymoron itself, the bustling metropolis of Geyser Falls.

The city had burrowed into the middle of the valley, near a crossing on a narrow river. The approach to the town snaked through a scrubby forest of cedar and bristlecone pine—I'd finally remembered the name of the twisty tree—at the higher elevations with sagebrush and creosote, I thought, lower down. Across the river, a snow-capped mountain backdrop appeared painted for the sole purpose of giving Geyser Falls a scenic view. A cornflower-blue sky reached from horizon to heaven, veiled with a single strip of clouds as thin as cotton gauze high above the frosted peaks.

Still no contrails.

I pulled up again a short mile from town, squinted, and scratched my ear. The thin trail led across the scrub plain to the town, appearing to morph into nothing more than twin rutted tracks as it approached the city limits. The town streets, too, were unpaved, as best I could tell. The haze of distance obscured a clear view, but the buildings appeared to be made from stacked rock, packing crates, and twisty planks cut from ugly trees, with a few larger structures near the center that might have been made of something more solid.

There were no cars.

Deep in Moorcock's saddlebags, I had found a pouch with six silver dollars and forty-two cents in US coins. None of the money had been minted later than 1886.

Evidence kept mounting that Birnbaum had sent me back to the 1880s American West. That truth seeped into my bones like poison from a tainted well, each little drop adding to the sickness in my belly. Hell, I shouldn't have expected less from a magician who could time travel. Second punch was first dead, and Birnbaum had obviously punched first. I knew something bad had happened in the mall, but I hadn't known what. Memories floated up, disjointed and out of sequence. I knew it had happened after the Rancor, but all I could remember were tiny bits and pieces, weird visions centered around being in a bubble.

A chill traced down my spine, and I jerked around, positive that a cold-fingered zombie had snuck up behind me, but nothing was there except weeds, trees, rocks, sand, buzzing grasshoppers, and chirruping birds. I couldn't shake the feeling that I was being watched.

I rolled my shoulders to loosen the black coat and caught another whiff of the former owner. My own juices had yet to overcome the imprint of the dead man's sweat stink, an odor similar to rancid goat cheese with a bottom note of wet ass. Moorcock's shirt rode high on my wrists, covering my sad, torn concert T-shirt. I'd tucked both pistols out of sight, along with my grenades, a Böker seven-inch dagger, a Benchmade Infidel boot knife, and a steel wire garrote. I'd concealed the latter inside the lining of my belt.

I twitched the reins to start Misery moving. A minute later, I swiveled in the saddle, hoping to trick whatever was watching me by catching it moving.

Still nothing. The high desert landscape—with its stunted trees, rocks for miles, and brushy stuff tall as Misery's belly—mocked me. Nothing stirred. The wind made a sound as faint as the memory of a childhood dream. It sounded like a laugh, and not a good one, but a sharp-toothed, blood-dripping clown cackle.

I kicked the horse hard in the ribs. "Move along there, little doggie."

For once, Misery listened and picked up his pace.

Native Americans occupied the first two dwellings along the road into Geyser Falls. Children in breech cloths played in the dirt yards of sod-and-twig huts, running among the dogs and chickens and aggravating the adults. The latter wore mismatched combinations of Western garb and buckskins. Bead necklaces ringed the neck of every person, from a withered grandma to a wobbly toddler.

I raised a hand in passing. The suspicious coal-dark eyes of the men followed me. No one waved back. Maybe if I stopped to explain my mixed heritage, that I, too, had the blood of the red man flowing through my veins, they would warm up. *Peace, brother. Indian power.* Instead, I kept riding.

Six dwellings of dubious construction wobbled toward imminent collapse on the outskirts of the town proper. They might once have been efforts at real homes or built for convenient storage of farm equipment, with their scrap timber walls, sometimes four of them, nailed together with neglect and standing by virtue of inertia, sheltering a collection of dirt daubers, spiderwebs, and four feral cats. The better homes were constructed of piled rocks that somehow defied gravity and stayed upright.

"Welcome back, baby, to the poor side of town," I muttered. "A Johnny Rivers song," I told the horse, "in case you were curious."

The quality of construction improved as the road continued. The main drag bisected Geyser Falls, and I counted six cross streets before the main street reached a bridge over the river. A few larger homes occupied the far side, but without getting closer, further gathering of intelligence was impossible. Toward the center of town, the buildings were made of brick, and the tallest reached three stories. Farther out, wood construction dominated, with false-fronted buildings that put me in mind of every Western movie I had ever seen.

Three men in dusty work clothes and slouch hats lounged in front of a shop. A barber pole had been crudely painted on the window glass. I pulled Misery to a stop—as in, I actively stopped trying to make him go forward—so I could read the sign posted next to the door. The loungers' stink-eyed gaze, thick as bubbling tar, spread over me. The sign listed services from a haircut (ten cents) to a tooth extraction (a half-dollar). Lettered in chalk at the bottom were the words "No Injuns or Nigers."

My lips twisted. "No 'nigers,' huh? Well okay, then, this should be fun."

None of the watchers seemed inclined to comment. I debated getting off the horse and giving the barber a spelling lesson, but discretion weighed in, and I reined my horse away, continuing toward the center of town. I had reached "civilization" but had no idea what the hell to do. I supposed I could hire on as a cowpoke and ride, boldly ride, in search of El Dorado.

After four days of sparing use, my amulet had charged about halfway, giving me enough power to deal with emergency situations, but the fact remained that I had no idea how to use it to get home. Birnbaum had the knowledge, and Birnbaum was roughly one hundred and ten years away from being born. My memory of the event that triggered the jaunt back to the nineteenth century was more hole than fabric.

So of course, of course, I asked the horse, "What now?"

Misery responded by dropping a smattering of road apples.

Failing to plan is planning to fail was one of my father's favorites, along with *Shut the fuck up and get to work*. I listened to the clopping hooves for a time, brain in neutral. Men—and a very few women—went about their business, trekking across the dusty street or thumping along the boardwalk. I received many slanted looks at me from under lowered hat brims, their eyes as narrow and suspicious as those of the Native Americans at the edge of town.

How about food, bath, bed for the night? A stable for the horse. Until your six dollars and forty-two cents runs out, anyway. There's your plan, Dad.

I found a low-slung building between a bank and feed store, the white facing hand-lettered with the word "EAT" in bold red paint. A smaller signboard posted by the door claimed the establishment as Maylene's and listed some prices for meals. Among them was a Lunch Special for twenty-five cents. I deduced there might be food to be had inside, and my belly rumbled an okay-let's-get-'er-done noise.

"Wait here, Misery." For good measure, I wrapped the reins around the hitch rail. Me cowboy, him horse.

Maylene's interior enjoyed the homey and welcoming feel of a prison mess hall. Two trestle tables with benches ran from front to back, long enough to seat twenty on a side, or more if they didn't mind sharing cooties. A central aisle ran the length of the place, from the front door to the kitchen. This time of day—midway between noon and dark—I had the place to myself.

At the jangle of the front doorbell, a squat woman in a flower-print dress and a flour-printed apron trundled from the kitchen. If God had taken a full-sized woman, pressed one mighty thumb on her head and squashed her to half-size, the result would look like this gray woman. Her pewter hair was torqued back so tightly that I was afraid her face might pop if a mosquito bit her.

"Lunch is over." The woman spoke with a German accent so heavy, I could taste the sauerkraut. "But I haf some food to eat, if that is what you want." ...*If zat is vhat you vhant.*

"Yes, thank you." I took a seat with my back to the wall. "Are you Maylene?"

"*Nein. Ich heisse* Gerda. This place, I have owned twelve years. People... slow to change, they are, ja?"

I laid a silver dollar on the table. "Keep the food coming until that runs out."

"Gut. Wait, I bring coffee." True to her word, Gerda brought a pot of coffee and a ceramic mug. In trip after trip, she served up a wheel of cornbread with a pot of soft butter, a bowl of leek soup, a pan-fried steak that lapped over the plate, boiled potatoes, pinto beans, carrots, and okra. As the final dish landed in front of me, Gerda wiped her hands on her grungy apron and said, "You finish, ja? I heff *apfel* pie in oven, to be ready soon."

"Newspaper?"

"Ja. I heff yesterday's paper. I bring."

Mouth stuffed with cornbread, I could only nod thanks when she handed me two sheets of folded, greasy newsprint. I cleared a space among the dishes and spread the paper open with fingers that shook with hunger, not fear—absolutely not fear. The header proclaimed the paper to be the *Geyser Falls Bulletin*, printed in Geyser

Falls, California. My eyes danced over the page for a moment, refusing to settle on the date until I forced myself to look at it.

According to the town paper, yesterday was October 21st, 1887.

"Well, damn," I whispered. No escaping it now. Speculation over. I was in the fucking past. The reality hit me hard enough that I swallowed coffee to break the logjam in my throat. No more denial. The truth was right there, in black and white. I was stuck in the nineteenth century. No phone, no car, no flush toilets. No Administrators of the Codex Magica—at least that I knew of—no Jurgens, Home Depots, Safeways, or even a goddamn 7-Eleven.

I looked up when the door jingled. A broad-shouldered, narrow-hipped lean wolf of a man in tall boots stood in the doorway, sporting a silver badge and an immaculate white hat. The lawman studied me with electric-blue eyes as he moseyed—and that was the only way to describe it—to the table and high-stepped over the bench to take a seat opposite me. He moved with the fluid, easy grace of a panther. The badge said "Sheriff" in block letters.

The sheriff remained silent while eyeballing me from across the table. I let my body go loose. My fight-or-flight sensors triggered a burst of adrenaline, and the fight portion rose to the ready. I was in no mood to be fucked with, and I could sense a serious amount of attitude radiating from the guy's Randolph Scott jawline to the tips of his pointy boots. My warrior brain cataloged all the convenient weapons and developed a flowchart for sudden violence. *If he does this, I do that...*

"Now, tell me—" Suspicion leaked out of the lawman's pores, along with aforementioned attitude. He spoke with the voice of command, much like my father once did. "Just who the hell are you, *boy?*"

I went cold, and my skin tightened.

The sheriff twitched back a tick, obviously not liking what he saw, and the lawman's hand fell below the table, presumably to the butt of his pistol.

Inside my head, Eric Clapton's "I Shot the Sheriff" clicked onto the turntable. "Here's the deal, Sheriff." My voice had the razor-steel calm it always did in the buildup to sudden death and smoking guns. "I'm quarter-Chinese, quarter-Black, quarter-Comanche, quarter-Irish, and one hundred percent American, so if you call me 'boy' one more time, I will beat you to a frazzled pixie stick and nail your dick to the door."

By his expression, the lawman had caught the gist of my statement, if not the fine points. His face transformed from ruddy tan to brick red.

"Now." I set my coffee cup down. "My name is Judge Calico Shivers, and you have one chance to start again before the ass-kicking begins."

Chapter Eight: Since You're a Judge...

Ten minutes in town, and someone already wanted to kill me. It was like my superpower. I didn't actively seek conflict—I had to admit that I'd thrown down the gauntlet, but he had provoked me—and yet somehow, I managed to rub people the wrong way, as though my pheromones marked me as an antisocial animal, the junkyard dog who didn't play well with others. Or maybe they sensed the killer inside and reacted at a cellular level with instinctive, atavistic anger toward a perceived threat.

By the glitter in the lawman's eyes, it was a close thing.

I picked up my coffee cup left-handed and flattened my right on the table, preparing for the first two moves: coffee to the face then shoving the table into the sheriff. It would buy me the second or so I would need to fire a magical lightning bolt down on the sheriff's Stetson. Game, set, match.

A corner of the lawman's mouth twitched up. The twitch turned into a grin, which evolved to a chuckle. I remained tense. I had seen guys laugh up a storm seconds before they blew a man's head off.

"Nail—nail my dick to a door!" the lawman said through his chuckle. "Now, that's funny. That's funny." He raised his right hand, a gesture of peace. "Not that you couldn't do it, and all. You look a salty old bo—ah, a salty feller, for sure. You might or might not, but let's say we don't find out right now. That all right with you?"

"Sure. Okay."

"I'm gonna have to remember that, for true. Dick to the door. Hah!" The sheriff extended a hand. "Let's try that again. I'm Sheriff Archibald Bridger. And you said you were Judge…"

"Shivers. Calico John Shivers."

"A judge?" The sheriff swallowed his disbelief with a visible effort. "You're a judge, huh? We don't normally see people of your… people of your age as judges."

"Emancipation. It's coming to a neighborhood near you." I had used my title as bestowed upon me by the Admins, yet I had procured a judge's robes and accoutrements, so my garb matched my title. One of God's cosmic chuckles.

"Yes, yes, I understand." Bridger cleared his throat and looked away. His lips pursed in a thoughtful frown, and he said nothing for a time. "I apologize for my rudeness. The town's a little on edge lately, and I get knocked into a cocked hat around strangers."

I toyed with my cup. The coffee was lukewarm, but it would still serve as a distraction if flung at Bridger's eyes.

Bridger returned his gaze to me, a speculative gleam taking hold. "Since you're a judge, and all…"

I cocked an eyebrow.

"Why don't you finish your supper and come on over to the jail. We have a need for a trial. The mayor was gonna preside, but maybe you'd like to take a whack at her, Judge Shivers."

"A chudge? Why not you are saying this earlier?" Gerda had arrived with a pot of fresh coffee and a blue plate covered with a wedge of *apfel* pie. "Mein Sheriff, would you like some pie?"

Bridger shook his head. "Thank you, Gerda, no. I have to get moving." He scooted back and put his hands on his thighs as if having to push himself upright.

"Who's on trial?" I stabbed a chunk of pie. My belly was stuffed tighter than a family car on summer vacation, but hey. Pie.

"Ach." The German woman gestured to ward off the evil eye. "Da vitch."

"Davitch?" I looked from one to the other. The first bite of pie melted in my mouth. Tart, sweet, cinnamony, with an air-light crust. I needed to find out if Gerda was married. "Who's Davitch?"

"Not Davitch." Bridger's blue eyes were deadly serious. "The witch. First one I've ever seen, but there's no doubt she's a witch. We've been waiting to have a trial so we can hang her, legal and all."

"Legal," I said after I swallowed. "Right."

"Think you could lend a hand?"

"Glad to help." A trial was nothing to me. I made a living by executing wizards without a trial. I was a paid assassin. "Due process" referred to how I cleaned and oiled my weapons before a job.

"Mighty whi—mighty kind of you, Your Honor."

"Just let me finish my pie."

The jail was five blocks away—two west, three south—and built entirely of stone. The upper floor had only narrow-slit windows covered in bars, while the downstairs facade included a picture window with "Sheriff's Office" painted in gold letters across it. A short, shaggy pony and a medium-tall bay mare occupied the hitching rail, leaving barely enough space for us to tie off our mounts.

I held Misery's bridle and focused on the animal's brown eyes.

Play nice with your new friends.

They hate me.

If you're nice to them, they'll be nice to you.

Misery snorted and tossed his head.

The jail contained two tables, both being used as desks, four chairs total, a gun rack, and a black potbelly stove. A framed map of the territory hung on the back wall. The stove's chimney leaked a thin ribbon of smoke from a joint near the middle, fogging the room with an acrid cloud. One man sat at each desk: on the right, a sheriff's deputy drank coffee from an enamel mug, and on the left, a round dandy puffed a submarine-sized cigar, adding a pungent stink to the rancid smog. The back door at the rear stood open, allowing a cross breeze to clear the air in fitful gusts.

"Mr. Mayor," Bridger said, "meet Judge Shivers. Shivers, this is Mayor Bunting."

"What!" The cigar-puffer hopped up and bounced around the desk, hand extended. His three-piece suit was wrapped around a body built like a globe, with stubby legs and short arms. A round head bobbled atop the globe, sporting slicked-down black hair and a waxed mustache more impressive than the spread on a longhorn bull. "Mayor Stokely Bunting, at your service." He goggled at me with eyes the size of hard-boiled eggs. "I say. You are a colored."

"And you're English." I shook the proffered hand, which Bunting snatched back and swiped against his vest. Another friendship died in childbirth.

"Judge Shivers, here," the Sheriff interjected, "ain't a colored man. He's a quarter-man. Quarter this and a quarter that. And if you sass him, he'll nail your dick to the door. Nail your dick to the door! And this"—Bridger gestured to the seated man—"is Deputy Potts."

The deputy touched a finger to his hat. "Call me Clay."

Bunting recovered his poise with the ease of a born politician. His look of dismay morphed into unctuous smiles and oily apologies. The sheriff perched a butt cheek on Deputy Potts's table and tilted his hat back. Bunting settled in one of the visitor chairs, insisting that I take the sheriff's desk chair.

"I must say, Judge Shivers," Bunting began, stopping to touch a fresh match to his cigar. "I must say, you're a very odd duck for a judge. Normally, men who've obtained the bench aren't quite so..."

"Dark?"

"Young, I was going to say." The mayor's eyes darted away, and he busied himself by picking tobacco bits from his lips.

"I want to see this witch. Where is this evil hag?"

The three townsmen looked at the ceiling. Bridger pointed up, in case I might not understand that the cells were upstairs.

"Bring her down here."

The men traded looks.

"What's wrong?" I demanded.

"She's sedated," Bridger said. "The only way we could keep her from getting out. Every time we locked the cell, she'd"—he whirled one hand in a twisted circle—"somehow get out. I never did see how. The doc gave us some stuff to keep her quiet. We figured she'd stay that way until come time to hang her, and all. I got a man upstairs, watching her."

Christ on a bicycle. "How long?"

"What?"

"How long has this woman been drugged?"

Bridger twisted to address his deputy. "What is it now, Clay? Four days?"

"'Bout that, I reckon."

I rubbed my eyes and counted backward from ten. These people... It was contrary, what with being a paid killer of magical people and all, but something about drugging an old woman and holding her in a cell didn't sit right with me.

Sooo, it's okay to kill her but not to get her high?

Shut up, brain, you're not helping. Besides, I don't have a conscience, so don't start acting like there's one hiding up there.

Something of my thoughts must have shown on my face. Bridger turned red, and Potts focused on the stack of papers on his desk. I stood and took a turn around the office, pausing at the map on the back wall. I found Geyser Falls after some determined searching. Turned out the river was the Owens, and the mountains I traveled through were called the Inyos. To the west lay the Sierra Madres, which at least I'd heard of. Treasure. Humphrey Bogart. *No stinkin' badges.*

"Look here, Shivers," Mayor Bunting blustered after a long silence. "You don't know what this woman has done. She's a witch, I say. A witch."

"Then we should hang her," I replied without inflection.

"Let me lay it out," Bridger said. He ticked off points on his fingers. "First, the Catholic church that all the Mexicans go to burnt to the ground, which ain't a real surprise, the way them papists is always lighting candles, but them that saw it says the thing whooshed up all in one go, like a bonfire soaked in oil. Then Pastor Allen, down at the Baptist church, grabs his throat midsermon, his face turns purple, and he keels over deader than Dick's hatband. I know 'cause I was there." Bridger's lips thinned. "Daniel Allen was a friend of mine."

"You see?" Bunting interjected. "You see the attacks are the work of the Devil!"

"And then," Bridger continued, "the bank is burglarized. Front door is found wide open, like somebody used a key, and the vault is the same. Wide open. About ten thousand dollars gone. Nobody saw a thing. Nobody heard a thing. Lucky for Ned Waterston, the bank manager, he was drinking at a saloon in front of a dozen witnesses the time it happened. Otherwise, I'd have arrested him for an inside job. An inside job."

I grunted. "So your atheist witch steals all this money then hangs around?"

"But that ain't all." Bridger ticked off another finger. "Three miners head out for their claim after stocking up on supplies. Two days later, their wagon is found, all the supplies untouched. No sign of the miners. They just disappeared. Then other folks start vanishing. The Blankenship boy, playing out in the scrub east of town. One minute, there, the next minute, gone. Then the Methodist church is burnt to the ground. Then a family of farmers, out north of here, up and vanishes, with food laid out on the table and animals left unfed. Then we find this here strange woman—the witch—out in the eastern foothills, wandering around, wearing a man's clothes and babbling strange things. We thought she was just addled, at first, but with all these other things… Ain't hard to put two and two together. Two and two together."

I stood and cracked my neck with a head twist. I wanted to twist somebody's head off, but I compromised. I could be reasonable.

A rush of footsteps pounded outside, and a man with a face like a Persian cat burst through the opening, wild-eyed and panting through the fur on his face. He blinked at the crowd of people then singled out Sheriff Bridger. "Archie! There's a crazy kid behind the Wheel. He's done killed two fellers—and tried to eat 'em!"

Bridger had his hat on and was stomping for the door before the last of Fuzzy's words were out of his mouth. "Potts, tell Barton to stay put upstairs, then come a-runnin'. Bring a scattergun."

A sick feeling took root in my guts. The image of Moorcock's flayed and filleted corpse flashed into my head. *Did Birnbaum send some of his menagerie to follow me back in time? Is that what I felt watching me?* Birnbaum created things that loved to kill. If the "crazy kid" was a Birny special, Sheriff Bridger had no clue what he was walking into.

"Shells," I demanded. I drew Moorcock's Colt and flipped open the loading gate. Potts, on his way to the rear stairs, tossed me a box from a drawer at the base of the gun rack. I loaded the two empty chambers while on the move. "Bunting, no more dope. I want that woman awake and sober."

"But—"

"I'm in a bad mood, Mayor." I paused in the doorway and favored the round man with a narrow-eyed look. "Don't fuck with me."

"Ah, yes. Yes, quite."

From several blocks away, the popping of gunshots peppered the night.

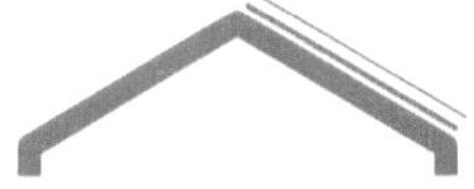

Chapter Nine: Shoot Low, Sheriff

I stepped outside and focused on the horses tied to the rail. *Where did the shots come from?*

From the sheriff's roan came a mental picture of a wooden building with an oversized false front. The horse couldn't read, but it conveyed the image of the words *The Broken Wheel*, painted in red, arched over a drawing of a cracked wagon wheel. Below the wheel, in smaller font, the sign read Beer, Spirits, Games of Chance. A general sense of direction filtered through as well, placing the building a short canter in the direction of the setting sun. I jogged that way, passing a gaggle of citizens emerging from doorways and side streets, all of them peering in the direction of the shots—and all armed with a collection of firearms, from a flintlock musket to a Henry Yellow Boy repeating rifle.

Geyser Falls townsfolk, I reflected, were not the quivering quislings depicted in Westerns galore, hiding under their beds when bad things came calling. These folks looked ready to shoot the devil a new asshole.

The sun had dipped behind the mountains, and already, interior lanterns illuminated shops and businesses. The clean air blew the stuffiness of the jail out of my lungs, and I inhaled deeply, enjoying the freshness.

The Colt felt snug in my fist. Moorcock had owned a well-built gun, with a six-inch barrel and walnut grips. Not my first choice of combat weapon, as the single action fired slowly and reloading required a steady hand and a time-out in the gunfight to go through all the fiddly actions it required. But I had only five rounds left for the Wilson, and once those were gone, that was that.

I had rolled my grenades in a gunny sack and tucked them into my saddlebags before riding into town, and I left them there on purpose. Exposing that level of tech to the locals could have gotten me hung alongside the witch. Besides, I grew up on *Star Trek*, and the Prime Directive required that I not interfere with the native culture... though Kirk always quoted it right before fucking over the native culture.

As I neared the saloon with the broken-wheel sign, the sheriff and Fuzzy raced around a corner and disappeared down a side street two blocks farther away. I loped after them and caught up as both men stopped at the open door of a barn-sized building. Whitewash paint had faded, but the name of the place remained visible: Bethlehem Stables.

What does that make us? Three wise men.

"He ran in there." Bridger pointed with his Colt to the dark interior of the stable. With the sun a golden glow over the western mountains, deep shadows swallowed the town, beaten back here and there by yellow globs spilling from open windows. Light refused to go more than a foot deep into the barn, darkness having kicked its ass, staking a claim to everything inside.

I squinted and saw nothing but a good chance to meet Jesus waiting beyond the threshold to Bethlehem. "Who went inside?"

"I'm... not sure." Bridger's face twisted as though he'd stepped in a pile of fresh manure.

"It was a boogeyman," Fuzzy said. The short geezer sported six good teeth and had a frizz of hair poking from under a hat worn by Noah while building the ark. "It was cutting strips off Ollie's leg, like they was tenderloin."

The sheriff confirmed this news with a nod. "Looks like Ollie Dunleavy was taking a leak out back of the Wheel when some... kid... attacked. Tater Grissom and Red Myers here stepped out to the alley on the same business, and... this kid killed Tater and nearly had Red."

"I'll tell you one thing," Fuzzy, aka Red, added, "I don't need to piss no more."

"A kid?" I squinted. *What had Birnbaum made that resembled a kid? A dwarf to go with his sex-elf? Did dwarfs eat people?* I would have to reread *Lord of the Rings* as soon as Tolkien got around to writing it.

"He ran off when I came up." Bridger scratched his head then re-settled his hat. "I shot at the, uh, the kid a couple of times. Must have missed. He ran away, and I chased him in here. In here."

All three of us examined the opening as if an oracle would appear and give us the secret to long life and sexual prowess. A half-dozen armed townsmen stormed up, and the sheriff explained that they had a murderer treed inside the stables—he left out the head-eating part. The group milled and grumbled, jaws clenched and looking ready to start blasting.

"We goin' in after him, Sheriff?" one man asked.

Bridger looked at the man then cocked an eye toward the open maw facing them. "You want to go first, Jimmy?"

"We can't wait for him to die of old age!"

"I wounded him," Bridger said, "I think. Back door to the Bethlehem is always locked. Hoping he'll bleed to death, nice and peaceful, and save us all the trouble."

"We should throw some lanterns inside," another citizen suggested. "Light the place up."

"And start a fire?" I said. "You'll kill the horses." The snorting and stamping of what I guessed to be three or four disturbed horses echoed from the interior of the building. I reached out with a mental question, but the horses were too disturbed to be receptive.

"The judge is right. But we aren't going in blind." The sheriff pointed to a man in the crowd. "Roy, would you be so kind as to bring me a lantern?"

"Make it two," I said. "I'm going in with you." Assuming the thing in the barn was Birnbaum's creation—and that seemed a good working theory—it was my problem.

Bridger nodded then held up a hand to forestall the rest of the group. "All right, but no more. We go in with a crowd, we'll shoot each other by mistake. Everybody, stand to the right of the door and don't shoot us if we come running out."

I amended my earlier unkind thoughts about the lawman's brain power. Bridger seemed capable and brave enough, though bigoted. Perhaps, I admitted, I may have judged the man through my twenty-first century perceptions. Maybe the sheriff's casual racism and his indifference to due process was the result of his environment more than his character. He had seemed more accepting of me since our pissing contest at Maylene's.

Roy appeared with two glowing lanterns and handed them off. Bridger lifted his in the stable's direction and checked me with a look. "You ready?"

I grunted.

The crowd had swollen to twenty men, and the townspeople sidled up behind them, the click and rattle of their weapons loud in the stillness. I wasn't sure which was more terrifying: the stomach-eating thing inside the stable or a score of trigger-happy townies at my back.

Evening sun lit the rooftops, and a night breeze swirled down from the mountains, chilling the air with the promise of night. The horse-manure reek of the barn killed any other smell dead in its tracks, leaving nothing for the nose but the pungent odor of fresh dung.

Our lanterns threw a double cone of light in front of us in a six-foot arc as we crept forward. I kept my eyes peeled for signs of movement. Inside the barn, a bouquet of competing scents competed with the manure smell: old hemp ropes, musty wood rot, weedy hay. A central aisle with stalls on each side ran the length of the stable. A high-wheeled farm wagon took up half the space from front to back, leaving just enough room on the sides to move horses in and out of the stalls.

Once across the threshold, Bridger and I paused then rotated to scan in opposite directions as if we'd planned it—the sheriff left, me right. Seeing by lantern light was tricky, as the burning globe tended to blind me when I tried to squint around it. I felt more like a staked goat under a spotlight than a keen hunter eying the darkness.

Bridger nudged me with a shoulder. "I'll take this side," he murmured. "You check the other. Look in all the stalls. Try not to shoot any horses. Don't shoot me. Or my dick."

I nodded and edged right. In the first stall, a black mare tossed her head and danced away from my light, her eyes rolling. Her agitation prevented any attempt at communication. There was no way to tell if anything hid in there with her. I twisted the wooden peg latch and let the gate swing open.

"Sending out a horse! Don't shoot it!"

The mare didn't want to leave her stall at first, so I streamed mental images of a snake under her hooves. The mare bolted for the exit and vanished amid shouts from the crowd outside. No one fired.

The stall was empty but for hay and horse turds. One down, seven more to go.

Sweat slicked my gun hand and patched my underarms and collar. The thick, close air weighed on me like an animal pelt. The lantern swayed and bobbed at the end of my extended left hand, painting every crack and crevice with light. I checked two more stalls at about the same speed as the sheriff, which put us on opposite sides

of the wagon, about midway along the central aisle. We inched farther toward the back, and my neck crawled with the sense of being
watched. This game of hide-and-seek felt much like hunting a rattlesnake by reaching down a blind hole.

The wagon bothered me—too tall to see into the bed and a forest
of wheels and shadows beneath. The thing loomed with a menace all
its own.

I paused at the fourth stall. This one also contained a frightened
horse, which I let loose after calling out to the waiting crowd. Bridger
did the same on his side, accounting for all the horses in the stable.
We had the place to ourselves. *Oh, yay. Go team.*

The lantern light did little to cut the shadows in the pockets and
corners of the cavernous barn. I gathered my will and reached out,
intending only to increase my lantern's brightness by a few lumens,
just enough to edge back the darkness a bit more and give myself an
extra second of warning.

Control had never been my strength, and after days of using magic only sparingly and with great need, I overdid it. Radiance flared
from the bell jar as if I'd transformed it into the interior of a hot
blue star. Brilliant luminescence washed the inside of the barn. The
Christmas Star had risen inside the Bethlehem Stable. Light blos-
somed, bloomed, flowered.

"Damn!" I flinched and dropped the overly bright lantern,
which thankfully did not shatter on impact. I stumbled back, face
in the crook of my elbow. Horror rode an express train from my gut
to my brain, arriving on platform Oh Fuck. As though frozen by a
photographer's strobe, a single frame of motion burned my retinas,
captured in the instant before they whited out. A nut-dark creature
with a bloody mouth, suspended in midair, leapt from the wagon
bed with clawlike hands extended.

The lantern died, and darkness swallowed me.

Chapter Ten: My Precious

I had been thinking about *Lord of the Rings*, so the first thing my mind latched on to when the thing jumped out of the wagon was that Sméagol himself had come back from Mordor. About the size of a preteen boy, ropy with muscle and oily slick, the creature was bare except for a loincloth around its hips. A mouthful of pointy teeth glistened. I gathered this vision as if from a snapshot, right before my eyes snapped shut against the brilliant aftereffects of the supernova lantern and the light died.

I backpedaled, tripped, and landed on my ass. The Gollum bounced off my chest like it was a trampoline, bounded high, and ran over my head and shoulders with bare, stone-calloused feet. The thing smelled worse than a dead fish in a dirty sock. It used my back as a springboard and shot toward the open barn door.

Confused shouting rose from the gathered crowd. A dozen or more shots banged out, followed by more yelling.

Peace returned at the same pace at which my eyesight recovered. My situation clarified with my vision, which was not to say it improved. Dampness from the floor soaked the seat of my pants. Best not to think of all the fluids that may have seeped into the soil of the Bethlehem Stables and saturated my britches.

The thud of bootheels announced Bridger's approach. The sheriff stood over me. "Are you all right?"

"Fine." I accepted his extended hand and hauled myself upright.

"What was that thing?" the sheriff asked.

"Something out of either *Lord of the Rings* or *Lord of the Flies*."

"Huh?"

"I don't know."

"You don't say much, but what you do say is odd as a sun-struck chicken."

"Did they get it?"

Bridger sighed. "No, 'fraid not. The kid moved too fast. Right now, I got a crowd of excited folks with guns, running around in the dark. I better go round 'em up before someone dies of lead poisoning. See you later, Judge."

My eyes adjusted, and I noticed the glint of brass where the box of shells had fallen from my coat pocket and spilled over the floor. I gathered and pocketed the loose cartridges, along with some grungy bits of debris collected in the process.

I ventured outside. Dogs from one corner of the town to the other barked in chorus. Men shouted, their voices attenuated by distance and impossible to locate. The night breeze brought a cooling draft and nothing more. The chase for the killer kid had left me far behind, and I could get no sense of direction or distance through mundane means. I checked for nearby animals and reached out to a tabby cat slipping along the sidewalk.

Hey, kitty. Did you see where the scary thing went?

Fuck you.

Cats. Go figure.

Nothing and no one else appeared to be within range. The chase for the thing—I had no ready classification, other than Gollum, which didn't feel quite right—had moved on without me, meaning the outcome was out of my control or influence. Running around in the dark in a strange town, looking for a crowd of gun-toting locals with edgy tempers, seemed unwise.

The light from the Broken Wheel's windows beckoned.

"I believe I'll have a drink."

Good idea. Getting drunk will surely improve your situation.
Shut up, brain.

The Broken Wheel proved to be everything I imagined a Western saloon should be. Here was something, at least, that matched my expectation of the Old West. A rough-hewn bar chopped from knotty pine ran along the left side. Stairs at the rear led to a second floor. A dozen tables filled the main space, many of them cluttered with abandoned glasses and suspended card games. A faro dealer spun his wheel in lazy circles—clickety-clickety-click-click... click... click—over and over again. The bartender paused in the middle of clearing a table when I stepped through the open door.

"H'ep you?"

I frowned at the empty room. "Everybody out chasing the... the killer?"

"Or in yon stockroom." The barman hoisted his chin in the direction of a closed door under the staircase. "Gawkin' at the dead'uns."

"You're keeping the bodies here?"

"Aye. Coroner's comin'." Shaved bald, with a walrus mustache to rival the mayor's, the bartender stood a shade over six-two, and heaping stacks of muscle strained his plain, collarless shirt. A tang of Scots peat bog flavored his speech. "Didna seem right to leave 'em in t'alley."

"Right. I'll have a Maker's Mark, straight up."

"Beggin' your pardon?"

"Ah, sorry." I surveyed the shelf of unlabeled bottles behind the bar. Many were filled with what I presumed was alcohol, either clear or tan in color, but without any external clue as to their contents. I fingered the coins in my pocket and tossed out a silver dollar. "Bring me whatever that will buy. If you have anything that may have at least heard of Tennessee or Kentucky, that'd be awesome."

"Aye. I'll see what I can do."

I took a seat at a clean table. The faro dealer left off spinning his wheel and started fiddling with a deck of cards, shuffling, cutting, and reshuffling. Riiippp-flutter. Riiippp-flutter.

"You'd be the judge, then?" The barkeep plonked an unlabeled bottle of rich amber liquid and a clean glass in front of me. He cocked a bushy eyebrow and extended a meaty hand. "Amos McKenzie."

"Mmm. Judge Calico Shivers."

"Aye, I know. I et me supper over t'Gerda's. She spoke of ye."

The door to the stockroom squeaked open, and a handful of subdued men—cowboys and farmers, by their clothes—trooped into the bar. They all looked a little green around the gills.

"Seen enough, boys?" McKenzie called.

"That was ghastly," a cowboy in leather chaps said. He shuddered. "Ghastly."

"Tater's neck was plumb chewed out," a frog-eyed man added. "And poor Ollie had a big chunk missing here." He demonstrated by cupping his clawed fingers against the side of his head, above his ear. "Head bashed in. I never."

"Ghastly," Chaps said again.

The returning men took their tables, and McKenzie got busy, refreshing drinks. Talk picked up, quiet and low-key. I tuned it out and addressed myself to pouring my own stiff drink. The bourbon tasted of oak and spice, not at all the backwoods corn mash I expected. I closed my eyes and recalled the still image of the thing that had jumped me inside the Bethlehem Stables. Brown as an earthworm. Dirty hair. Naked except for a loincloth. Sinewy muscles stretched over a small frame.

And shark teeth lined a bear trap mouth.

Admittedly, I had only a brief glimpse of the... creature... person... thing, but I had the distinct impression it was not something created in a lab. The thing's body looked too lived in. I didn't know. I just couldn't see it as something I brought back from the future, which created a whole other level of creepy, as I had never heard of pygmy tribes inhabiting the Southwestern US. Maybe I had been asleep when they covered that in history, but it seemed unlikely that I would miss something that odd. And where were the pygmies in the old Western movies? *Roy Rogers and the Attack of the Little Indians. Fort Lilliputian Apache.*

I dropped my borrowed flat-brimmed hat on the table and scratched my sweaty head as if I could ease the itch on the inside. I slurped a mouthful of whiskey then coughed as the liquid fire burned my esophagus. My eyes watered, and I suctioned life-giving oxygen through my open mouth. Then, proving I had no ability to learn from past mistakes, I chased the first slug with another. It appeared cauterization improved the taste. I poured another shot.

A hand touched my back, and I jerked. Only a quick reaction prevented me spilling my drink, thereby saving a nasty hole burning through the floor to the center of the Earth. The heat of a warm body and the smell of perfume, along with a gentle touch that trailed across my shoulders, stopped me from reacting with sudden and explosive violence. A girl eased into my lap with the sinuous suppleness of a boa constrictor sliding around its next meal. Dark, almond-shaped eyes regarded me from close range. Her lips were as plump as ripe berries. A mass of tumbling black hair graced the girl's bare, honey-toned shoulders. The top of her gown revealed a breathtaking amount of her apple-shaped breasts when she leaned into me.

I grunted as her weight settled onto my lap.

Her cinnamon-toast voice tickled my ear. "Hola, señor, can you help me, please?"

"Help you?" I arched an eyebrow. "I think I'm the one in trouble here."

"I have been stranded, señor," she said with a sad pout, "with no one to help me. I just have been trying to get home for so long..."

"You too?"

A tiny flicker of a frown came and went. "But the travel, it is so-o-o-o expensive."

"You can borrow my horse."

"I would—excuse me, señor, what did you say?"

"Never mind. Please continue." I shifted her to a more comfortable position. My predictable reaction to her wiggling rump made its presence felt.

"I would be so, so grateful for any act of kindness, señor." She clung to me as if I alone stood between her and a desolate end. Lustrous black hair tickled my nose. Her bottom managed to squirm against me even more insistently. "So very grateful."

"Esmeralda." McKenzie appeared at the table, hands on hips. "The judge"—he made a point of emphasizing the word—"is no rube to be conned by the likes o' you. Leave the man be, fer the love o' Christ."

"We're good," I said when the young lady stiffened. "How old are you, Esmeralda?"

Esmeralda lowered her eyes and looked at me through her lashes. Her lower lip trembled. "I... I am so very young, Señor Judge. I no have the... experiences with the men. I am so sorry to have offensed you."

I let out my first real laugh in a while. My aches and pains faded, and I felt better than I had in days. "Oh my. You're good." I patted her back. "Hop off and pull up a chair. I have a half-dollar that's all yours if you'll just sit there and look pretty for a while."

"Are you sure, now?" McKenzie said. "I'll run her off if she's a bother."

"No bother." I leaned back. "Bring another glass and one for yourself, if you'd like. I'd like to hear about the town of Geyser Falls." *And catch up on the year of 1887.*

"Of course, Your Honor. T'would be a pleasure."

The bartender left, and I spun a half-dollar across the table to Esmeralda, who made it disappear faster than any magician, real or stage, I'd ever seen. She regarded me with cat's eyes, outlined in kohl. A wicked smile touched her satiny lips. When she moved to take a seat, she half hopped, half stepped. I frowned and glanced under the table, letting out a grunt of surprise. One shoe, one wooden stump.

"A wolf, señor," Esmeralda said with such perfect sincerity that I knew she was lying. "I was lost in the woods, and a wolf ate my foot."

I sat back for a moment to allow my brain to run after the departing reality train and latch on to it. It was surreal. I was sitting in a real saloon, a six-gun tucked in my waistband, a beautiful Mexican one-legged maiden—well, not a maiden, per se—and a bottle of whiskey on the table in front of me. My own personal cowboy movie. *Eat your heart out, Gary Cooper.*

If not for the whole issue of temporal displacement, I could see Geyser Falls as a cool place to hang out and chill. Ride horses, shoot guns, mosey into saloons... Didn't every boy want to be a cowboy at some point?

Here, I had no worries. No responsibilities. No mission to accomplish. No terminally ill sister. No one I had to execute—except maybe for a few wild pygmies.

I downed a shot and let the whiskey burn my throat.

You have no magic. Don't forget that.

But maybe that wasn't such a bad thing. For six years, I had manipulated energy like I was some kind of demigod, beholden to no one and nothing but my own conscience. No law bound me, other than a loose set of rules established by old farts who claimed superiority by virtue of longer exposure to magical power. I had signed on as their enforcer almost gratefully. They had given me a mission when I needed one, a purpose.

That purpose was to kill people who needed killing. Somebody had to do the hard thing, right? It was just an extension of being a soldier, protecting the homeland from those who would harm it.

"Tell me," I said to Esmeralda, whose dark eyes had studied me while I brooded. "How did you happen to get to Geyser Falls?"

Before she could answer, the door to the saloon pounded open, and a short man with a drinker's red nose and ruddy cheeks paraded in, carrying a black bag. Given his wavy blond hair, mustache, and goatee, he was the separated-at-birth twin of General George Custer, except in a black suit instead of an arrow shirt. He stomped up to the bar and slapped it with an open palm.

"Where's the stiffs, Amos? I need to get 'em planted before the stink kills what few customers your rotgut swill hasn't already separated from this mortal coil. Although come to think of it, more dead people means more business for me. So I guess I'm in no hurry, after all. Give me a shooter of your rotgut swill to fortify me for the task ahead."

"My rotgut is better than ye deserve, Mallory," McKenzie boomed in response.

I leaned toward Esmeralda while I poured another shot. "The coroner, I presume?"

"Sí, Señor Judge. He is the undertaker too."

"Call me Calico."

The Spanish beauty smiled, and her lost-waif act evaporated. "You can call on me anytime, Señor Calico."

I laughed again and realized I felt almost... happy. And talkative. Where was all this conversational ability coming from? "Why hasn't some handsome cowboy carried you away?"

"For me to live in a bunkhouse? Or a hole in the dirt?" Esmeralda's exaggerated shudder suggested that the idea lacked appeal. She bit her lip, and her eyes took on a wicked gleam. "No, señor, I think I will wait for a man of means to rescue me from this horrible place." She made a point of looking me up and down. "A man with big, broad shoulders and curly dark hair."

"Good luck with that."

"Here's to the dead!" Mallory shouted. He knocked back his drink and clunked the empty shot glass on the bar. "Long may they rest. Now, where the fuck are they, McKenzie? The night's a-wastin' away, and the cards are calling my name."

"In the stockroom," the barman said. "You should know the way. You've slept there often enough."

"Indeed I do." The coroner-slash-undertaker picked up his bag and marched toward the stockroom door. "Let me pronounce 'em dead as the Devil's dick, and we'll get the shindig rolling."

Chapter Eleven: Off to See the Witch

The saloon doors swung open, and Sheriff Bridger trooped in, followed by a cluster of six civilians. The townsmen babbled loudly over one another, smiles all around. Bridger spotted me and altered course toward my table.

A look I couldn't read passed between Bridger and Esmeralda, and the girl slipped away in a swirl of green, stroking my arm as she departed. A rush of warmth bloomed from the place she touched and infused me with a silly sense of pleasure. She moved well on only one leg. Bridger glanced at her swaying rear end then settled into a chair opposite me. He dropped his hat onto the table and finger-combed his salty-brown hair.

McKenzie appeared at the same time as the sheriff and plonked a glass on the table. "I'll be leaving this with you, then, Archie. Hafta see to me patrons at the bar, so I shan't tarry. Maybe next time, Judge."

I poured both glasses full then capped the bottle, mentally calling a time-out on drinking. The whiskey had loosened me up more than was safe in my current situation. I forced down a strange wave of euphoria. I needed to stay sharp, focused. My dad's voice played in my head: *No time for that foolishness, son.*

"Did you get him?" I asked.

"Nope. Never saw him again." Bridger knocked back a shot, grimaced, then helped himself to the bottle. "Reports from all over town, people saying they saw the kid, but nothing solid."

I stifled a yawn. "Is there a hotel open around here?"

"The Bannerworth. Over on Sixth Street. I have a room there, on the top floor."

"I'll go see this witch of yours, then I'm hitting the rack."

Bridger tilted his head and studied me through narrowed eyes. "I have to say—no offense intended—you are the strangest damn judge I ever met. You stepped right into that barn like you done it every day. I've seen men, salty as a cracker, who would've shit their drawers when that little terror come out the wagon. Shit their drawers, and all."

What am I supposed to say to that? I tilted my head in a slight nod.

"And then there's this thing with you being quarter-this and quarter-that." Bridger raised his hands, palms out. "Again, no offense intended. I like my dick where it is. Right where it is." The sheriff knocked back another shot. "In my experience," he said, obviously choosing his words with care, "only men of... a certain fairness of skin make it to the bar examination, let alone the bench."

"Is there a question in there?"

"No. No, not really. More like... an observation. An observation." Bridger squinted at me through one eye, as though lining up a gun sight. "There's more to you than you're lettin' on, Judge Calico Shivers. Uh-huh. Don't know what, but something."

My chair screeched as I stood. "Right. Good talk, Bridger."

I waved to the barkeep on the way out. McKenzie lifted his chin in response, his attention being claimed by the crowd at the bar, telling and retelling how they'd chased the Monster of Geyser Falls. The sound of their happy voices faded as I pushed through the door.

I oriented on the jail and set off. Time to see this witch for myself. McKenzie must have packed a big wallop of kick ass in his whiskey, as I wobbled on jelly legs for a couple of steps. I shook my head to clear the cobwebs. I smelled faintly of Esmeralda's scent. The old Eagles song "Witchy Woman" sprang to mind when I thought of the Latina beauty.

"Spanish hair and swaying hips," I crooned. "While walking on her wooden tip. Sultry accent, full of fight. She's a wanton temptress... and I'm high as a kite. Wooo-hoooo, witchy woman."

From somewhere, a dog howled.

I quieted the singing and concentrated on walking a straight line.

My sad little pony, Misery, remained tied at the rail in front of the sheriff's office. Guilt snuck up and stabbed me in the chest. The horse had been standing there for well over an hour, actually closer to two, still saddled and without food or water. And I didn't need the horse's accusatory mental image—a pile of dried horse bones bleaching in the sun—to remind me that I needed to care for the animal.

"Let's go to the stable," I told Misery. "At least you'll have the place all to yourself."

Alone again.

Naturally.

I was dragging ass by the time I saw to the buckskin's stabling and returned to the jail. I slumped under the weight of the judge's saddlebags, and yawns kept forcing their way up from the place where yawns were born. The town appeared to be rolling up for bed. Very few people remained on the streets, and businesses were shuttered. Even the dogs had settled to only rare outbreaks of barking. The crescent moon touched the mountain peaks to the east, and a cool breeze rolled down the valley.

I found the lower floor of the sheriff's office deserted and the door unlocked. I dropped my saddlebags, crossed the plank floor, and opened the door to the staircase leading to the second story. At the top of the dark tunnel, a dim yellow light flickered.

"Hello?"

"Yo?" a man's voice called out.

"Deputy, ah, Barton?" I clomped up the stairs, trailing one hand on the wall. My head felt stuffed with cotton. "Judge Shivers coming up."

"Come ahead."

Barton turned out to be one of the ugliest men I had seen in my life. The Rancor had been prettier. The jailer's round face, scarred by some dread disease, had a lopsided, out-of-kilter appearance. Between the gourd-shaped nose and the V-neck of his plaid shirt, the deputy sported a mat of dense facial hair. The first word that popped into my mind was "troll."

"You ever meet a guy named Birnbaum?"

"Huh?"

"Never mind."

Barton occupied a single chair at the end of a wide hall, cradling a shotgun in his lap. A row of three cells lined the wall on the right. The only light came from an oil lantern hanging near Barton's head.

"Where's the woman?"

"Right here, right here, Your Honor." Barton scrambled up, bumping the lantern with his head and making it sway. "In here."

"In here" turned out to be the last cell in the row, a six-by-twelve box with three stone walls, fronted by bars and with high, narrow windows open to the elements. On the narrow cot, a small form huddled under a blanket. A strong odor of urine and unwashed human punched me in the nose and watered my eyes.

"Gah. Is that you or her?"

"What, Your Honor?"

"Forget it. Open the door and go get a cup of coffee. I need to question the prisoner in private."

Barton hesitated. He shifted from foot to foot and glanced from the prisoner to me and back. "Ah, yes, sir. What—why do you—"

"Go on, Deputy," I said in my command voice.

He nodded and jangled the keys loose from his belt. He unlocked the cell and nodded again. "I'll be just downstairs, then," Barton said, though he remained in place, clearly reluctant to leave.

"Go. I'll be fine."

"Not you I'm worried about."

He's being chivalrous, you ass. I took a breath and modulated my tone. "I mean the woman no harm. I just need a few minutes."

Barton dry-sniffed and glanced around as if he'd forgotten something. "All right, then." He walked away.

I plucked up the deputy's vacated chair and the lantern and carried both into the cell. The smell inside the tight space was stronger, answering the question of who stank worse. The woman on the bed sat up when I entered, and I got my first good look at her. Her face was puffy from drugged sleep, and a bad case of bedhead spiked her hair on one side.

I laughed for the third time in one night, setting some kind of laughter record for me. "*You're* the Terror of Geyser Falls? You're not big enough for the kiddie rides at Six Flags."

The woman's hooded eyes examined me. Her confusion showed on her face. "Who are you?"

"Let me ask you a question first: When were you born?"

"I—what? What did you say?" Her voice came sluggishly, her words slow. She had obviously not shaken off the laudanum or whatever the medieval quack had dosed her with.

"If I had to guess by the blue-dyed streaks in your hair, the Mickey Mouse tattoo on your neck, and the red dots from old piercings in your earlobes, I'd say you were recently a Magical from Columbus, Ohio, who reported a wizard named Dustin Birnbaum to the frogdicked Admins for further investigation. If I remember the case file correctly, your name is, um, Lillith Kathryn Krawczyk?"

"I…" She blinked and scrubbed her hair. "Yeah, that's me. Who… How did you…"

"Judge Calico Shivers." I settled back in the chair. "I, ah, caught up with Birnbaum, and… it apparently didn't go well."

"A judge? A Magical Judge? Oh, that's… great. Welcome to the Dark Ages, Your Honor. Call me Kat," she said through a yawn. "Man, I'm out of it."

Kat Krawczyk could easily have played Peter Pan on stage. I guessed her at a ham sandwich under five feet tall, with cropped blue hair and tiny facial features. On the other side of her neck, another tattoo rose above the collar of her shirt and curled below her jaw-line—either a dragon's wing or a butterfly, I wasn't sure which. She wore a man's shirt, and her bare feet poked from the rolled-up cuffs of denim jeans. There was a pair of clodhopper shoes under the bed.

"How're they treating you?" I asked.

"Ermal's okay." Krawczyk palmed one eye and stretched. "Potts likes to watch when I pee. I think he came in here and was doing stuff after they drugged me, but Ermal shooed him off. It's all hazy."

"Ermal?"

"Barton. Ermal Barton."

"And the sheriff?"

Krawczyk's gaze sharpened for a moment. "His aura is bad. A lot of negative energy around him. All smiley-smiley, then wham! Hit me on the back of the head when I wasn't looking. Been doping me ever since." Her eyelids drooped again. "Can't concentrate long enough to magic the dope out of my system." Her jaws cracked wide in another yawn, keying the same from me.

"'Magic the dope out'? Are you a healer?"

"Uh-huh."

Healers were rare and tended to hide their gift, lest they be mobbed by sick and dying people. I would have long since grabbed one and threatened murder until they healed my sister, but, one, the Admins forbade healers from curing mundane people, lest they expose the Magical community to scrutiny. Two, I had never run across one with skill sufficient enough that I would trust my sister's life to their care. If Krawczyk... *No, best table that thought for now. More pressing problems.*

I rubbed my gritty eyes. "Sit tight. I'll be back in the morning."

"That'd be... nice," Krawczyk murmured. Already, she was fading, sinking onto the cot and closing her eyes. In seconds, deep breathing signified that sleep had claimed her.

I rubbed my face and forced my sluggish brain to engage. First, Kat Krawczyk found and reported Birnbaum then got zapped back to the past. Then the little snotball punted me, the mighty Judge Shivers, to the same time and nearly the same place. Birnbaum may or may not have sent some of his toys back to 1887, just to cause a ruckus or to chase down his two least-favorite Magicals. I had strong doubts, but whatever the case, I was way too tired to figure out an answer that night.

I covered the sleeping woman with the blanket and left.

Chapter Twelve: Monster Blood by Moonlight

I only half listened to Barton's directions to the Bannerworth Hotel. As a consequence, I got lost. Hey, at least I asked for directions.

I hummed "Horse with no Name," the song by America, as I wandered from street to street to alley and back to street. I even sang a few bars, keeping it low and quiet so I wouldn't upset the dogs. Singing at a whisper was a habit ingrained in my teen years, since my father hadn't been a fan of music in general and found his son's interest in it particularly irksome—"Shut the fuck up and focus, John." He also thought the name Calico was frivolous and refused to use it. My mother gave me that half of my name, and he never let me forget it.

Very few lights remained on, and those were invariably inside the buildings, not out on the street where signposts might be revealed so lost strangers could be spared a walking tour of the town. Not that there were any signposts either.

"Oh, come on," I said after the third road I tried ended at the river. "This place ain't that big!"

I tried going north for a time and was rewarded by a store sign: First Street Butcher Shop. If logic held, Sixth Street would be five blocks farther north, perpendicular to the river. Down by the water, a cool breeze blew, so I charted a course upstream. I skirted the edge of town, walking along a sandy, weedy strip between the riverbank and where the buildings petered out.

The crescent moon rode high overhead, so bright that looking at it almost hurt. Night birds called over the river's rush, and bats darted and dipped over the silvery water. Frogs by the dozens added their chirrups and grunts. Jangly notes from a piano—played with zest if not talent—added a zip-a-dee-doo-dah counterpoint to my low-voiced destruction of the classic song about riding through the desert on a nameless horse. Shadows pooled in places the moon couldn't reach, and darkness in those sheltered niches congealed, flowed, and merged as though composed of liquid ink rather than a lack of light.

In honor of my mighty steed, I changed the lyrics on the fly. "I've been through the desert on a horse that's so lame, made me want to put him out of his pain."

I passed an alley between Fourth and Fifth Street. It reeked of outhouses and rancid trash, which I was finding pretty typical of alleys in the nineteenth century. With only one town to go by, I admit it was a small sample size, but still...

A shadow detached from the alley. A figure groped from the darkness and wrapped its arms around me. My overactive imagination, combined with my sludgy, overtired thought process, threw up an image of a zombie about to eat my face. I grabbed magic and threw a punch of kinetic energy at my assailant. As punches went, it ranked in the lightweight division—more of a sharp jab than a Rocky Balboa body shot. Nevertheless, the zombie sailed backward and thunked into the side of a single-story building on Fifth Street, rattling windows and setting off a small dust storm.

The zombie said, "Ugh."

I had the Colt in hand, hammer back, ready to blow zombie brains all over the wall. My index finger squeezed the trigg—

"Wait. What?" I stopped squeezing. I imagined the sear engaging the hammer and preventing it from striking by the pressure of a fly fart. "What did you say?"

"Oh, hell. That hurts," the creature replied in a wheezing slur.

I decocked my pistol and edged closer to the groaning figure in the dirt. Using a dry twig as a match, I kindled a little magic and lit the end. Feeble light showed a man in the advanced stages of alcohol abuse—bird-nest hair, whiskers, and a hodge-podge of clothes. The fumes wafting off him warned me to blow out the flame so I didn't immolate the geezer.

"You all right, old-timer?" I checked the man's pulse, made sure all the drunk's fingers and toes responded per specification, then helped him sit up.

Bleary eyes peered at me from under scraggly brows then slid away, unfocused. "Who're you? Wha' happen'?"

"A little misunderstanding."

"Oh. Okay." The man's wandering gaze tracked back to meet mine. "Hey, can you he'p outta vet'ran?"

I fished out a quarter. "You're sure nothing's broken?"

The drunk assured me he'd be right as rain, as soon as he bought some "medicine."

I moved on, shaking my head in disgust at myself. I was burning through magic as if I had an endless surplus. The energy source here was limited, and as I'd already proven to myself, I had gotten soft as my dependence on magic had grown. It was time to kill that bad habit and get back to the old-fashioned way of doing things—in other words, manually inflicting bodily harm and mayhem.

I rounded the corner on what I hoped was Sixth Street and headed east, into a much nicer part of town from the dirt-and-spit hovels I had passed earlier. Two-story houses in post-Colonial or Victorian style lined the street—bulky things with columns and wraparound porches and gabled windows. Lights shone from behind windows, and people rocked on porch swings, enjoying the evening air. No one waved as I passed, which pleased me just fine.

Forty yards ahead of me, a man in a business suit passed through a spill of light from somebody's parlor. I twitched at the man's sudden appearance, until I figured out the guy was no threat, merely someone walking in the same direction. I'd missed him earlier due to the darkness, as he only revealed himself when he passed through the light. I noted the bowler hat and round body, thinking I had found Stokely Bunting. But no, this man was thinner and slightly taller than the mayor of Geyser Falls.

Houses gave way to a more mercantile area made up of small shops fronted by a boardwalk. I stayed in the middle of the street—better to have dusty boots than blow up some innocent farmer because he happened to bolt out of an alley at the wrong moment. I moved aside for a late-working teamster driving a four-horse hitched wagon, who said something neighborly I didn't catch and didn't care about anyway.

And you wonder why people don't like you.

Shut up.

At a crossroad, a rare street sign confirmed I was on Sixth. All that remained was to locate the elusive Bannerworth and find a bed for the night. Would they have a bath? Or would that be asking too much? How about a shower? One thing was for sure: if I was stuck there for any length of time, I was inventing indoor plumbing and air-conditioning. Maybe I would go to Texas and hunt for oil or invest in a start-up company run by Alexander Bell or Henry Ford. Being from the future wasn't all bad. At least I would know not to hitch a ride on the *Hindenburg* or the *Titanic.*

I closed the distance to the businessman walking ahead of me. The fellow opted for the boardwalk over the street, and his footsteps bonked along in a steady cadence. Too irregular a beat to set to lyrics, though. He stepped off the end of the boardwalk and crossed in front of an alley—

Something lunged from the shadows and snagged the businessman by the suit. A small gang of somethings.

"Ack!" the man squawked as he disappeared into the darkness.

I gaped, making noises like "hah, huh, whuh?" before my whiskey-soaked instincts kicked in, and I sprinted to the mouth of the alley. I froze at the black tunnel between the buildings, reached for magic, and found only a sip left in the bottom of the cup. Not enough to do any fancy hocus-pocus.

A grizzly crackling sound rolled out of the dark. A choked gurgle followed. I hesitated, eyes straining. My night vision had been ruined by the pool of light in the street, and only shades of black loomed ahead.

Light. I needed light. A match wouldn't do. I needed—*there.*

A stick.

A thin, triangular piece of a boardwalk step had cracked loose. I snapped it free with a quick tug. Bracing myself, I cocked the Colt revolver and tossed the broken piece of board into the darkness. At the height of its arc, I reached out and hit the wood with a blast of superheat. The chunk burst into flames. Like a torch, the fiery board turned end over end, arcing in a burning parabola.

A gaunt, grisly thing crouched over the neck of the businessman, holding a knife black with blood. Other figures scuttled away from the light. The remaining... thing looked the same as the one who'd attacked me in the stables. The scrambling forms of his pals looked much the same. *What the ever-loving fuckitude is this? A whole gang of Gollums?*

The businessman jerked spasmodically, heels kicking in death.

The size of a young boy, the pygmy had flat, dead eyes, lit with an inner glow. Mouthful of jagged teeth. Same expression of malevolent hatred as the thing that jumped on me from the wagon. In the moment before the fiery board hit the dust, the monster's internally fired eyes fixed on me with a look of malice so powerful that it rocked me. I lined up the Colt's front sight and squeezed. A stream of fire blazed from the muzzle. The gun bucked, and I rode the recoil to thumb back the hammer. I chased the first shot with a second. Powder smoke fogged the air. I had forgotten how much black powder smoked.

The last flicker of fire from the kindling I had thrown guttered out to a single ember.

Ears ringing, eyes dazzled from muzzle blast, I cocked the Colt and squinted. No way did I plan to race into a black-as-a-mineshaft alley and tackle a goblin horde with only a six-shooter and my Wilson. I braced for an attack, expecting to see a leathery-skinned monster rushing me from the darkness. A second passed. Then a few more. I let out a breath and waited. Shouts and running footsteps added to the clamor of my pounding heart.

"What is it? What happened?" The first man to reach me held a Smith & Wesson breakover revolver. His muttonchop sideburns came together to form a mustache.

"Something attacked a man," I said. "Watch my back."

I edged forward, twisting my head to use the better light receptors in my peripheral vision. A shadowy form lay on the ground. I knelt and confirmed it was the cooling body of the businessman in the bowler hat. I wrinkled my nose at the raw-iron stink of fresh blood. The creatures were gone.

I had missed, or my shots hadn't been enough to bring it down.

More citizens pounded up to the alley mouth. Some brought lanterns, and one even had a by-God-actual flaming torch. Voices were raised in anger and not a little fear.

"Great jumpin' Jesus." The man with the Smith had followed me down the alley. "Did you do that?"

"No. It was the same thing that killed Ollie Dunleavy and Tater Grissom. Bring a light over here!" I shouted to the crowd.

Several folks came forward, and the shadows retreated. The light revealed the businessman lying in a lake of blood, a ragged chunk torn from the flesh under his jaw. Glassy eyes stared at the night sky. I grabbed the nearest lantern and held it close to the ground. Outside of the blood pool, which even soaked into the dust, spatters of liquid beaded the dirt like so many scattered black pearls. The onyx fluid sprayed out in a fan, suggestive of the blood splatter from a bullet wound.

"I hit it at least once," I said. Stepping around the crimson mud, I held the lantern low and walked in a crouch, like a man in a tunnel, studying the ground. A trail of opalescent drops led away from the scene. "It's wounded and running away."

"What are you looking at?" said Muttonchop. "What's that black stuff?"

"Monster blood." I stood and addressed the crowd. "One of you, go get the coroner. What's his name? Mallory? Somebody go find Bridger, or his deputies. The rest of you, come with me."

I hadn't taken two steps when a woman's scream reverberated down the alley from the direction the creatures had fled.

Chapter Thirteen: A Merilee We Will Go

I dashed through the alley and into the avenue beyond, a half-dozen armed men at my back. I stopped, and my posse surged around me, churning dust as I scanned the street. Nothing. Shuttered businesses and no activity. The townsmen with me seemed equally at a loss.

"Where did that—" I started.

A second scream split the night.

"Next one over!" someone shouted.

I was already moving. I ran through yet another alley. A pile of trash appeared at my feet, half seen in the darkness—I leaped it more by instinct than skill. Some of my companions weren't as lucky. Crashing and cursing echoed behind me. The lanterns bobbed and wobbled in confusion, splashing the alley with pulsating blooms of yellow light. My jittery, elongated shadow capered ahead of me.

I thundered at full gallop into the next street. It should have been Eighth Street, if logic applied to Geyser Falls's numbering system.

Twenty yards to my left, on the other side of the road, a woman's petticoats and fashionable shoes disappeared in the narrow gap between a drugstore and a cobbler. Her small feet drummed a tattoo in the dirt. Judging by the volume of her curses, she appeared to be putting up a good fight.

"This way!" I yelled and raced to the gap where I'd last seen the woman's feet then barreled around the corner.

Light from a second-floor window revealed a vegetable garden packed into a fenced yard behind the two buildings. Not one but three of the small people, along with their scrabbling, kicking victim, had torn through a trellis of runner beans. They plowed a crosscut ditch across neat rows of squash and tomato vines.

"Hey!" I yelled. "I've had enough of this shit for one night. Drop the woman and come die like good little monsters."

The ropey-muscled things stopped dragging the woman. She twisted free with a rip of cloth and rolled away, crashing through another dozen tomato plants. I stalked closer, keeping my gun ready and my attention fixed on the creatures. The posse arrived and fanned out behind me, all dust and raised voices, bringing more light and a better look at the vaguely manlike beings.

A gaggle of Gollums. Sméagol and his twin brothers.

"Holy God," one man sputtered. "What are they?"

The Gollums glared at the line of men who fanned out to either side. One of the three trailed blood from a split scalp. Leaves and bits of debris clung to its slick, damp skin.

"I've never seen…" said the lantern carrier.

The trio of goblins growled and backed away while the woman clawed through the vines, struggling with a pile of skirts and petticoats to get upright.

"Hold your fire," I ordered. "Let the lady get clear."

The lady in question marched to stand next to me, holding her torn blouse up with one hand. She pushed her tangled hair back and said, "When you gentlemen are quite through dithering, please feel free to shoot the ever-loving holy hell out of those… those things."

I blinked. "Are you all right?"

Her off hand moved, and I could have sworn she tucked a stiletto into a skirt pocket. The woman sniffed and swiped dirt across her forehead with a sleeve. "Quite fine now, thank you, sir."

"All right, boys," said Muttonchop, who'd come up on my right. "You heard the lady. Let's get to killin.'"

Guns rattled as levers were cranked and hammers cocked. The woman gathered her skirts and stalked off.

The Gollums had backed away, their heels almost touching the fence. There was no way out. High fences surrounded the yard on three sides, and a line of men with guns held the fourth. We had the things trapped. An old saw about cornered animals came to mind. Trapped might be the last place we wanted them.

Except the Gollums apparently had clawed fingers and toes and could climb like Spiderman. Before I could aim and fire the Colt, the three creatures sprang high, twisted and scrabbled over the fence in a scurry of brown limbs. A couple of poorly aimed shots barked wood, but nobody managed to come close. In an instant, the little monsters were gone, leaving nothing behind but their rancid smell, a piquant bouquet akin to unwashed armpits and unwiped asses.

"Huh," I grunted. "I'll be damned."

"Are you injured?" I asked the woman when I caught up to her. The wild mass of her brunette tresses swished when she shook her head—and yes, I said tresses. Calling the wavy waterfall that reached the middle of the woman's back "hair" would be like saying Stevie Nicks was a gal who could sing.

"No, thank you, sir. Some bumps and bruises." She slanted a look at me. "To whom do I owe my rescue?"

I noticed that while sliding the dirk into her stocking, she had also sheathed her London-based, grimy-coal Cockney accent and replaced it with a more refined, upper-crust, so-glad-you-could-come manner of speech.

"Shivers. Judge Calico Shivers."

"Gerda mentioned we had a new judge. She didn't mention... Ah..." She paused as if to add something then reconsidered and held it back.

"Gerda gets around," I noted. "And you are?"

"Merilee Soames," she said.

We walked on the dusty road side by side, in an odd parody of a strolling couple: she held a pledge-of-allegiance pose to keep her torn blouse from falling open while I reloaded my pistol and watched the shadows. Merilee Soames held herself upright, eyes straight ahead. She appeared remarkably composed for having been attacked and dragged toward a certain death by a nightmare come to life.

I was to the point of asking if the name started with a Mrs. or a Miss when she preempted my question.

"What were those things?" A tremble in her voice revealed Miss Soames wasn't as cool as she'd have me believe. The top of her head came to about nose level, putting her at above-average tall, with a slender waist and an impressive bust, which she failed to conceal behind a neck-high blouse that was torn from shoulder to waist, revealing a scandalous amount of bare flesh, no matter how hard she worked to keep the flap closed.

I dragged my eyes away with an effort. "I don't think they have a name," I said. "If I had to guess, I'd call them Gollums."

"A golem? As in Jewish folklore?"

"Um, I suppose. If Tolkien was Jewish."

"Excuse me?"

"Never mind. Where are you headed?"

"The Bannerworth."

"Me too," I said. "Are you a guest there?"

"No, I own the place." Merilee cast me a wary look, as though waiting for a comment. A few steps later, she added, "Though more accurately, I work there in servitude to the mortgage."

We reached the hotel steps moments later. A broad light shining from its windows revealed that Merilee had suffered some bumps. A split lip puffed up the corner of her mouth, and her chin had a bad case of road rash. A dirty hand held up her blouse, the nails chipped and scratched. With all that, she walked tall and kept her chin up. Nice poise. Effortless grace. Rolling hips.

Just the right-sized hips for a two-handed grip.

Stop that, dick.

It was not until we reached the top of the stairs that I noticed a broad-shouldered man in a three-piece black suit. His bony, angular face was half-masked with a black chin beard, no mustache, resembling a young Abe Lincoln in a round-brimmed hat.

I hitched my chin by way of greeting. Thought I'd try my Western lingo on him. "Howdy, partner."

"You bastard! What have you done to this good woman?"

"Huh?"

The Abe lookalike stalked forward, fists clenched. "Damn your kind. You're all the same!"

I glanced at Merilee, who seemed as thunderstruck as I. "What the hell are you—"

A bony fist obliterated my vision. There came a moment of weightless flight before my back hit the dirt with a bone-rattling thump. Sight and sound seemed as if from a distant planet, crude signals full of static.

My cognitive processes wandered into the twilight zone, lay down, and took a nap.

The acrid stench of ammonia burned my sinuses, penetrated my foggy dreams, and jerked me back from la-la land. My eyes snapped open to the face of a middle-aged man with slicked-down hair. Basset hounds looked happier than this guy. When he saw I was awake, he skinned on a mask of mild interest, the type of expression worn by doctors everywhere.

"Ugh." I waved away the bottle under my nose. "What happened? Where am I? Who're you?"

"To answer your second question first, in a hotel room, Judge Shivers." The man I presumed to be a physician straightened and crossed the room to a black case on the nightstand, capping the brown bottle. "As to the first, you took a nasty knock on the head following a solid right cross to the orbital bone of your left eye. As to your last, I'm Doctor Halperin. James Halperin."

I surveyed the room. The yellow light of an oil lantern revealed an iron-framed bed with stiff, scratchy sheets and a musty quilt. A water pitcher, covered by a weighted lace doily, waited atop an antique dresser. White curtains curled in the breeze, revealing the darkness of night beyond. My coat, pants, and other gear lay piled on a chair near the bed.

The dull ache in my face demanded attention. I touched my cheek and hissed.

"You'll have quite a shiner." Halperin brought the lamp over to the bed and held it close to my face, moving it back and forth and examining my eyes. "But both pupils seem to be reacting normally. What do you remember?"

"Abe Lincoln sucker punched me. Asshole."

"Your memory seems a bit displaced, though your judge of character is spot on. You were struck by the Reverend Weeks, not a dead president." Halperin set the lamp down and cradled my head with probing fingers. "Does it hurt when I do this?"

"Ow!"

"I'll take that as a yes. Hold still, as this will definitely sting a bit." The doctor felt along the bones of my left eye, ignoring my butt cheeks walking across the bed to get away. "Nothing broken, I believe."

"You're quite the sadist, aren't you?"

"You should see how I treat men with the clap."

"Is Miss Soames all right?"

"Fine, fine, fine. I believe *Missus* Soames reprimanded the reverend quite forcefully." Halperin grinned. "The lady has quite the temper when provoked and a command of some very colorful idioms." The doctor pulled up the room's only chair and sat next to the bed. "Now. Tell me about the late Mr. Mulligan and his attackers."

"Mulligan?"

"The man killed in the alley tonight."

"Oh." I related the things I knew, leaving out everything about Birnbaum and his chemistry set from the future, which made for a short story. I ended it with "The last I saw, the pygmies were headed over the fence."

A light tap at the door stalled Halperin's response. From the hall, Merilee Soames asked, "Is everybody decent?"

The tired line "no, but I'm dressed" crossed my mind. "Yes, come in."

In the time since I'd last seen her, Merilee had washed up, changed clothes, tamed her wild hair with a brush, and pinned it up. The fierce lady tiger who fought the Gollum's attack was now hidden behind a schoolmarm's look of cool objectivity. She paused in the doorway, clasping her hands in front of her.

"How is he, Doctor?"

Halperin stood and offered a small bow. "He's fine, madam, or will be once the swelling goes down. I would advise a cool compress for the eye and bed rest for the bump to the head." He checked me with raised eyebrows. "I have some medication to help you sleep, if you'd like."

Since any sleep medication the doctor suggested would un-doubtedly contain opium, I declined.

"Well, then." Halperin grabbed his bag and snapped it closed. "I'm off to take a look at Mr. Mulligan. Perhaps a postmortem will reveal more details of his killers."

I grunted a thank-you.

The doctor nodded, snagged his hat off the bedpost, and said his goodbyes. Merilee stepped into the room but left the door open. Of course it would have been improper to be alone in a man's bedroom, no matter his condition. People would talk, after all. I pulled the quilt up to my chin and kept my expression neutral, fighting my twenty-first century sensibilities.

"Mrs. Soames, I intended to rent a room but not to check in quite like this."

She glided to the foot of my bed. "Do not concern yourself, sir. It's the least I could do, after your poor treatment by Jonathan—ah, Mr. Weeks, I mean."

"Mr. Weeks was the asshole on the porch, right?"

Merilee stiffened. "Breakfast service begins at seven. Just downstairs. Good night, sir." With a brittle, professional smile, the hotel owner swept from the room, closing the door as she went.

Wow. Stepped in it there, didn't you?

I touched my eye gingerly and winced.

Damn your kind. You're all the same! Weeks had said right before he punched me. *Your kind.* My nose was straight, lips average, and hair curly but not kinky. My skin tone was no darker than a Latino's or a well-tanned surfer's, yet the sheriff and the reverend had me slotted into a racially inferior category at first glance. Except for EEOC check boxes and the odd crank racist fuck, I had rarely given my mixed heritage more than a passing thought. Here, I was *your kind*.

My mother thought Calico a name that suited me—a cat of many colors. She'd defied Old Hardass to stick me with it. Calico John. She'd loved that name.

My father called me John.

A thought pulled me up short: my mother wouldn't be born for another seventy-two years, in a county hospital in Lawton, Oklahoma, daughter to a Cherokee woman and a Black corporal from Fort Sill. Dead forty-three years later. Done in by streptococcus, which she contracted in a different hospital while staying overnight for a mild case of pneumonia.

Killed by damned strep throat.

When I was thirteen years old, the day after my mother's funeral, my Chinese-Irish dad said to me, "Your mom's gone, John. Time to stop being a fuckup. Focus on your future, define your goals, and realize your full potential."

"Well hey, Dad," I said to the empty room. "No job, trapped in the past. No magic, wrong color, no money, no friends, and no mission. How's that for a life achievement?"

I turned out the lamp, rolled over, and went to sleep.

Chapter Fourteen: Colleeta and the Wolf

An hour after first light, Colleeta Fae Dalrymple tossed the last of the breakfast slop to the farm dogs. She stretched her back, and it crackled like a fresh pine log thrown on the fire. Colleeta meandered across the yard to the cottonwood in front of their three-room farmhouse and settled on the cutting block Mr. Dalrymple used to split fire logs. Resting her bones, Colleeta ruminated long and hard and in great detail about the strips she planned to tear off her lazy husband when he came moseying back from wherever he'd gotten to.

Colleeta shaded her eyes, more from habit than need, and studied the trails leading to Geyser Falls, which lay several miles down the valley. Low-hanging clouds shrouded the mountaintops, and long shadows extended away from every bump in the terrain. The Dalrymple homestead covered forty acres, abutting a steadily running creek in the foothills of the Inyos, and their front yard commanded a good view down into the Owens Valley. Anyone coming up the road from Geyser Falls could be seen a ways off, and she kept expecting to see the lanky form of Mr. Do-it-when-I-please Dalrymple.

But no. The road remained stubbornly empty of traffic, as it had for the past two days. Mr. Dalrymple had hared off after a chicken-stealing coyote, rifle in hand, and she hadn't seen a lick of him since. Likely the man had snuck off to town for a jolt of Who Hit John and a game of cards down at Murphy's Saloon. She half expected him to come slinking up the road with his rifle in one hand and a hangover in the other. Colleeta gritted her teeth at the thought. Every hour he stayed away added another chapter to the book of hurt she planned to beat him with.

She quashed the worry pecking her heart. "It aren't like him to be gone this long," she muttered aloud.

Marcus and Anthony raced through the yard, which set the hens to squawking and clucking. The boys took after their father when it came to chores, which meant they treated breaking a sweat the way they would opening a barrel of snakes.

"Marcus," she snapped at her oldest, "water the mules and get 'em hitched up. I'm a-gonna take the wagon to town, see if I can't find your daddy. If I have to pour that man out of a bottle—"

Already, Marcus, at fourteen summers, stood taller than any doorframe built—the boy was constantly bruised on his forehead—and had feet too big for any Montgomery Ward's shoes ever made. Though not the brightest lamp in the dark, the boy had a natural, easy way with animals. The youngest, Anthony, looked more like a stick drawing than a human, skinnier than a body ought to be. Both boys towered over their momma, which truthfully didn't require a great deal of trying. Most folks agreed Colleeta could walk upright under a cat's nose and not tickle a whisker.

"You think he got that coyote?" Anthony asked.

"It weren't a coyote, pissant!" Marcus swatted his brother on the head with his hat. "Daddy said it had feet like a damn Injun kid."

"Watch your mouth, boy," Colleeta warned. "Or I'll take a willow switch to your backside, you hear? Anthony, go get some of them peach preserves out of the root cellar. I promised Reverend Weeks I'd deliver him some special, and his camp's on the way to town."

"Yes'm." Her youngest dashed off to the house.

Colleeta dried her hands and went to draw some water to wash up. She'd have to change into her go-to-town dress and pinch her feet into her Sunday shoes. Driving the wagon ten miles to town would get her all dusty and sweaty, and by the time she reached Geyser Falls, it wouldn't make a pickle's worth of difference what she wore—everything would wind up looking like it belonged on a scarecrow instead of a person. But appearances were important.

"Damn you, Mr. Dalrymple," she said then looked around to see if her boys had overheard. "I find you, you're gonna wish that coyote et you right up."

Colleeta went into the house, washed her face from her bucket of fresh well water, changed her dress, and knotted the tie on her good bonnet. She stepped out onto the porch and found three jars of peach preserves next to the door. She picked them up and tucked them into a canvas poke. Both boys had vanished, which was not surprising, as she had a list of chores longer than the Book of Genesis, and they had a knack for avoidance of labor akin to miraculous.

More to the point, no mule-hitched wagon awaited her.

"Marrr-*cus*!" Colleeta could pitch her voice to carry into the hills and start a rockslide. She waited, listening to the quiet. Hens bobbed around the patchy yard, gossiping and pecking. A passing cloud provided a moment of shade while cicadas sang and a mockingbird carried on as if delivering a sermon.

"Where the hell—heck has that boy got to?" Colleeta shaded her eyes with a hand and turned a slow circle. It was as if the Earth had swallowed up all the people, leaving her alone with her clucking hens. "Anthony! Marcus! Where are you?"

No answer.

Colleeta gritted her teeth and set off for the barn. "Them boys think they've gotten too big for a whipping. I find them lollygagging around, I'm gonna cut me the biggest willow switch I can find..." She crossed into the dark interior of the barn, stomped down the center aisle, and stopped.

Anthony slumped against Betty's stall, sitting with his legs straight out. Somehow, he'd managed to splash his chest and belly with a bucket of red paint. Had the bucket hit him on the head and knocked him cold? Anger mixed with worry, and Colleeta ran to her youngest.

"Anthony, I swear if you've gone and—"

The smell of raw guts and iron blood stopped her cold. The paint covering Anthony's shirtfront wasn't paint at all. A hideous, gaping hole in his throat dripped blood into the soggy mess on his middle. The mule, Betty, was down as well, milky-eyed and with her tongue flopped out.

A sound to her left dragged her eyes to Sally's stall. Crouched over Marcus's twitching body, a tiny little Indian with a stone knife glared at her. Two eyes as sulfurous as a demon's raised from a fiery pit in the deepest level of hell burned from beneath shaggy brows. Just a skinny thing, wearing naught but a scrap of cloth around his privates, but packed with such evil intent—he fairly seethed with it.

The Injun sprang at her.

Colleeta cracked the thing across the head with her poke sack. Glass crunched. The Injun sagged and dropped to his knees, and Colleeta bolted for the barn door then skidded to a halt.

In front of the door, blocking it with countless bodies, an entire tribe of midget Injuns gathered. Some had little-bitty bows and arrows, some had knives, and some others had clubs. All of them had a hateful expression, and their eyes seemed to glitter with demon fire. More appeared at the edge of the loft, and others crept from stalls and out of the bales of hay stacked in the back.

Colleeta was fair surrounded by people no taller than her bosom, which meant they were pretty damn short indeed. But there were dozens of them. And when they came at her, Colleeta fell to her knees and sent up the fastest prayer she could manage.

The Injuns fell upon her, stabbing with their spears.

She smelled peaches and then... nothing.

I followed the smell of bacon and the sound of clanking cutlery to the dining room attached to the Bannerworth lobby. The breakfast crowd filled the modest room's twenty tables nearly to capacity. I hustled between the tables and cut off two well-dressed banker types, beating them to an open table by the window. I smiled sweetly at their glares.

Merilee Soames flashed me a professional smile from across the room but continued on her way to the kitchen with a tray full of dirty dishes. She was flushed, with a lock of curly hair bouncing over her brow, and more curls had sprung loose at the nape of her neck. Her magnificent bosom caught my eye, and I allowed for a moment of pure appreciation. Although many of my fellow men belonged to the Bigger is Better Club when it came to a woman's breasts, I believed in a total-package approach and preferred women with a good mix of characteristics, body and mind. My gaze dropped to Merilee's hips as she swayed through the restaurant and lingered there long enough for an indecent thought to take hold.

I looked away with an effort. The work had been heavy lately, and I had had very little time for dating. When I did manage to connect, it had rarely gone well.

"What do you do for a living?"

"I hunt magical people and kill them. But only bad magical people."

"Uh-huh. Uber, please."

That left things like Tinder and other apps for quick hookups. Fun, sweaty exercise but all the emotional connection of an oil change.

And this bothers you how?

Not a damn bit. The fewer emotions, the better I like it.

I very firmly put thoughts of a naked Merilee Soames out of my mind and concentrated on feeding my face.

The restaurant stayed busy throughout my breakfast, and Merilee raced from kitchen to tables without a pause. If I didn't know better, I would say she was avoiding me. Her eyes slid away without meeting mine, and she stayed on the far side of the room unless duty carried her closer. On one of those rare occasions that she came close, I spoke up.

"Morning, Mrs. Soames."

She whipped on by me, fake smile on tight, and somehow failed to hear me.

Avoiding me. Just as well.

Still, I marveled at the woman's energy as much as I admired her body. It was no wonder she stayed so slim, the way she charged around from kitchen to table. Only last night, she had been dragged through the streets by a gaggle of Gollums who were in the mood for some British takeaway. A short night's sleep after that, and here she was, back to work at full speed, smiling at the customers, serving, cleaning, pausing to exchange pleasantries with everyone... except, of course, me.

Merilee Soames carried an aloofness that hinted of thick walls protecting her privacy, and I guessed it would take a long-term siege to breach those ramparts. I much preferred the drawbridge be down and the castle ready for occupation. I had no time for entanglements.

"Focus," I growled to myself. "Stay on mission."

Yes, we must stay Oscar Mike at all costs. Remind me, what was the mission again? Kill Birnbaum? How's that working out?

Shut up.

After springing Kat Krawczyk, I intended to be long gone. She could come or stay, though if she were a decent healer, I would have preferred to bring her back to our time over leaving her here. There was no magic in the vicinity of Geyser Falls, and if I intended to get back home, I'd need a heaping helping of it—not to mention a memory boost to recall the events surrounding how it was done in the first place. I needed to break it down to manageable parts. Objective one, find a huge, dog-slobbering mess of magic. Objective two, figure out how the whole time travel thing worked, which only one wizard in history, at least to my knowledge, had ever done. Objective three, get back to the Mall of Wondrous Creatures and turn Dustin Birnbaum into a charcoal briquette. Call him Cinder-fella.

Use his tech to grow Alizandra a new liver, or convince Krawcyzk to heal her, whichever could be done most efficaciously.

As good a plan as any, I supposed.

"Shivers!" Mayor Bunting called from the restaurant doorway, interrupting my thoughts. The round Englishman tap-danced through the breakfast crowd to my table. He sat down without waiting for an invitation. "Oh, I say, Judge Shivers!" Bunting daubed at his splotched red face with a handkerchief. His bow tie hung askew, and the top button of his vest had popped loose. A sweat ring had formed midway along the crown of his derby hat. "Judge Shivers, a moment, if I may."

"Bunting." I forced my face into simulating mild interest or at least not hostile distaste.

"Do you intend to hang the witch today, sir?" The mayor's mustache twitched as if something lived within it. "That is to say... I mean, ah, try her first, of course. By all means. But will you be setting a date for the hanging?"

"No."

"I... What?" Bunting cast about as though seeking support. No one in the dining room paid us the slightest interest. "No, you don't intend to hang her, or no, you don't intend to hang her today?"

"No hanging at all. Period."

Bunting goggled like a fat owl. "I say!"

I must have been losing my touch. Normally, when I pitched my voice to executioner level, people paid attention. Not Bunting.

"But you must," he all but howled. People looked our way, and I glared them down, so maybe it was just Bunting who was oblivious. I cranked up the intensity of my take-no-prisoners attitude to—I hoped—penetrate the granite skull of the town's mayor. My eyeballs hurt, my pride was chilled by the Soames woman's cold shoulder, and my I-Hate-the-World-powered engine was overheating, so it wasn't hard to come off as ready to kill something.

"Listen up," I said. "There is no statute in the penal code of California that addresses witchcraft, Bunting." I had checked this, flipping through Moorcock's law books before breakfast. "If she actually did set someone's church on fire, through either mundane means or something arcane, then she's guilty of arson." I paused and fixed him with a dead-eyed stare. "Can you prove arson?"

"Ah... no."

"Murder?"

"N-No."

"Assault? Robbery?"

"No, but—" He gaped and goggled, reminding me of a fish with a mustache.

"Well, there you go." I stood and donned my hat. I touched the brim in salute to the mayor, and not with my middle finger, so extra points awarded to Calico Shivers for anger management. "Have yourself a lovely day."

I found Sheriff Archibald Bridger at his desk in the jail, frowning over a ledger and scratching at it with a pencil. Today, the Marlboro Man wore a gray hat, a stiff white shirt with a string tie, and a brocade vest in red and gold tones. None of the deputies were present. A blue-steel pot sat atop the stove and filled the room with the aroma of coffee.

"He'p yourself," Bridger said without looking up.

I declined and snagged a chair across from the lawman. "Tell me about Reverend Weeks."

"I hear he walloped you a good lick."

"Guy has a fist like a five-pound sledge."

Bridger's mustache crooked up in a grin. He looked up from his paperwork and fixed me with his smoky-blue eyes. "Guess he nailed your dick to the door, huh?"

I swallowed the acid response that bubbled up. Anger management, level two. "Hmm. So what's his deal?"

"Merilee Soames, I'd say." Bridger's chair creaked when he leaned back. His expression turned sour. "Man's like stink on a skunk where it comes to Mizz Soames. Has been ever since he showed up a couple of months ago and moved into a room over at the hotel. Two doors down from mine, in fact."

"You don't sound happy about it."

"Yeah, you could say that." Bridger's mustache twitched, and he appeared as though he wanted to spit. "Before he showed up, I had a feeling Merilee and me... well, I was callin' on her. Calling on her."

"And now there's another dog in the hunt, huh?"

"Not just that, but she seems to be—what's the word? Ah, *receptive* to his interest. More than to mine, any which way."

"So when I show up at the hotel with Mrs. Soames, and her blouse is torn, and she's all rumpled up..."

Bridger nodded. "Weeks thought you were plowing his pasture and punched your lights out."

"And what about Mr. Soames? Where is he in all this?"

"I don't know. Don't know. She arrived in Geyser Falls before me with enough cash for a down payment on the Bannerworth, they say. Claimed to be a widow, and nobody's learned any different. Or cares, for that matter. People's past is their own business around here. Their own business."

"And what about the little people who attacked Mulligan and Mrs. Soames? Any clues on who they are or where they come from?"

"Nothing. They vanished like smoke. Some tracks led off into the scrub east of town, but the ground's dry, won't hold a print for shit. Potts and Barton are out, quartering the ground between here and the mountains, hoping to pick up the trail."

I tilted my chair back on two legs and tried ordering my thoughts into an action plan. I had objectives, but what I needed was a tasking, or a to-do list at the very least. I had always been good with clear, concise orders, typed out in neat bullet-point objectives. See target, hit target. Move to point A, execute option three. If option three unavailable, go to option four. Muddling around in unfamiliar territory, without a plan, bothered me at a cellular level.

"What's that you're humming?" Bridger asked.

"Hm? Oh... 'Land of Confusion' by Genesis."

"Genesis?" Bridger's face scrunched up. "Like in the Bible?"

"No, not quite." I could just imagine what Dad would have said if he could have seen me. *Whining about what you don't have is for losers. Work with what you do have and go from there.* "Are the church attacks and the little people connected in some way, do you think?"

Bridger inhaled hard and long. He glanced at the open door to the street, and his eyes took on a hooded, guarded look. "I have my suspicions about the church business, but given what I said earlier, you might think I'm a tad... predispositioned to suspect certain things."

"Try me."

The sheriff rubbed a finger across his mustache. "See, this trouble started about six weeks ago. First the Catholics, then the Methodists, then the Baptists, right? One church after another."

I nodded for Bridger to continue. I saw where he was going, and I liked it so far.

"Now, I ask myself—" The sheriff's voice dropped a notch, and he hunched forward, as if imparting a grave secret. "Who stands to benefit?"

"Follow the money."

"Exactly! Follow the money. I like that. Follow the money. So whose church do you think has been gaining converts, now that it seems that God has smote all the others?" Bridger touched a finger to his nose. "Think on that a second."

"Weeks. Has his congregation been growing?"

"Like a teenager's dick at a barn dance."

"I can see why you'd be wary of confronting him. Could look like bad blood over a woman."

"That and I got no evidence," Bridger confessed with a sigh. "Which is a thing you judges seem to like."

"I didn't think you'd bother much with evidence, Sheriff, given what you planned to do to Miss Krawczyk."

"Well, hanging a strange little strumpet like her is a whole different pot of stew. You seen her, right? Hair like that, and the way she acts. The things she says. Such a foul mouth, it liken to make a body faint, the way she talks. A lot of people want her hung for that alone. I've been keeping her locked up for her own protection. Her protection." Bridger leaned forward and lowered his voice again. His bland expression showed no chagrin at having completely switched positions on Krawczyk being guilty of witchcraft. "She told Merilee, she said she don't like men. She does it... the other way. We don't truck with that kind of perversion in this town."

I let that one go. No time for bringing sexual enlightenment to Geyser Falls. "How could the Methodist minister be choked to death in his own pulpit, with nobody seeing anything?"

"That was the Baptist, Pastor Allen, what got choked. I dunno that either. Poison, maybe?"

I shifted to cover the sudden bad thought that came to mind. Instead of poison, more likely a dose of magic. Was that it? Was Weeks a nineteenth-century Magical, running around and putting his rivals out of business with magic? And did he have any connection to the pygmies, who seemed to be attacking townspeople at random? Or was it random at all? One thing was true: if Weeks had that much magic, I wanted to know where he got it.

There you go. Task A under Objective 1.

Yep. I'd have this planning thing licked in no time. "And the bank?" I asked. "The other missing folks?"

"No idea. Nobody seems to have seen a thing."

Krawczyk was a Magical, but she had no reason to go rogue and start choking Baptists and burning down Methodist churches or disappearing miners and small boys by the job lot. And robbing banks? Well, there was always that temptation for someone with power, no matter who they were. But it didn't square with the woman I'd seen in the jail cell. My instinct said she had nothing to do with the crime wave in Geyser Falls. Besides, she had not been in this time period long enough to be responsible for every crime.

"Mulligan and the others," I said. "Any connection to Weeks?"

"Ahhh..." Bridger scratched his head and stared at the ceiling for a bit. From outside came the sound of a blacksmith's hammer tanging on an anvil. "You know, now that you mention it, I believe Mulligan was a member of Weeks's congregation. He was an attorney but all fired up on God most days. I'd have to check on Ollie and Tater." The sheriff slanted a look of speculation at me. "I never thought of that. Could be there's a connection after all."

"You say I can find Weeks at the hotel?" I touched my sore eye socket and forced myself not to wince. One more reason to pay the reverend a visit, only this time if he swung, I would see it coming and give him the opportunity to meet God in person.

"Not always," said Bridger, "and not regular like. He spends most days and some nights out at his revival tent, due north of town, alongside the river. About two miles or so. Thirty minutes on a slow horse."

"A slow horse is the only kind I have." I stood and started for the door but stopped halfway with a snap of my fingers and turned. "And cut Miss Krawczyk loose."

Bridger grimaced. "Are you sure? A lot of people are going to be mighty nervous."

"She have anywhere to stay?"

"Actually, Merilee took her in when they first found her up in the mountains. Gave the gal a spare room in her suite."

"Take her back over there," I said. "Let her get cleaned up and eat, but tell her to stay put until I get back. Out of sight, out of mind."

Bridger's grimace seemed permanently affixed. "If you're sure..."

"I'm sure. She's not the cause of the problem here."

"That's not what Reverend Weeks says. He says a woman like her has to be straight from Hell." Bridger's eyes widened as a thought struck him. "Say. You think maybe he's trying to shift the blame? Make it look like she's the one done all the crime?"

"Wouldn't be the first time somebody tried framing a patsy." I touched my hat brim—I was getting pretty used to the cowboy thing—and headed for the door, thinking about the ride out to Weeks's camp.

Oh boy! More time on horseback. Ugh.

Maybe a nice, warm stable had improved Misery's attitude.

When did you become an optimist?

Shut up.

Chapter Fifteen: A Weeks's Worth of Trouble

By the time I hit the street after leaving Bridger, a golden sun topped the Inyo Mountains, burning away the coolness of early morning. Commerce bustled in the town of Geyser Falls. For a place in the middle of damn-near nowhere, it was busy. Given my overheard breakfast conversations, silver and copper were mined from the nearby mountains, and the streets were crowded with mules and wagons headed east, filled with picks, shovels, raw timber, and all the myriad bits and bobs needed for operating a mine. Several of the big mercantile outfits near the center of town seemed to be geared toward nothing but supplying hopeful dreamers with the right equipment to dig deep into the earth in search of El Dorado. I passed Owen's Valley Dry Goods and Hardware, Big Nate's Mine and Sundry Shoppe, Schoenbeck's Emporium on my way to the Bethlehem Stables, and all of them were packed with customers. Wagons lined up in front of docks, and men in knee-high boots and floppy hats stomped around, loading supplies, jawing at each other, and inspecting their animals while they waited.

I obtained directions to Reverend Weeks's encampment from the stable owner when he went to retrieve my sad excuse for a horse. Spending another couple of hours in a saddle appealed about as much as sitting in a nest of fire ants, but the alternative meant a many-mile round-trip hike. Yay, me. Time to ride my pony like a real cowboy.

But if Weeks had magic, I needed to know. And if he was killing people with magic, that meant he was in violation of the Codex Magica and therefore was subject to summary justice from a Judge. Like me. It would be justice, then, not revenge for my black eye.

If a Judge is sent back to a time before there are Judges, does that make him still a Judge?

Um, sure. I think so. Shut up.

Misery must have picked up a hint of the question, for he came back with his inevitable answer.

Who cares?

"I had a vinyl LP once, was a lot like you," I told the horse. "Stuck in the same groove. Harry Chapin, 'Cat's in the Cradle.' I hate that song. Saddest goddamn song in the world. It kept playing 'know when, know when, know when' over and over."

On the ride through the north end of town, Misery plodded past the shell of a house that I imagined was once the home of a working man and his family. The current occupant of the termite ranch sat on the porch in overalls and no shirt or shoes, taking his ease on a three-legged chair. He balanced by leaning against the wall of the rickety dwelling, displaying a devil-may-care lack of caution, considering the amount of dry rot undermining his support. A second guy, a rough man with a ginger fringe of hair that failed to cover his one-and-a-half ears, lounged in the blank space where a door once hung. I made a wild-ass guess that the last honest labor the two gentlemen performed was straining to fill a diaper while plotting a breakout from behind the bars of their cribs. The aura of distrust and malice they projected would curdle milk inside a cow.

In an open lot between a barn and a collapsed house, another trio of shifty characters passed a bottle. They squatted in a circle around the smoking remains of a fire, the charred bones of an unidentified animal scattered about. Three pairs of hooded eyes tracked me from the shadows of weathered, sweat-stained hats.

If Geyser Falls had a set of railroad tracks, this section of town would be on the wrong side of it.

The houses petered out as the road became a two-rut trail paralleling the Owens River. Wheel marks cut through rye grass and thick sedge. Cottonwoods, willows, and the other green things with leaves shaded the trail. I welcomed both the shade and the rare breeze off the river, as the climbing sun had turned the day warm.

Air-conditioning. If I invented air-conditioning, I could make a fortune. I knew the principles, mostly. Something about the expansion of gas removing heat, which led me down the rabbit hole of how I would need to make freon. Chemistry. Ugh. That occupied me for all of thirty seconds before I gave it up as a waste of time.

"Let's review," I said to Misery. "Objective one, task one: find out if Weeks has a magic amulet. Task two: learn if Weeks is using magic to kill. No. Scratch that. Task two: learn how much magic Weeks can store in his amulet and if he has found a quick way to charge it." I touched mine and found that in a day and a half, I had regained almost a full charge. "Calico Shivers, Power Ranger!"

Misery snorted.

"Task three, you ask? Task three: punch Weeks in the nose as hard as I can. With my fist. Into his nose and out the back of his head."

Thirty minutes later, I found Weeks's revival tent set off to the left of the road, down by the river's edge. The once-white tent fabric had weathered to the color of dirty dishwater. Longer than a barn but not as tall, the tent faced the road, the opening pulled back and tied off. An area of beaten-down, hard-packed grass separated the tent from the trail. I supposed this area was set aside to park parishioners' wagons and horses. The smashed and hoof-printed horse droppings clued me in.

The rigorous pounding of a hammer resonated from inside the canvas structure.

On the tent's left side, a one-story farmhouse was a heavy breath away from imploding. All four walls leaned north, whereas the roof leaned south, as if the place couldn't decide which way to collapse. Sheets covered the two empty sockets of the front windows, and a plank door had been added to the entry—it was the only part of the structure that stood straight, its rectangular shape only partially covering the parallelogram opening.

I pulled Misery to a halt under a cottonwood and wrapped the reins around a low-hanging branch.

Is this where you leave me to die? the horse asked.

"No. Stop being such a big ninny."

You hate me.

"Not true." I shook my head. "See, I parked you over some nice grass. Eat some."

There are burrs in it.

I straightened my coat, resettled my hat, and strode to the tent, following the sound of pounding. The hammer wielder turned out to be a Black man old enough to have dandled baby Moses on his knee. He stood a hunched six feet tall, with skin as dark and gnarled as dried persimmon and a fringe of snowy hair. At a glance, he appeared to be building a new set of pews from milled wood, replacing the bare-bones backless seating with proper chair-style benches. Intent on his task, he didn't notice when I stepped through the opening.

"Good morning, sir!" I yelled over the banging.

The old man bobbed up with a look of surprise, a pair of nails dangling from his lips. "Mawnin', boss."

"Reverend Weeks?"

"No, sah. He—oh, he right there." The worker pointed with his hammer to a space behind my left shoulder.

"I'm Reverend Weeks."

Jumping Jesus! I started and twisted in surprise to find Abe Lincoln right up in my personal space. "I didn't hear you."

"And how could you, over Enoch's incessant hammering? You were seeking me?" The reverend bore only a superficial resemblance to our mumble-teenth president.

Yeah, slept through history too. In fact, let's cut to the chase—the only classes during which I paid attention were music and gym. Okay? Picture rebellious teenager, overbearing father, blah, blah, blah.

Weeks was a darkly handsome man in his late thirties or early forties, with thick black hair combed straight back, heavy brows, and a strong jaw. More Josh Brolin than Abe Lincoln. He inclined his head in invitation and led me from the tent. "Perhaps you would like revenge for my unfortunate loss of temper. Let's go somewhere softer, shall we, so when I fall, I won't break anything."

After he offered refreshments, and I declined, and he offered a seat inside the helter-skelter home, which I likewise declined, we ended up strolling along the riverbank. The sun sparkled off the water and baked me in my long-tailed black coat. Sweat slicked my hatband. I churned through several ways I could start the ball rolling and accomplish task one of objective one—find out if Weeks had magic—without going straight to task three and punching his nose through the back of his head.

"The boys in Sunday School," Weeks said as if reading my mind, "call it trading licks."

"Hmm?"

Weeks smiled without showing his teeth. "One boy punches first, as hard as he can, then the other boy gets a turn. The one who hits the hardest wins the contest. Though I imagine it's more about bravado and a test of courage than actual combat. Since I struck you first, I'm now offering to trade licks."

"Yeah, I know what trading licks means. Tempting, but..." The man's openness flummoxed me a bit. He seemed as inoffensive and meek as a lady's knitting circle. "Let's just move forward."

"Very Christian of you, sir." Weeks favored me with a thin smile. "And which church do you attend, Judge Shivers? Have you accepted Jesus Christ as your Lord and Savior?"

That was exactly why I hated talking to preachers—invariably, this question came up. A thousand answers came to mind, the kind of reflex smart-ass remarks that always got me in trouble with Old Hardass, pastor of the Church of the Leather Belt. But I needed to learn if Weeks was a Magical, not get into a religious pissing contest. I was there for information, not confrontation.

Everybody likes Methodists. Go with that. "I typically attend Methodist services."

Weeks seemed to relax. His hawk gaze slid back to the river, and his smile dropped away. Not much of a smiler.

"I came here to ask," I continued, "about Miss Krawczyk. You have suggested she might be using witchcraft?" Wherever the fuck that question came from, I had no idea, but I liked it. It got the conversation moving into the area of magical stuff, which had to have been good. I admit that I wasn't much of a detective.

"She has often been observed speaking in tongues, Judge Shivers. Babbling phrases in odd languages and demonstrating the mind of someone clearly possessed by a demon."

"I see. You have a lot of experience with magic users?" *Subtlety, thy name is me.*

That tight-lipped smile appeared again. "She has also shown a complete lack of deference as befitting a person of the fairer sex. She often argues with or belittles men, many of them gentlemen of stature in our community. She has no decorum befitting a lady and often uses foul language. She does not accept... admonishment."

Anybody used to the casually salty language of the twenty-first century would have thought nothing of sprinkling their speech with epithets. Not surprising people of an earlier era would find that unsettling.

"The woman's skin is marked with signs and sigils." Weeks added after a pause, "Plus, it is rumored... she has made reference to having an interest in both men and, ah, women."

"Oh, for God's sake—"

"Do not blaspheme, sir," Weeks snapped. The quiet demeanor of a back-country pastor fell away to reveal an underlayment carved from gravestones. "This woman's behavior is simple for a man like me to interpret, beholden as I am to the God Almighty and His son, Jesus Christ the Redeemer. When Christ returns and takes us to the Kingdom of Heaven, blessed are those who have washed their robes in the blood of Christ, for they shall know the tree of life and may enter the Kingdom by its gates. Outside will remain the dogs, sorcerers, the sexually immoral, the idolaters, and everyone who practices falsehood. Revelations, chapter twenty-two. Woe to those who scheme iniquity and who work evil in their beds. It is God's law that a man or woman who is a witch shall be put to death. They shall be stoned, and their blood shall be upon them. Leviticus, chapter twenty."

Yikes. Full on biblical wrath incoming. Shields up. "The law—"

"The law is not made for a righteous person but for those who are lawless and rebellious, for the ungodly and sinners, for the unholy and profane, for those who kill their fathers or mothers, for murderers and immoral men and *homosexuals* and kidnappers and liars and perjurers, and whatever else is contrary to sound teaching, according to the glorious gospel of the blessed God, with which I have been entrusted." Weeks drew a breath before continuing in a thunderous voice, "For behold, the day is coming, burning like a furnace; and all the arrogant and every evildoer will be chaff; and the day that is coming will set them ablaze, says the Lord of hosts, so that it will leave them neither root nor branch. Malachi, chapter four." Weeks leaned forward, putting his face close enough that I smelled lunch on the man's breath. Or maybe it was sulfur.

"Taketh this lesson to heart, young man," the preacher grated. "That woman shall die. Make no mistake, there is but one outcome that will satisfy the Lord, our God, in this matter. She will die, die, die. Hanged by the neck, then her body burned and the ashes buried in a pit of lime. Should you decide to spare the little bitch's life, you will be condemned to an everlasting torment and burn forever in the fiery belly of the lowest hell. And I shall see to it you meet that fate sooner rather than later."

Heat bloomed in my chest. Adrenaline spiked.

Ah yes. I know the lyrics to this song very well. I wrote it. See "Problem, Hit Problem," by Calico John Shivers.

I opened my symphony with a percussion instrument. Hard. I launched a fist that began as a throat punch and morphed to a palm-strike to the chin at the last second. The throat punch would have crushed the preacher's larynx and killed him slowly, whereas the chin strike merely rang the bell in his steeple. Moderation, thy name is Shivers.

Weeks stumbled back, a look of shock flash freezing his face.

I forced Weeks onto his heels. "You need to back the hell off. If you so much as sneer in that woman's direction, I'll blow you into mouse turds. I can promise you one thing: you'll be the devil's ass boy if you come after Kat Krawczyk. Are... we... clear... on... that?" I punctuated my final sentence with a finger jab to the preacher's chest at each word. I filled my will with magic, sucking dry my amulet and holding the power ready. I itched to use it, to lash out and blast out a wall of force that would catapult Weeks into the river. All I had to do was focus and—

No. Stop it, dumbass.

I squeezed down with an effort and shoved the genie back into its bottle. It felt like capping a geyser or a volcano.

Weeks's shocked expression relaxed, and he held both hands in a palms-up gesture of peaceful intent. Sun broke through the clouds, the fitful river-born breeze died, and the twitter of birds resumed.

"I deeply regret my choice of words, Judge Shivers." Weeks worked his jaw then spat blood. His words came thickly, as if he'd bitten his tongue. "Sometimes my zeal at doing the Lord's bidding overcomes my... normally humble nature."

I took a breath and tried out a tight smile of my own. "Uh-huh." I drew in a lungful of air. Blew it out. "I know how it is to be passionate about your work."

"It's true. I feel deeply passionate about purging evil wherever I find it."

"I need to get back to town."

Weeks didn't volunteer his hand for a shake, and I didn't care. I left the preacher under the willow tree. As I returned along the riverbank to the tent site, my back crawled with the sense of the preacher's brooding, dark eyes boring into the space between my shoulder blades, assessing, I was sure, the right spot to plant a knife. I kept hold of my magic, ready to throw up a block of solid air or ignite a miniature sun inside Weeks' skull, whichever seemed most appropriate. It occurred to me that offering my back to a magic-user might prove fatal if the man were inclined to get frisky. My scalp itched all the way back to the clearing.

I found Misery tied to the tree where I left him. The horse dozed, swishing his tail at the occasional fly.

Enoch squatted on a nearby stump, gnawing a fried chicken leg.

"Taking a break?" I said.

"Yassah. Getting on to lunchtime for the likes of me."

I hitched my thumb at the tent. "Why the new benches?"

"A lot of folk lately come to hear the reverend preach the word." Enoch wrapped his bare chicken bone in a ragged piece of wax paper, which he wadded and stuffed into a tow sack. "More and more peoples coming, and we need somewheres to sit 'em down. Else when the spirit moves in 'em, they pass right out and fall over." He clapped his hands like an alligator shutting its mouth.

"The reverend's getting a lot of new parishioners these days, huh?"

"That be true, boss. More ever' week." Enoch grinned. "Ever' week, more for Weeks, now."

I quirked my lips in a near-smile. The humor died when I spotted the preacher standing next to the tent. It was the second time Weeks had appeared without me sensing the man's approach. Magic? Or was the man just naturally stealthy?

I prodded Misery. "Wake up. We need to move on. I don't think the preacher likes me."

Who does?

Chapter Sixteen: Call Me Kat

"**S**o I'm on house arrest, is that it?"

Lillith Kathryn—"Call me Kat"—Krawczyk sat across from me at a table in the Bannerworth's dining room. The lunch crowd had drained away, and we had the place to ourselves. The waitress had left a pot of coffee and two cups, along with a plate of biscuits with a jug of honey. I brushed at the crumbs littering the tablecloth, which were all that was left of the biscuits. My hands were sticky. Punching preachers made me hungry, or maybe it was all the healthy outdoor activity.

Riding back from Weeks's camp, I had reined Misery off the trail and into a stand of willows next to the river. In the cool shade, I watched the river flow and let the breeze blow away my anger. I had to admit to myself how close I had come to planting Weeks under greener pastures. A week's worth—*har-har, fuck you, pun*—of frustration, helplessness, and fear of the unknown had built inside me like heat in a nuclear reactor, triggering a meltdown that nearly led to an exploding reverend.

There on the riverbank, I sat and threw myself a grand old pity party, complete with sulky hats and pouty cakes. Of course, I made sure no one was watching—it would have been uncool for a fierce fucker like me to have been seen having a tantrum.

If I had only taken a breath and backed out at the mall, pre-Rancor, and called in some backup, none of this shit would be happening. But no, I let my balls rule my brain and drove on, right into...

whatever the hell had happened. And there I was, stuck in 18-fucking-87, in the prehistoric Stone Age of the Old West, where the people stank and the transportation crapped on the road. Simple as that.

How long had it been since I had last failed a task set before me? I executed missions. They didn't execute me.

And yet, here you are.

Cue the deep sigh. FIDO, as we used to say in the Rangers. Fuck it, drive on.

The strange little Gollum creatures were a distraction, noise I was using to white out my sense of failure. Stamping out an infestation of pygmies—unless they were indeed Birnbaum's gift to the nineteenth century—was not in my job description. Weeks was a distraction—the man had about as much magic as a pogo stick. The mystery of the open bank door and the dead preachers was not mine to solve. The sooner I got back on mission, the better I would feel. Hanging around Geyser Falls was counterproductive.

Conclusion: un-ass the town and figure out how to get home to help Alizandra.

"Helloooo," said Kat Krawczyk, waving a hand in front of my face. "Paging Judge Shivers. Please return to Earth, Wandering Spirit."

"I'm here. Thinking."

"Don't hurt yourself." Krawczyk's boyish, blue-dyed hair had been washed. The roots had grown out as sandy brown, leaving her with a two-toned look. If she stayed much longer, she would outgrow her blue hair after the next couple of cuts.

"You need a horse," I said. My coffee had gone cold. I pulled a face and put the cup back on the saucer.

"A horse? Why?"

"Unless you want to walk."

"Walk?" Krawczyk held her palms up and glanced around. "Where're we going?"

"The US office of the Administration of the Codex Magica is based in San Francisco. Start there."

"Do you know when they were formed into a body? Is there such a thing in this time and place?"

"Don't know."

"Have you figured out how to do the time-travel trick? Get us back?"

"No."

"How much magic will it take you to figure it out?"

"Don't know."

"By the Goddess, your aura is soooo tight," Krawczyk said. "Enough negative energy radiates from you, you practically glow dark red."

I frowned. *Aura? What kind of New Age nut is this?* "How good are you?"

"Excuse me?"

"Magically. You said you're a healer. How good a healer are you?"

"I'm good, Judge Shivers. Very good." Krawczyk's expression remained grave, much like a mechanic with a balky engine. "And I can see people's auras. My reading of yours suggests it's not healthy for you to repress your emotions so strongly. You need to loosen up, Mr. Shivers." Her grim look changed, and a sly smile curled her lips. "As a healer, I'd suggest maybe... ah... find someone nice and go fuck like bunnies? Sexual intercourse holds great healing power as well as being good aerobic exercise."

As if cued by the gods, Merilee Soames exited the kitchen and crossed the dining room, throwing us a quick glance and the thinnest of professional smiles before heading into the hotel lobby.

"For example," Krawczyk said. "Start with her. Boobs like pillows. If you don't hit that, I will."

"I'm not her cup of tea."

"What? Guy like you, with that curly dark hair and that brooding-bad-boy look of yours? You look like some kind of Bedouin prince or something. She ought to be melting in her knickers. Hmm... maybe we can all hop in the sack together?"

"No. Stay focused. I only have a couple of dollars left. Not enough to buy a horse. I need to earn some cash. There's a faro game at the Broken Wheel, but it's low stakes. Might take a while to build up enough cash."

"I'm ashamed of you, Judge Shivers. Cheating like that."

"Objective two, acquire horses, camping gear, weapons."

Krawczyk arched a formerly pierced eyebrow. "You know there's a stagecoach, right?"

"Objective—excuse me, what?"

"There's a stagecoach that runs right through Geyser Falls. It's packed with prospectors on the way down, and it runs from the railhead in... can't think of the town name. Somewhere north of here. You can buy tickets there and take a train direct to San Francisco. Cheaper than horses. Faster too." She waved a hand in the air. "Although I'm not pleased by the size of the carbon footprint. Have you seen how much smoke those trains put out?"

I sipped from my coffee, remembering too late that it had gone cold.

"But it's a good plan," Krawczyk said. "All those objectives and everything? Very well-organized. We can still totally do that, if you want."

"How do you know this? About the stage?"

"You're not the only one who knows where the Admins hang out. Hung out. Will hang out. I checked it out last week, but then I got framed for all the hoodoo in town. End of exploration. Go directly to jail. Don't pass Go." Krawczyk made a noise like a game show buzzer.

The sound of banging pots rang from the kitchen. The desk bell dinged, followed shortly by the sound of Merilee's voice, raised in query. On the street outside, two miners started a shove fight, upsetting their mule, who brayed and kicked the air.

Krawczyk watched me choke down my pride, her head cocked to the side like a spaniel.

"We'll take the stage." I forced the words out past my ego.

"What was that? Couldn't hear you."

"Stage," I said, louder.

"That's a great idea! But we still need a bankroll, oh Brooding One." Krawczyk winked. "I think you should go rip off the faro dealer. Objective one and all that shit."

Intermission
Billy Minor and the Canyon

Billy Minor led his pack animals, Junior Mule and Dorothy Mule, along a narrow trail. Steep, rugged hills rose to either side, dotted with tough, prickly bushes clinging to the rocky soil. He had no particular destination in mind. He trusted his nose to find a good spot to set up camp, somewhere with water, shelter from the wind, and a ripe place to start digging.

Forty years, he'd traipsed the Madres, the Inyos, the Gabriels, the San Jacintos, and others with names only an Indian could pronounce. Strikes had been rare, good veins even rarer. The money, when he had it, had pissed through his fingers and soaked into the pockets of card sharks, faro dealers, whores, and con men. Didn't stop him from digging in the mountains for more, hiking deep into the lonely places, risking his scalp, braving mountain storms, freezing his keister off, melting it in hinges-of-hell heat, hunting for scarce water and scarcer riches.

It was what he knew. It was what he did.

Even had the right name for it. Minor. Miner. He'd been born for it, one might say.

Right now, his nose led him higher into the Inyo Mountains, along a dry wash canyon trail. *Ahead*, his nose said. *Keep on going this'a'way.*

The sun walloped him like a ten-pound hammer. The giant, burning ball had always felt so much closer the higher Billy ventured into the mountains, the air so thin and hot, it was like breathing from a fire. At night, the temperature would plummet so low, he'd lie under three blankets and still not feel warm enough.

Clumps of yellow rabbitbrush and thick stands of creosote hemmed the trail he followed. Grasshoppers fizzed away at his approach, and dragonflies darted about.

Billy paused at a narrow gap in the vegetation to his left, promising either a cut into a new canyon or a dead end. His nose was saying to take the cut and see where it led. His gut was telling him to stay the hell out. He never understood where such feelings came from—God, or the Devil, or gas from a sloppy plate of beans and tortillas—but he'd never gone wrong in trusting either his nose or his gut. When they disagreed... well, he couldn't recall the last time that happened.

"That old Paiute's got you spooked," he told Junior Mule. The young bluenose rotated an ear in his direction and reserved comment.

Two days before, Billy had come upon a Paiute family trekking out of the mountains with all their worldly goods packed on their backs. They all stopped, and Billy had commenced to palavering with the old man of the family, a dried-up geezer with more wrinkles than teeth and a better command of the English language than most of the Injuns he knew—better than many a white man. Billy had shared his salt pork and coffee, whereas the Paiutes offered up some cornmeal and wild onions. Mama Paiute had cooked up a meal while Billy and Papa Paiute squatted for a smoke and a talk.

"Where y'all headed?" Billy asked.

"Away. Far away."

"Better hunting grounds?"

The old man's lips thinned, and he shook his head like a doctor pronouncing the patient dead. "Mountains bad. Always bad, now many bad."

"Bad?"

"Inyo angry. Many angry. Nimerigar many."

Billy knocked the dead wattle out of his pipe and fished for another pinch of tobacco from the pouch at his waist. "The mountains are angry?" he asked, thinking, *Earthquakes? Rockslides? And what the hell's a nimmereggar? Another word for colored folk?*

"Inyo angry. Inyo is Paiute word." Papa touched his chest. "Inyo is spirit. Long time spirit live in mountain near Paiute. Bad spirit. Paiute... ah... peace with spirit. Peace with Nimerigar. Paiute stay away deep mountain. Nimerigar stay away Paiute."

"He don't mess with you, and you don't mess with him."

Papa Paiute inclined his head and accepted the lit pipe. He sucked in a lungful of smoke and let it dribble from his nostrils.

"What's this spirit look like?" Billy asked. "In case I run into him."

"No go deep mountain, Bill-ee. Spirit many angry. Bill-ee go deep mountain, Bill-ee die."

Mama Paiute shrieked. A six-foot rattler swirled out from under a brush near where she'd been rooting around for firewood. It came right at her like it had a personal grudge. When she ran, the snake chased her across the camp. At least that was what it looked like at the time. Billy surmised that the snake was more likely trying to get away and picked the clearest path to freedom. Billy blew it in half with his single-barrel twelve gauge, ending its snaky plans, whatever they may have been.

He offered to skin it and fry up the meat, but the Paiutes were having none of it.

"Inyo angry, Inyo angry," they kept saying.

The family wolfed down their bacon and corn cakes, packed up, and vanished quicker than fried chicken at a church social. Billy grilled chunks of rattlesnake over the open fire, but it tasted funny, so he threw it out. The next day, he ignored their advice and continued his journey deeper into the mountains.

"And now look at us," Billy said to his mules as he studied the cleft in the trail. "Spooked by an ignorant savage and an addle-pated snake. Well, come on, then. Let's go see what's up this'a'way."

He tugged the lead, and Junior Mule followed, pulling Dorothy behind. Billy sidled between the bushes, scraping and scratching through dry limbs and prickly thorns that caught on his clothes and seemed to pull him back. He forged ahead, ripping away from the brush and fighting his way through the vegetation. And he was rewarded, by God, with a split in the canyon wall, revealing a trail into a deep-walled cut. In his experience, such hidden cuts led to higher elevations and remote, untouched valleys with water and good spots for digging up silver or copper, sometimes even gold. A pessimist would have said they led to a blank wall and a long trip back to where he started.

Billy was an optimist at heart.

However, night was coming on, so he pitched camp.

"Come tomorrow, Junior," he told his lead mule, "we'll go see if Mr. Inyo's got some gold he wants to share."

Feeling restless, Billy broke camp at first light, loaded his mules, and resumed the narrow canyon trail he'd been following the previous night. As he walked, he caught glimpses of a pocket canyon, just like he'd figured there'd be, whenever the trail topped out on a rise. By midmorning, the mockingbirds competed with the jays for who could tell the best story.

Billy felt *it* was close. What *it* was remained to be seen, but Billy had a good feeling that morning. His gut had ceased its moaning about unseen problems and seemed to be in agreement with his nose. Somewhere up this trail would be a strike. He knew it all the way down to his bones.

That high up, the air held a chill long into the morning, and breathing came harder. He forced himself to pause now and again to let both him and the mules blow a little and catch their breaths. Jagged, red cliffs of sandstone rose to each side of the trail, which was choked in places by sage and thorny little wait-a-minute bushes. Sand burrs dotted the hems of his trousers, and one had somehow snuck its way into his boot, causing Billy to have to stop and pick it out. A tiny waterfall of sand poured out with it.

After a dogleg right and a push through a twisted maze of cholla cactus, he found it. Like the neck of a bottle, the trail opened without warning, and the sight was enough to give Billy a pause. He'd seen some things wandering the mountains for four decades, but this sight took his breath away.

Far from where he'd abandoned the main trail, what first appeared as a spot of green in the distance had emerged as a full-fledged oasis in the arid landscape. Aspens and elms and pine trees all backed up against a ridgeline, from which a stream of water streaked a white line down a sheer cliff. He'd found a miraculous little pocket canyon buried deep in the Inyos, as rich and fertile as the surrounding mountains were arid and harsh. It was like the tales of Shangri-la.

"We made it," he told his mules.

Junior dragged back against the lead rope. He'd been acting balky and foolish all day, and Dorothy wasn't much better. Normally the more placid of the two, Dorothy had brayed and danced around in eye-rolling nonsense at every bottle fly and yellow jacket that passed her nose.

Didn't matter how stupid the critters were being. The enticement of water meant no turning back. Both skins and all three of his canteens were dry. With nothing but sand and shed snake skins behind him and a waterfall directly ahead, Billy had one choice of direction. It was sultry and hot down in the narrow canyon, and his throat was parched. The sight of free-flowing water was enough to make him a little cranky.

"Come on, dammit," he snapped.

When he looked again, something registered that he hadn't noticed at first. Thin trails of smoke arose from several spots in the dense forest growth—the kind of smoke that only came from campfires. Several of them.

"Dad-gummit!" Billy stomped his foot. "Somebody beat me to it."

A sense of motion to his right startled him. The lead rope jerked out of his hand as Junior brayed in fear and Dorothy bucked and kicked. Billy whirled—or at least he tried to. Turned out his whirling days were far behind him. He stumbled, off-balance.

A blow thudded on the back of Billy's head, and the lights went out.

Chapter Seventeen: And Then You Get to Bang the Judge's Gavel

The Broken Wheel was doing a gold rush business. Men crowded the bar, telling tales at full volume, with exuberant profanity and flailing hands. The bartender, McKenzie, topped off shot glasses with fluid speed. I caught the man's attention and gestured for a bottle, then Krawczyk and I found a table in the corner, away from the action.

McKenzie hustled over and plonked a bottle and two glasses down. He gave Krawczyk a hairy stare, obviously started to say something, but decided against it. He pocketed the coin I handed him and left with a nod.

"Tactically unsound," I said to the blue-haired woman. "You being here, in a saloon. In this day and age, decent women didn't come into saloons."

"Neither did people of color. So there you go." She arched an eyebrow and directed a meaningful look at the faro table. For a Magical, obtaining cash was rarely a problem, as long as there was gambling available. A little tip of the wheel or a nudge on the dice was all it took to gain a road stake. Cheating at gambling was perfectly acceptable to the Administrators, as was lifting cash from drug cartels and committing other fiscal felonies, including tax evasion. Even petty larceny was overlooked. In fact, assuming a Magical avoided big, splashy crimes that brought unwanted scrutiny or harmed civilians, pretty much anything was fair game.

"What are you humming?" Kat asked.

"Hmm?"

"Just now. You were humming a tune. It sounded familiar."

"I was?"

Krawczyk held her empty glass out for a fill. "Under your breath, kind of."

I paused in the middle of pouring. I honestly couldn't remember—"Ahh... The Who. 'Boris the Spider.'"

"Nope. I was wrong. Never heard of it."

"From the album *A Quick One*. 1966." I knocked back my shot and poured another while molten lava cauterized my throat.

"What do you think about Birnbaum?" Krawczyk asked.

I cocked an eyebrow in a silent question.

"Dustin Birnbaum, Wacky Wizard of Ohio." She sipped her drink, pulled a face. "Gah. That's disgusting. I need a mojito. You said maybe some stuff of his came back. You think maybe he sent the Gollums."

I shrugged and sipped my next shot with greater care, checking out the rest of the saloon. Krawczyk studied me with her dark-eyed gypsy stare.

"No, I don't. But I don't remember much," I said after deciding she wouldn't be put off, "about the... trip through time." I rested my elbows on the table, and my chair squeaked when I shifted weight. My glass was empty—small glass. "Images, mostly. In none of those... flashes... do I see what Birnbaum did. Can't describe it, but he felt like a long *when* away."

"But you don't think these things are his, right? Birnbaum didn't make 'em? I mean, who else but a nerd from our time thinks of a *Lord of the Rings* character, for the Goddess's sake? And those elves and fake movie creatures you mentioned? Think about it: why else would all this caca be hitting the propeller now if it wasn't connected to you and me? And probably more you than me."

"Caca?"

"Or you know, he could be sending gifts from the future, drop-ping a little torment back in the past to keep us busy. Pour me some more of that shit, would you? It kinda grows on you. But hey, listen. We need to be sure, right? We should probably go up into the moun-tains and look for the little sonofabitch. Make sure he's not around, making more creepy-crawlies for fun and amusement. Put a... ah, put a stop to him. You know"—she made a helpless gesture—"bring him to justice and all that. Do that thing you do."

"'That Thing You Do.' The Wonders, 1996. A fictional band for a movie of the same name."

"Huh?"

"Never mind." I leaned back in my chair. "But no. The answer is no."

"Why not?"

"Time."

"So?" Krawczyk shrugged. "We're stuck here, in this time, unless you can remember the way to get back home. We shouldn't leave these people with monsters on account of how we're in a rush to get back. I mean, we brought 'em, right? The Gollums?"

"Again, I don't think so. More importantly, not our job."

"Not our job? Are you kidding me? What the hell, Mr. Magical Judge? Aren't you all about hunting down Magicals gone wrong and murdering or terminating them with extreme prejudice or whatever it is you do? That is what you do, correct? Assuming we can't find them a safe place to relocate, we need to somehow stop the Gollums from hurting people. As reluctant as I am to kill, even I see that as a distinct possibility. How can keeping people safe not be your job?"

I flicked a glance at her and refilled my shot glass. "No proof."

"What?"

"No proof the Gollums are Birnbaum's. I think they're actually pygmies."

"So what if they're not?" Krawczyk scrunched her face, evidently dismayed by my lack of emotion. Wow, like I've never seen that before. "You—"

"Judge Chivers!" Esmeralda cried out from the top of the stairs. She bounded down the staircase, agile even on one leg, and rushed through the room in a sensuous wiggle of satin and lace.

I put up a stop signal with an open palm. Esmeralda clutched my extended hand and pulled it between her breasts, overacting an expression of relieved distress. "Oh, Judge Chivers, I'm so glad you have came—"

"I wouldn't count on him coming, dearest," Krawczyk snarled. "Coming would take too much time."

"I had such a dream of you," Esmeralda said, ignoring the interruption. "It was dark, and I was all alone, surrounded by the biggest wolves I have ever seen! And then you came with your big *pistola* and shooted the wolves all dead." Esmeralda crooked a forearm over her brow, as though about to swoon. "It was horrible. I was so ascared. Then you picked me up in your strong arms and carried me away, and I was all safe again." She tugged my hand tighter into her bosom, treating me to the sensation of a firm breast under my palm. Esmeralda blinked coal-dark, liquid eyes. "What do you think it means, *mi hermano*?"

Krawczyk's jaw fell open. "Is she for real?"

Getting my hand away was like pulling off a wet glove. "She's whatever you want, for a price."

"Little sister," Krawczyk implored, "you shouldn't have to sell your body to make a living. You're more than a tool to be used and thrown away like a disposable washrag. We are all sexual beings, and there's nothing wrong with seeking pleasure, but it should be *for* pleasure, not commerce."

Esmeralda's brows knitted together in a frown. She swiveled her eyes back to me. "What is this woman saying?"

"You don't have to fuck for money, if you don't want to."

"But... I *like* fucking for money."

"Hey." I pointed at Krawczyk as if I'd just remembered something. "Didn't you just tell me I should get laid?"

"Not with a... a victim of sex traffickers!"

I stood and tossed back the last of my whiskey. "Come on, Esmie. Come show me how to play faro. I need to win some money."

"And then?" the Latino woman asked with a hopeful inflection.

"And then you get to bang the Judge's gavel, I bet." Krawczyk spoke through clenched teeth, her neck blotchy red. "I'll be at the hotel." Her eyes flared at the way Esmeralda rubbed against me like a cat marking her scent. "You and I are going to have a talk about women's rights, Esmeralda."

The tiny woman stalked away, stiff-legged, her borrowed pants rolled up at the cuffs and her farmer's boots clumping the floor.

"I heard that woman is a witch," Esmeralda said. "Is true?"

"Yes. Just not how you imagine."

The faro table at the Broken Wheel played a low-stakes game, and I took care to win only a little above average. As a consequence, I was up only by forty dollars after three solid hours of playing. Might have been fifty but for Esmeralda, who sat next to me and squealed when I won and moaned when I lost. Every time a grimy miner or a dusty vaquero sidled up to the one-legged woman, I slipped her a dollar, paying her to stay with me rather than go off and earn a living the old-fashioned way. She stuck on me tighter than a rusted jar lid.

I cut a look at Esmeralda, her body so close I could tell she had an innie and not an outie. "How'd you lose your foot?"

"A bear trap," she said without blinking an eye.

"A bear trap?"

"Si." Esmeralda demonstrated by clawing her fingers together. "Is a steel trap, to catch the bear."

"Ah. You shouldn't step in those." It was the fourth time I'd asked her how she lost her foot, and the bear trap was her fourth different answer. First, wolves. Then a mountain lion had eaten it. A horse spooked with her foot caught in the stirrup. And now, bear trap.

I yawned, and my eyelids drooped. I needed a bed, and I would honestly have considered inflicting grave bodily injury on the entire offensive line of the Detroit Lions for a long, hot shower. My skin itched and felt greasy and gritty. I laughed at my own fussiness. *When did you become such a priss?* In the army, I had gone days, sometimes weeks, without a proper bath, but in the years since, as a Magical and a Judge, it had been much different. Showers every day, sometimes twice. Deodorant. Safety razors, ten in a package, all nested together with plastic guards over the blades.

Esmeralda's fingers tickled my neck, jerking me back to reality. "Wass wrong, *mi hermano*?"

"Nothing. Sorry, just tired. I'm calling it a night."

"Ah yes, let's go upstairs." Esmeralda jumped up, eager as a puppy. "I've been waiting soooo long."

I stood and stretched. Joints popped. I pocketed my winnings and peeled the young woman from my side. "Not tonight. Here's another dollar. Go to bed and get some sleep."

"But my bed is so cold and lonely." She pouted her full, red lips. "I need you to keep me warm at night."

"How old are you, really?"

"I'm... nineteen," she said while watching me through her eyelashes.

If Esmeralda was over eighteen, I'd eat Misery raw, without salt. I had no illusions that she would go to bed and sleep. The night—by a prostitute's clock—was still very young, and given the high count of randy men in the saloon, she would have customers lined up before I reached the hotel.

You're not a social worker, big fella.

No, that was true. I'd done what I could. It wasn't my job to uphold the woman's virtue—or anyone else's, for that matter.

I touched the brim of my hat. "G'night, ma'am," I said in my best John Wayne voice. *Lookit me, Ma. I'm a cowboy!* By the next day, I'd probably be walking bowlegged, punching cattle, and riding the purple sage with a big iron on my hip.

You have to get out of this place, Calico.

Yeah? No shit.

I returned to the Bannerworth, nodding to the desk man on the way to my room. He looked up from his paper and nodded right back at me. The lobby was empty, the only sound the ticking of a grandfather clock against the wall next to the cut-through to the restaurant. Krawczyk was nowhere to be seen, and I didn't bother looking for her. She told me Merilee Soames had invited her to stay in her personal suite, in a spare bedroom, which she thought was mighty generous and I thought was mighty suspicious.

"You're judging people by your own paradigm," she had scolded me. "People of this era are more generous and neighborly than in our time."

"Not to people of color, lesbians, or supposed witches," I had fired back.

That had shut her up. Score one for Team Shivers.

I was just as happy to leave her be. Weariness dragged at me, and I trudged up the stairs, looking forward to my narrow little lumpy mattress. My eyeballs grated as if sand coated the sockets, my left eye worse than the right, due to Weeks having sucker punched me there.

Though even as I thought of the pain, I realized it had diminished somewhat since I last noticed it. I felt only the memory of pain, not the reality of it. Same for my other aches and ouches. Maybe there was some natural analgesic in the rotgut served at the Broken Wheel.

The room had cooled somewhat, and a nice breeze stirred the curtains. I locked the door behind me and started the process of disarming. When I undressed, I recoiled from the smell wafting from my armpits, so I poured water into the basin and washed up as best I could. With a towel around my waist and slightly damp, I felt almost chilly, so I turned out the lamp and flopped into bed, drawing the covers over me with a feeling akin to bliss.

Sleep, however, filed a restraining order and refused to come near me.

Though feeling much better, my eye still ached a bit, my thighs were rubbery from horseback riding, and the ankle I had sprained during the mall fight pinged me with little daggers of annoyance whenever I turned my foot the wrong way.

I needed an ibuprofen, modern fucking medicine. Some Magicals, like Krawczyk, were healers. Magicals with that skill could manipulate the body's energy to speed healing and ease pain, sensing the damaged areas in a body through their magic and intuiting how to repair them. I wasn't a healer—not even close. If I tried something like that, I'd blow out an artery or turn my eyeball to jelly, which is what was so frustrating about my sister's situation. I knew there were people who could heal her, but the damn Admins refused to break the Codex and allow it.

You could go see Kat. Maybe she'd heal you.

I snorted. Yeah, sure. Probably chant a mantra and burn some aloe vera over me. God, I hate New Agers.

You hate everyone.

They typically hate me first. Now go away, brain, and let me sleep.

The curtains belled inward, and the scent of sage drifted on the breeze, overlaid with a tang of manure. Geyser Falls was a mining town, and the saloons would be packed by now, but this end of town was quieter and more upscale, and the streets rolled up early. Sounds were muted, distant.

My head had sunk into an overheated pit in the down-filled pillow. I punched it up and rolled over.

Birnbaum. Dead Wizard Walking. I kept coming back to that.

By now, Jurgens would know I had failed and had probably dispatched more Judges to take care of the problem—hopefully several, given how tightly dug in Birnbaum was, behind his circus of homegrown freaks. Would Jurgens take the time to figure out what happened to me and Krawczyk and maybe convince the Admins to set up a rescue op?

Ha. He was more likely to wear a fruit salad hat and dance the merengue.

No, the Admins were, at their core, giant pricks—ego-driven, self-appointed rulers of the Magical community. They would protect humanity from the rogue wizard who flagrantly disobeyed the law and brought attention to himself, not out of altruism but from a strong sense of self-preservation. Magicals who flaunted their power could prod the mundane humans to notice us and take action. They say you never heard the cruise missile that killed you, and Admins didn't want to live in a constant state of fear and paranoia.

They would sacrifice the life of a sixteen-year-old girl to protect the secret of magic from the general population. The Admins would easily write off the loss of a Judge and a Magical from Ohio—especially one as contentious as I—without raising an eyebrow.

It was late. After midnight. I grew too warm under the covers and tossed aside everything except a thin cotton sheet. Perspiration soaked my scalp. A five-thousand BTU window unit would have done nicely. I would have set that baby on frigid and chilled the room until icicles formed on the bed frame.

The Old West sucked. The Westerns I had eaten up like pudding had left out a lot of reality—the smell, for one. No plumbing. Rare bathing. Wood or coal for fuel. The streets stank, the animal dung stank, and the outhouses were places only a maggot could love. Krawczyk had a rosy-eyed view of the people of that era, whereas I had a totally different take on them as being suspicious, ignorant and bigoted.

Truth be told, staying there would deeply and voraciously have sucked donkey balls.

I missed three-ply, downy-soft toilet paper, moist cotton wipes, minty-fresh toothpaste, and multilayer soft-bristle toothbrushes.

Tooth decay. Jesus. What if you have to go to a dentist?

Well. Shit. Who can sleep now? Thanks.

But what if...

If I wanted, I could have rewritten a shitload of history. I could have traveled to Austria and thwarted the assassination of Archduke Ferdinand, assuming I could remember where and when it would take place. Sarajevo? 1914? I'd dozed through history class.

Oh, I know. While in Austria, I could have tracked down a skinny kid born to Alois Hitler and Something German Schicklgruber. Maybe convinced the little shit to move to Iceland or Tahiti or to take up farming. I didn't need to kill Hitler, just divert the kid to a path other than megalomania and genocide.

Think bigger. Krawczyk was a healer. With her willing help—and I could recognize a born do-gooder from a mile away—we could start a hospital and "invent" modern medical techniques. Maybe we could develop a flu vaccine by 1918 that would mitigate the Spanish Flu, thereby saving the lives of forty million people.

I could even bypass the rule about Magicals healing regular people. Wouldn't that have been a kick? It had to have been easier to avoid Admins in that day and age, before cell phones and the internet.

What if… I ran for president? Could I exert enough influence on Wall Street to stop the margin buying of stocks and prevent the Great Depression? Lay the groundwork for defeating communism before the Cold War? Avert a couple of World Wars and maybe put off the development of nuclear weapons for another dozen years or so?

Exactly how much history could I fuck up? Or is the butterfly effect real? Would I, by screwing around with the cosmos, eliminate my birth from ever happening? Would I vanish the instant I stepped on a cockroach? Alter history so much that my parents never met? I had always avoided reading fiction, especially science fiction—*"Stop wasting your time with those trashy books, son! Focus on your math."*—but I knew a paradox was not something one wore to keep their feet warm. From what I recalled, time paradox implied that if it didn't happen, the time traveler didn't do it. Or something like that.

So, taken to its logical conclusion, I never altered and could never alter my personal history because, *tah-dah!* There I was, stuck in 18-fucking-87.

Yes, I get it. Poor you. Can't find your way home. Awww, cry me a river. Quit whining and go to sleep.

For once, I tried to take my brain's advice.

Chapter Eighteen: An Invasion of Pygmies

I jolted awake.

The night lay dead in that deep, funereal quiet that came an hour before false dawn. In Ranger school, it was the hour of the day I most wanted to quit, the time when my eyes burned, my body ached so badly that the pain became a separate, evil spirit infusing my muscles, and even simple tasks required monumental effort. Years later, whenever I happened to be up and about at that time of the morning, I still felt the pull of defeat sapping my strength. Which was why I hated waking up at that hour and didn't do it unless there was a damn good reason. So in short: WTF?

The curtain shifted, stirred by a thin, dry breeze. The town was quiet. No tinny piano music, no gunshots, no laughing, cussing, or screaming. I lay awake and concentrated on listening.

A floorboard creaked, followed by the patter of stealthy feet from the hall. Faint shuffles as quiet as mice on cotton sheets. Nobody who was up to anything good skittered around like that.

I snatched the Colt from its holster hanging from the bedframe and pulled on pants in the darkness. Then I ghosted, barefoot and shirtless, to the door. I put my ear to the rough plank. The back of my neck itched, a sure sign that my early-warning radar detected a threat.

The Bannerworth was three stories tall, and my room was on the second floor, midway along the corridor. All the rooms on the second floor opened onto a railed balcony overlooking the lobby. A staircase on my far right led to the top floor, while the one opposite curved downward to spill out near the front desk. If I stepped out, I would have a view of the hotel's front doors directly ahead, the check-in desk to the left, and the dining room entrance to the right.

More pattering, scuffing sounds, and a guttural growl that might have been words echoed from the lobby.

A straight iron key with a wooden number tag protruded from the lock, as I'd left it when I came in. The mechanism grated like a rusty winch when turned, so stealth was out of the question. As soon as I twisted the key, I would announce my presence to the world.

So be it. Subtle is to Shivers like intellect is to a Marine.

I twisted the key, yanked open the door, and stepped into an invasion of pygmies.

Ten or twelve of the Gollum people roamed the second-floor hall. They appeared to be sniffing at the doors. Others pattered up the stairs toward the third floor, disappearing with a flash of tiny bare feet. The lobby crawled with two dozen or more, as industrious and active as a kicked-over anthill. Loincloths appeared to be the uniform of the day, and at first I thought the invaders were all male until the detached, analytical part of my brain—*so now you want me to get involved?*—registered some with nubbin breasts and slightly wider hips. The Gollums ranged in skin tone from nut brown to ghostly white, and all had greasy, lank black hair. Diversity in miniature.

A singular creature in the center of the lobby stood apart from the rest, in a cleared circle as though the others were loath to come too close, and I couldn't blame them. The Gollum was a giant among his people, standing a head taller than his minions. The Big Chief, High Kahuna, HMFIC—whatever his title, the tallest pygmy left no doubt that he was the boss. Necklaces and armbands festooned his body, and he wore a band of vicious claws around his forehead and gave off a me-point-you-do aura.

All the Gollums froze as one when I popped out, and dozens of angry, twisted faces fixed on me. Big Chief Ugly Butt met my stare with a pair of bloodred eyes that glowed like the coals of the devil's toilet seat. If all the hate, meanness, bigotry, and human suffering in the world could have gathered into a ball of greasy evil, boiled in a giant pot until only the singularity of its essence remained, and then swallowed by a living creature so that the corruption and malevolence soaked its soul and sent it on a murder spree through the entire school district of New York City, that creature would be a fuzzy kitten compared to this shit blister.

Designate: Target One. Range, thirty meters. Fire at will.

I cocked, aimed, and fired in one smooth motion. By bad luck or deliberate self-sacrifice, a pygmy stepped in front of the chief and caught the bullet that should have punched through the leader's chest. The gunshot galvanized the Gollums. The little people surrounding me in the hall rushed me with stone weapons raised. An arrow hummed past my cheek and thunked the doorframe behind me. I pivoted, left-right-left, firing at each twist. Three shots, three down. Only a hundred more to go. Gunsmoke clogged the hall. Another arrow, fired from the lobby, deflected off the banister and wobbled over my head. Gollums closed in from both sides.

Time to un-ass the hall.

I ducked back into my room, slammed the door, and locked it. The wood shuddered from impacts. Adrenaline jittered my hands as I punched spent rounds from the Colt's loading gate. I reloaded from the box on the dresser—a fiddly-fucking operation. Damn, I missed my semiauto—and jammed a handful of shells into my pocket. From my saddlebags, I dug out both grenades, flash-bang and frag, and added them to my pockets. I tucked the Wilson into the back of my pants. Only five rounds in the pistol, but if I died from lack of firepower, I would never forgive myself.

Shouts and the bang of gunfire reverberated throughout the hotel as other guests woke to the danger. A very feminine scream pierced the commotion.

Merilee Soames lived in a suite located somewhere behind the front desk. Assuming she had given Krawczyk her spare room in the suite, both women were at the center of the Gollum storm downstairs. Although Krawczyk had her scrap of magic for defense, it wouldn't last long against the horde of miniature Mongols. Merilee seemed fierce when cornered and may or may not have had a dagger at her disposal. Neither woman was prepared for the kind of battle we were in.

My door reverberated from multiple impacts. I twisted the key and tugged it open. Two Gollums with stone axes stumbled in the doorway, suddenly swinging at open space instead of a hotel door. I shot one before the warrior could recover and side-kicked the second one into the banister. I charged the reeling Gollum, snagged his loincloth left-handed, then pitched the pygmy over the balcony.

Both sides of the hallway seethed with pandemonium. To my left, a hotel guest was surrounded by Gollums. They were pressing so tightly against him that he was using the repeating rifle in his hands like a club. A porcupine of small arrows sprouted from his nightshirt. The man went down in a pile of writhing bodies. On the opposite side, more Gollums flooded the stairs from the lobby, charging the second floor in a wave attack.

I raced to the head of the lobby stairs as the first of the pygmies reached the landing. The Colt bucked in my hand with the precision of a metronome. Smoke fogged the hall, and the Gollums on the stairs leaped the bodies of their dead comrades and ran at me. I swapped hands with the empty revolver and snaked the Wilson .45 from my waistband. The semiauto barked. Its Glaser ammunition smoked less and punched harder. Gollums flew backward with each shot, their blood and viscera decorating the carpet and splattering the next wave of attackers. One round overpenetrated, blowing out the skull of the first pygmy and traveling on to kill the one behind him. A twofer, as my fellow Rangers liked to say.

Twelve down in half as many heartbeats stunned the remaining attackers. They faltered in the face of such devastating firepower, eyes round and clearly hesitating.

"Yeah!" I yelled. "Come get some!"

Before they could regroup and recover, I tossed my only fragmentation grenade into the pack bunched on the stairs.

"Frag out!" I yelled from habit and dropped to the floor.

Crack!

From the bloom of fiery smoke, the shattered component parts of small bodies fountained. Red rain pattered the stairs. Stunned Gollums outside the blast zone shrieked and covered their ears.

I gathered up some magic and prepared to zap a whopper of a lightning bolt if the Gollums had any fight left in them, but it appeared as though the small people had had enough. The Big Chief disappeared into the dining room, snapping orders, and I missed my chance to barbecue his ass. His warriors melted back toward him, flowing outward in a motley tide. Some carried their wounded fellows while others backed away, weapons held in defensive postures. They may have been retreating, but they were doing it in an orderly, disciplined manner.

I let them go. Using a grenade was one thing, as such devices were not unheard of in the nineteenth century. Blazing away with magic would have created a whole other level of "holy shit—who are you?"

Then the boss man came back for a second look. I knelt by the newel post and locked eyes with Big Chief. The force of the taller pygmy's enmity sent a chill down my spine. That look promised a lot: dismemberment, torture, torment, anguish, and—eventually—death. I locked up for a second, more deeply disturbed than I'd ever been in the face of an enemy. I had fought Taliban, terrorists,

Magicals, and murderers, but never in my life had I seen such butt-clenching hate as I did right then.

The chief's piggy eyes shifted minutely. A distant bell fired a clamor of warning. In the heat of action, I had somehow forgotten about the pygmies behind me, the ones who had charged for the third floor.

I pivoted.

Six Gollum warriors had crept to within spitting distance while their chief had kept me pinned with his Jedi mind trick. The six approached in a semicircle, pointy teeth bared and stone weapons raised. Far behind them, at the base of the stairs, Sheriff Bridger appeared, wearing red long johns and carrying a revolver. He tentatively raised the pistol in his hand. The Gollums were too close, and firing meant probably hitting me. The sheriff queried me with a look. *Should I shoot?* I twitched my head. *No.*

The Gollums snarled and charged.

You shouldn't use magic—

Well, fuck, what do you suggest I do? Send a letter of protest?

I focused and converted energy into electricity. I was good with electricity.

Actinic flashes of jagged lightning converged on the Gollums and flash-fried them. Discharging electricity bored vacuum tunnels in the air, which collapsed with a crack of thunder so loud that the light sconces rattled and dust filtered from the ceiling. Like so many charred logs, the Gollums timbered into a messy heap, giving off a burned-bacon stench.

"Everlasting Mother of Jesus." Bridger gaped, dangling his revolver at his side.

"Don't blaspheme, Sheriff." Reverend Weeks appeared at the lawman's shoulder, wearing black pants with suspenders over a gray undershirt. He carried a pepper pot revolver and a look of moral superiority. I met the preacher's narrow-eyed look and read suspicion mixed with more suspicion.

In the lobby, all the remaining Gollum-people had vanished. Kat Krawczyk and Merilee Soames pushed through the curtain behind the front desk, still wearing their nightclothes. There was no mistake this time—Merilee carried a slim-bladed dagger, wicked and sharp as an evil stepmother. Krawczyk held a fireplace poker as though it was a Louisville slugger. I cracked a smile at the disheveled warrior queen and her court jester, ready for battle, with fire in their eyes. Lucky for Big Chief that he retreated when he did.

"What was that?" Bridger pointed at the burned heap at my feet.

"Static electricity, I guess," I said with a straight face. "You can work up a real spark on the carpet in here."

"What the bleeding hell have you done to my hotel?" All trace of upper-crust, faint British accent had disappeared from Merilee Soames's speech. What came out was pure East End Bow Bell Cockney. *Wot the bleedin 'ell have you done't me 'otel?*

"What have *I* done?" I gaped and struggled to articulate a response. Part of the problem was that Merilee wore nothing but a nightdress of cotton fabric, thin and translucent with repeated laundering. The garment appeared suspended on the twin peaks of her breasts, which threatened me like two nuclear-tipped ballistic missiles. She also carried that damn dagger, held low by her thigh. I stepped back out of range of the dagger—the boobs had an infinitely greater field of fire. "What have I done? I defended myself against an attack of... of pygmy people invading your hotel. And you're welcome."

"You wot?" Merilee jabbed at the stairs with her dagger. "Look at that mess! Didya hafta blow up half me hotel, ya daft bugger."

I had to admit, the stairs were... a mess. A big chunk of banister had blown out, several treads were damaged, and a great gaping hole was torn through the plaster. Blood and gore bedecked the stair runner and painted the wall in a Rorschach of dripping blackish wetness. Dead Gollums and Gollum parts littered the hotel as though thrown about by a gibbering mad bellman run amok.

Bridger and Krawczyk looked on, with an inscrutable look of calculation and a smirk, respectively. No doubt she was enjoying this public dressing-down. We were gathered in the lobby, along with the reverend, next to the dead body of the night clerk whose name I hadn't gotten.

Other guests ventured onto the second-floor landing, as though in the gallery of a gruesome stage play. Some were carrying valises and suitcases, the night's activity having cooled their desire to remain guests of the Bannerworth.

"There, there, my dear." Weeks tried putting an arm around Merilee, but she shrugged him off and stalked up to me, using her double-edged blade as a pointing finger.

"Look here, you. You're a curse, mate. These... these fings t'weren't here till you showed up. Now, we're bloody infested! Piss off, you bugger, d'ye hear me? Piss off!" She spun on a heel and stamped away.

"Gladly!" I tossed at her retreating backside. The word bounced off and rolled to the floor, unnoticed.

Krawczyk rolled her eyes and followed Merilee through the curtained alcove, presumably to the owner's suite beyond, probably hoping to console the distraught hotelier by spreading a little Sapphic love around the Bannerworth.

Krawczyk's so little, she'll get lost between those boobs.

I almost smiled.

"I need to go check the town," Bridger said, "and make sure those things are gone."

"You'll need to gather some men with guns."

"Why didn't I think of that? Damn, are all you judges so smart?"

"You want company?"

"Sure," Bridger said with a snort. "The way you shoot? I'd be a fool not to."

"Fine."

"I gotta pull some pants on," Bridger said. "Man can't kill hobgoblins in his undie-wears."

I hitched my chin at Weeks. "What about you? You good for anything other than sucker punching people?"

Weeks stirred and looked away from the alcove where Merilee had disappeared. "No. No, I believe I could better serve by caring for the injured and departed." With a wave of his hand, he indicated the dead clerk lying in a pool of blood. A thin, humorless smile appeared. "And praying for your success, of course."

"Success? Is that how they say 'untimely death' where you're from?"

The wind picked up, and a suctioning draft pulled through the hotel. The front door, which had been hanging open, slammed shut with a loud bang. I jumped at the sound. Weeks did not.

What an asshole.

Agreed.

I meant you, dumbass.

Chapter Nineteen: A Borrowed Dog

The morning after the hotel battle, Kat Krawczyk and I demolished—well, I demolished, and Krawczyk nibbled—a plate of Gerda's biscuits big and soft enough to be pillows. Cups of strong, bitter coffee helped the biscuits on their way, as did a pot of runny butter. The breakfast rush was over, and we had the room to ourselves, except for an old man sweeping the floor. Gerda, the German owner of Maylene's, had disappeared after dropping off the plate of biscuits and pot of coffee. The scritch-scritch of the old man's broom kept good time. *It's a steady beat, and you can dance to it.*

Krawczyk had been standoffish and cool until I admitted I paid Esmeralda *not* to have sex with me. She acted like she mostly believed me or was at least willing to give me the benefit of the doubt.

"Remember? I came out of my room alone during the pygmy attack. No strange women."

"And you didn't find *anything* of the pygmies?" Krawczyk asked for the third time.

I waved it off, my cheeks full of biscuit.

"Do you think they could all have come from Birnbaum?" Second time for that one.

"Not a chance in hell."

"You're probably right," she admitted. "They seemed to have a strongly developed sense of community, with a hierarchy and a division of duties I would not expect from a bunch of vat-grown creatures." Krawczyk poked into the ceramic pot of soft, lumpy butter with a dull knife. "You think this stuff is pasteurized?"

"It came out of a pasture, yeah."

"Good thing I'm not vegan. I'd starve here."

I leaned over the table and pitched my voice low. "I picked up forty bucks last night at the faro game. Once I sell Misery, we can go."

"You can sell misery? I wish it were that easy."

"Huh? No, Misery is my horse. Long story. Don't ask."

"Oh. Okay." Krawczyk skimmed a thin layer of butter on a biscuit half. "Wait. Leave now? Are you kidding me?"

I narrowed my eyes at her. I could tell I wouldn't like where this was going.

"You'd just up and leave?" Krawczyk said. "Run off and leave these people with the evil whatsits crawling all over the place? And they could be Birnbaum's evil whatsits at that."

"They're not." I pictured Big Chief. "The boss wore necklaces and trinkets that looked old and worn. And all those stone weapons weren't grown in a vat. Somebody had to make those weapons. Dustin Birnbaum didn't pick them up at Pygmies R Us."

"Even so." Krawczyk punched a finger on the table. "They're attacking the town and killing people. Burning churches, for some reason. Before I left to come find you, a rider came into the hotel and said a family up in the hills east of town had been slaughtered and pieces of them left hanging in the barn. The guy said they looked like they'd been butchered... for meat, Shivers. Butchered for *meat*. Who the fuck does that? And why here, why now? Right fucking now when two people from the goddamn *future* are in the same place!"

"Keep your voice down." I glanced at the old man with the broom, who had moved farther away and appeared to have no interest in our conversation. Scritch-scritch. Scritch-scritch. His sweeping sounded like the slow start to "Stand by Me." My jaw tightened, and a mulish stubbornness took root in my neck. "Short version: I have a... mission unfinished." I aborted mentioning my sister. I did not like to speak of her with strangers. "If you recall, there's a rogue Magical in Ohio who's capable of doing any stupid thing that plops into his brain. My mission is to end him, and I intend to get back and do just that."

"Your *mission*?" Kat hissed. "Are you out of your gods-damned mind? First, you don't even know if you can get back. Two, if you can get back, by the time you do, other Judges will have settled Birnbaum's shit. Oh, no wait. Scratch that." Krawczyk pulled up short, holding up a finger and biting her lip. Her tone changed from the temperature of melting steel to cool speculation. "If you're time traveling, I don't guess it would matter because you could come back whenever."

"Exactly." I said it as if I had long ago figured that out. *Actually, doesn't the same logic apply to Alizandra's condition? Shut up.* "I intend to pop in before he leaves his house and blow him off his skateboard."

"But still," Krawczyk continued, "what about these people? You just gonna leave them to these pissed off little pixies? Is that your idea of how a Judge should act? No, scratch that too. Is that your idea of how a human should act? I never took you for a coward, Shivers."

Cold splashed through me, followed by heat boiling up into my face. I controlled my voice with an effort. "Tread carefully, Krawczyk."

She let out a breath. "Yeah, sorry. That was out of line. Here." She filled both coffee cups from the cooling pot on the table. "Anyway, changing the subject, I got Merilee chilled down about you staying at the hotel. She knew it wasn't your fault. She was just pissed it happened and took it out on you. I think she likes you," she added with a slanted look.

"I'm pretty sure she doesn't."

"No, I think she does, but she can't admit it, you being of racially ambiguous descent."

"'Cause I's part darkie?"

"Yes." Krawczyk sighed. "The bigotry in this age is awful."

I huffed a sarcastic agreement.

"But she's a product of the times, Shivers. You have to cut her some slack."

We drank coffee in silence for a time while I picked at the crumbs dotting my plate and the table. I held off at picking any off the floor, as a man had to have some limits. The old man finished his sweeping, and the absence of scritching made the quiet more pronounced. Despite the coffee, my eyes drooped. I cracked a yawn.

"Been meaning to ask you something," I said.

"What?"

"Every Magical I've ever seen has to be in physical contact with their amulet to channel the energy. Mine's on a chain around my neck, but you don't wear a chain or a ring..."

The corner of Krawczyk's mouth lifted in a wicked grin. "Not all piercings are visible, Shivers."

The penny dropped, and I nodded. "Got it."

"What about the pygmies? Are you really just going to leave?"

I sighed. Nothing was ever easy. I sniffed and looked out the window, then words came out of my mouth before I could think them through. "I'll try to track these pygmy bastards down. I have an idea how I can do that. I make no promises. However, I do not think they're involved with the arsons and the preacher getting killed and the bank robbery and stuff. That smells more like a Magical than it does little Gollum people, and a Magical with a grudge against organized religion. Could be the upstanding Reverend Weeks, even."

"I'll keep an eye on Weeks." Krawczyk paused and narrowed her eyes in a look I had come to recognize as concern for others, the same look people used for abandoned kittens and cancer patients. "If Weeks is using magic illegally, what will you do?"

I grunted. "What Judges always do. I'll kill him."

I navigated to the stable, my throat parched by the dry air. The morning sun peeked over the eastern mountains and shot the sky full of golden beams of light. Even under the flat brim of my hat, I was forced to squint against the glare.

Bridger had said he was going to organize a search party, promising to scour the town from basement to bell tower for the little people, and while the sheriff's strategy was sound, my gut said the search would prove fruitless. No matter how small the Gollum people were, a horde of them could not hide in somebody's cupboard. I suspected Big Chief had pulled his warriors back to the desert or even to the mountains to rest and regroup before attempting another foray into town.

But what the hell did they want? At first, it had appeared that the Gollums were sniffing at doors. Were they tracking somebody? Looking for something? Hunting like hound dogs?

That triggered an idea. There was a lot of territory to cover out there. Blundering around witlessly wouldn't be a productive use of time. It was my third day in Geyser Falls, and I had not made one inch of progress toward returning home, and wasting days by wandering the mountains would be worse than stupid. *Lack of planning is planning to fail.* Dad-ism number one million twenty-three.

I needed a little help.

The stableman, George Bethlehem, dozed in a chair tilted back against the inside wall of his stable. Both front and back doors were open, catching a rare cross-breeze and keeping the interior a bearable temperature. A black-and-tan hound curled at Bethlehem's feet and eyeballed me without lifting his head. The dog's tail thumped the ground with a lazy greeting.

"Wake up, George."

The stable owner snorted and cracked one eye. "Mornin', Judge."

"I need my horse." When the hound stood and sniffed at my feet, I added, "How good does your dog smell?"

"Like a dog. Worse when wet."

I closed my eyes, counted to four. "No, George. Track. How well does he track?"

Bethlehem settled the front legs of his chair to the ground and frowned at the mutt. "Don't know. Never seen him trail nothing."

"Can I borrow him?"

"Borrow my dog?"

"Yes. Borrow your dog."

"I don't loan out my dog, Your Honor." Bethlehem scratched his nose. He smiled through yellow teeth. "But you can rent him, if you want."

Of course. I sighed. "Okay, whatever. Put it on my bill. What's the dog's name? Scalper?"

"No, I just call him Blackie."

"Original." I knelt and rubbed the dog's ears. The mutt butted his head into my armpit, tail whapping hard enough to wiggle his entire rear. I held Blackie by the cheeks and looked into his eyes. Communicating with dogs was tough. Their attention span—squirrel!

I need you to find some people, I projected into the dog's mind.

Okay, okay, okay. Blackie's tail beat in time with his thoughts.

"Have my horse ready," I told Bethlehem. "I have an errand to run."

I jogged back to the Bannerworth. In front of the hotel, the bloody and burned pygmy corpses were being stacked in a wagon like cord wood. Undertaker Mallory, the Custer lookalike, supervised a team of laborers as they tossed bodies on the pile with the *one-two-three-swing* method.

"I need some of their clothing," I told the undertaker. "Personal effects, whatever."

Mallory brewed up a thunderhead expression. His florid face turned even redder. "I beg your pardon."

"It's for the dog," I explained. "I need a scent for him to track."

"Ah. Of course. You there... yes, you. Strip some of those diapers off 'em. C'mon, man, don't be so damned squeamish."

When I returned to the stable, Bethlehem brought out Misery, bridled and saddled. The stableman handed off the reins and flopped back into his chair with the sigh of a man who had done a day's work with little appreciation and less compensation. He had kicked back against the wall and closed his eyes before my butt hit the saddle.

Misery rolled his eyes at Blackie and snorted. The horse danced away as if frightened.

"Easy, now," I said.

If a horse's thoughts could be said to mutter, Misery muttered something like, *Mangy, ankle-biting, stupid, noisy shit factory.*

I bumped the horse in the ribs with my heels and guided the buckskin eastward at a canter. Blackie loped ahead, happy thoughts of butterflies and steak bones flitting through his mind. I registered the strong impression this grand adventure was making on him. Nothing more fun than being a dog on a mission.

I could empathize.

Chapter Twenty: Kat and the Reverend

Intermission
Kat Krawczyk and the Reverend Weeks

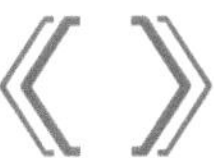

Kat Krawczyk clomped along the dusty streets of Geyser Falls on her way back to the Bannerworth Hotel, ignoring the stares from the uptight citizens she passed. In her miner boots, men's jeans, and plaid work shirt, she felt a lot like a girl playing dress-up in her daddy's clothes, which she decided would be a kinky fantasy to play out with Carrin Andover, her on-again, off-again girlfriend back in Columbus, Ohio. The thought of never again seeing Carrin's athletic body stretched out across her king-size bed, bowing up like a suspension bridge while singing "Yesyesyesyesyesyes!" in high soprano filled Kat with melancholy both foreign and unwelcome.

Until her untimely jaunt back to the past, Kat believed herself to be a generally happy person. Chronic sinus congestion, religious fanatics, and people who farted in elevators were the only things that ever turned her smile upside down. She was brash, loved to party, loved to laugh, and loved kittens. She was a sexual being who enjoyed the pleasures of both male and female companions. She was a one-time Wiccan, believed in the healing power of Mother Earth, and could use magic—although she avoided using the word "magic." To her, magic was another form of the natural energy of the universe, in a state a few lucky souls could recognize and bend to their will. Magic was energy, energy was matter, and matter was energy, may the Goddess bless Albert Einstein.

Those qualities were trouble enough in the twenty-first century, but transplanted to the puritanical early-America of 1887... well, she found it no wonder that the people of Geyser Falls wanted to burn her at the stake.

She promised Shivers she would keep her head down and her opinions to herself until he got back, which was really freaking annoying because she shouldn't have needed a man to protect her, but there it was. She was very alone in a strange time and stranger place, with mores she barely recognized and social norms she found archaic, ignorant, and stifling. Kat hated guns and had no desire to learn how to use one. As for magic, she believed it to be a power for good and would never use it to hurt anyone... well, except for that one time she started a fire in the pants of a bigoted blowhard in line at the movies.

She was good with anatomy. Healing required converting the body's energy to repair cellular damage, increase blood flow, oxygenate tissues, stimulate glands. Kat could navigate around a person's bloodstream, neural network, and lymphatic system as easily as walking to Stern's Market on the corner of her block. Intellectually, she knew a million ways to switch off a living being—stop the heart, freeze the brain, blow out an artery... the list went on.

But that wasn't her. Kat caught bugs in her apartment on a dustpan and deposited them outside rather than kill them. She'd joked with Shivers about not being vegan, but she wasn't far from it. Even when Birnbaum had her trapped in his invisible force field, she'd been unable to pull the trigger, metaphorically speaking, on blowing his brains out his ears with a force bubble.

It took a cold-hearted asshole to do that job—killing. It took someone like Shivers.

Shivers. What an apt name. Light-colored, green-tinted eyes with a very slight tilt, hooded brows, a bold, Roman nose, and sensuous lips—his odd heritage was evident in a few simple features. Dark, deadly, and dangerous like a panther suspended in a tree over a jungle trail, waiting for a tasty meal to cross his path. The man reminded her of one of those high-end precision German chef's knives. Cold, honed steel.

Capital punishment disgusted her. Capital punishment without due process made her insides twist into knots. That Shivers used his power as judge, jury, and executioner made her skin crawl. *If only there was a way to imprison Magicals who went rogue, instead of murdering them without a trial...* She'd thought about it often, coming up with solutions like knocking them out and taking their amulets. When she had brought it up to the Admins, they had brushed her aside. The old fogies did things the way they did them, and that was it, staying with the theory that fear of ultimate punishment kept people honest.

Kat snorted. *Asshats.*

She rounded the corner of Sixth and Main and stopped dead in her tracks. The Reverend Jonathon Weeks strolled from the entrance of the Bannerworth and turned west, toward the river. Kat scrambled in reverse and put her back to the Bunting Law Office building. She risked a peek around the corner. Weeks strode away, his gaze focused ahead, a man with purpose, on his way to do something important.

Burn a church, maybe? Rob another bank?

Kat slipped around the corner and kept pace with the tall reverend, double-stepping to every one of his long strides.

"Okay, Nancy Shrew," Kat told herself. "Let's see what the preacher man's up to."

I followed the dog east, tapping into Blackie's mind at odd intervals. The mongrel quested back and forth without a hit. He sniffed bushes and dirt and grass and bugs and all manner of furry critters. The animal was excited by the profusion of smells but also held the Gollum's scent focused in his mind. When he drifted, I reminded him with a gentle nudge.

We crisscrossed the flats between the town and the mountains in broader sweeps from north to south, but the long treks through thick, scrubby brush accomplished nothing more than giving me a headache. Cutting the Gollums' trail was proving harder than I anticipated. Maybe they had gone to ground somewhere in Geyser Falls, after all. Maybe Bridger would turn up a nest of them in some barn loft and have a Custer's Last Stand of his own. Archie Bridger and the Mini-Indians sounded like a rock band from the fifties.

Meanwhile, Blackie and I would be trekking around in circles until we reached Nevada.

"How about a song for the journey?" I said to the horse. On my own, with no one listening, I could sing without criticism or judgment. "Bob Seger, 'Turn the Page' or 'Night Moves'? No, something more melancholy. Hmm. Peter, Paul, and Mary, maybe? 'Blowing in the Wind'? Perfect choice, Misery." The horse tossed his head, which I interpreted as permission to proceed. "How many roads must a man walk down—"

Misery nickered plaintively.

"That's it! Now, you're in the spirit." I patted his flank. "Stay on key now."

The sun topped the mountains, and the heat intensified as if a giant magnifying glass focused the rays directly on me and the plodding horse. I mentally thanked George Bethlehem because the man had filled a canteen and hung it from Misery's saddle horn. I sucked down a long pull of the brackish water between stanzas.

"I'll probably get the shits," I said.

Misery sent me a mental image of a dried-up husk, an empty skin sack with my face.

"Very funny. I'm not full of shit, you nag."

We were on the far north end of our sweep when Blackie paused and threw his head up. His wet nose tested the wind, and he let out a short woof as though confused. The dog continued northeastward, and I drew a breath to call him back then hesitated. Blackie seemed more focused than he had been all morning, making a beeline for the mountains. I shrugged and decided to follow the dog.

When Blackie reached a rutted trail, he bayed in full voice and bolted. I caught a bit of his excitement from our mental connection. *This way, this way!*

"Come on, horse. Let's giddyap."

Miraculously, Misery broke into a full-out canter. I was so surprised, I nearly fell off.

If horses could laugh, Misery was having a giggling fit.

Intermission
Archie Bridger and the blue-haired witch

Sheriff Archibald Bridger paused in the doorway of an abandoned dwelling on the north side of town and examined the dusty interior. Empty. He removed his hat and mopped sweat with a sleeve. His deputies, Potts and Barton, squatted in front of the house, under the shade of a diseased elm, its leaves twisted and brown rather than the expected lush green of spring. Everything on the north side of Geyser Falls past Eighth Street and down close to the river seemed to be diseased, dead, or abandoned. What the place needed was a good fire to burn out the rats and spiders and scorpions and leave some ruffians homeless in the bargain.

When Bridger turned from the broken porch of the two-room house, his deputies shot expectant looks his way. Bridger shook his head. *No.* No trace of the ugly little bastards that attacked the hotel. He and his deputies had swept the north half of town while the ass, Bunting, had led a contingent from Main Street to the south. In the absence of their prearranged signal, three shots fired in the air, Bridger had to assume Bunting's party had achieved the same lack of results.

"What a goddamn nuisance," Bridger muttered to himself. "Like rats in the corn. I've had about enough of this shit."

And right when he was so close to solving his problem with the Bible-thumper. A few more days without distraction, and he might have been able to pin the preacher with all the mayhem happening around town. He had been so damn close. Then the blue-haired bitch had shown up and knocked him into a cocked hat, followed by that damn uppity darkie, quarter this and quarter that. Bull dookie. "Part Sambo is all Sambo," his daddy used to say.

Bridger had been cock of the walk before Weeks and now Shivers had arrived in town. Merilee had dropped him like a hot coal as soon as Weeks crooked his finger, and now, this Shivers acted like he was running things. To Hell with that nonsense.

Shivers was a full-on asshole, no two ways about it. And there was more to both him and the perverted little bitch than met the eyes. The darkie had done... something... on the stairs back at the hotel. Bridger had a pretty good suspicion what it was too. Blew the jiminy-Christmas outta a whole buncha half-pint Injun bastards and a big chunk of hotel, too, and lit a bee in Merilee's bonnet, that little stunt. Bridger smiled at the memory. Cherry on top, she'd given Weeks the cold shoulder right after that. Could be maybe she was seeing the light where that sanctimonious holy roller was concerned.

Well, I've tried doing things sneaky-like, and look where that's got me. Maybe it's time to cut loose and let the bronc buck. Time I showed people who's boss hog in this sty.

A flicker of motion from across the street caught Bridger's eye, and he stepped back into the shadows of the building.

"Well," he said to himself, "think of the devil, and here he comes."

The long strides of the Reverend Jonathon Weeks ate up the ground as the preacher marched out of town along the northern road. For some reason, the man preferred walking to riding, more evidence that there was something wrong with him. Weeks stepped along as though he owned the world, a Bible tucked under one arm and his broad-brimmed hat shadowing his face. He looked neither right nor left, his eyes fixed no doubt on God's holy light shining somewhere only Weeks could see. Goddamn uppity bastard.

Bridger spat in the dirt. His palm itched with the desire to pull out his piece and blow a hole in Weeks big enough to lodge a fence post. In the short time Weeks had been in Geyser Falls, he had grown from a pimple to a boil on Bridger's ass. Bridger couldn't take a shit without the preacher telling him how bad it smelled.

Oh, hello. What is this sneaking along behind him? Bridger stepped deeper into the shadows. *Lookie, lookie here. If it ain't the blue-haired witch herself, creeping along after the preacher like an Apache after his scalp.*

Bridger held himself still and watched them pass. Neither appeared to take note of Bridger or his deputies on the opposite side of the street, so focused they were on their personal business, stalker and stalked. How easy it would be to slip out of town on their trail, shoot them both, and solve at least two problems at the same time.

Except he didn't want to kill Weeks. He wanted the man in jail first then properly hung by the neck until his pretty face turned purple. Or gone, bags packed and headed out to Bible-thump some savage Mongoloid race on a continent far away from America. Ambushing the man would make him a martyr for Merilee to grieve, and that was a complication Bridger didn't need. No, Merilee had to see Weeks for the dastardly coward he was, no fit mate for a woman of her quality. Her infatuation with Weeks's broad shoulders and blocky chin needed to die of natural causes of its own accord, else Bridger would never get himself situated between the woman's satiny thighs the way he wanted.

That was the elegant solution. The intelligent solution. Much more satisfying than just chopping down all the weeds and reaping the fertile fields left behind.

No, best to leave them be for now. Mayhap Weeks and the witch would get up to some mischief that would see them both dead of their own devices, leaving Bridger in the clear and Merilee needing comforting. And he knew just how to provide such comfort, which was by repeatedly using his stiff dick to pound her with doses of sweet succor.

Bridger smiled and waited in the shadows until Krawczyk disappeared. He rolled his shoulder to loosen it up. The damn thing ached something fierce ever since an ornery horse had thrown him into a pile of rocks.

Time to go see Esmeralda and have her ease my pain in more ways than one.

He stepped into the weedy yard and told his drowsing companions, "C'mon, boys. It's comin' on lunch time. Let's call off this hoedown and go to the Wheel for some ham and boiled eggs. First beer's on me."

Intermission
Billy Minor and the Indian

Billy Minor peeled back gummy eyelids and discovered he was tied to a tree. A thick rope of braided sinew circled his upper body six or eight times and held him upright against the trunk of an elm. The glitter of sunlight off a lake pierced the trees, and along with it, the muted rush of a waterfall hissed in the distance. Woodsmoke itched his nostrils, smoke and the smell of meat cooking over an open flame. Sawdust stuffed his brain cavity, heavy and thick, and thinking happened with the sluggishness of sugarfied honey oozing from a jar.

He studied this predicament for a time. It didn't get any better with studying. Billy shifted the oversized pumpkin on his neck toward the meat-cooking smell. Through the trees a goodly few yards away, the torso and haunch of some animal had been skinned, dressed, and suspended over glowing coals. Fat dripped, hissed, and smoked when it hit the fire. The blackened carcass rotated, turned by a scrawny youngster in a nappy, a bird's nest of black hair, and a smushed-up, brutal face.

That is one ugly dang kid, by gosh.

Billy's stomach took a bad turn when he recognized the carcass over the fire.

It was a mule, for damn sure, and he would bet almost a whole silver dollar that either Junior or Dorothy was being roasted into somebody's dinner.

"Dad-raspit," Billy moaned. "Eat a man's mule. That's low."

His stomach grumbled from hunger, which seemed a betrayal of his good friends. Dorothy and Junior meant more to him than pack animals, both having been companions of his long years of prospecting. They'd spent many a winter night high in the mountains, fighting frostbite, cougars, and wolves. Didn't seem right he should be hungry for them now that one of 'em was a-cooking over there. But there he was, stomach betraying his pals by growling and gurgling for some mule meat, same as any starving wolf.

And he had to piss like crazy.

Older he got, the more peeing became a dadgummed chore. Three or four times a night, he would have to roll out of his blankets, traipse off a ways, unlimber the pump handle, then stand there and tease the stream to starting, drizzle a bit, and tease some more before his bladder was happy enough to let him go back to sleep. Only he was tied to a tree and couldn't reach his dingus, nor could he stand, and he darned sure could not traipse off anywheres. If he was gonna pee, it was gonna happen right here, right now, and then he'd have to live with it for God knew how long.

"Hey," he croaked toward the stump-ugly cook tending the fire. Then louder, "Hey! Untie me so I can go take a call of nature!"

The kid doing the spit-turning may have grunted, or Billy may have imagined it. Either way, the response was less than a brass band and a parade.

"Hey there, padnah! I'm a-fixin' to water this here tree if you don't come cut me loose."

"It will do you no good," said a nearby voice.

Billy swiveled his head the opposite direction and spotted an Injun in white man's clothes, tied to a tree, in the same predicament as Billy. The Injun looked hard-used, his fancy Eastern-cut suit dusty and rumpled, torn at one shoulder. A purple knot over the man's right eye trailed dried ribbons of blood down his cheek, and the wire-framed glasses perched on his nose were bent askew. He wore no hat, and his lank, black hair hung below his ears as if it had been cut around a bowl on his head.

"Who're you?" Billy asked.

"My American name is James Snow. My Paiute name is"—he gargled some syllables in Injun—"which means something like Little

Owl, so I am sometimes known as James Little Owl." The Injun shrugged. "It depends upon the company."

"Oh," said Billy. "How'd you come to be here?"

"Same as you, I'd expect. Wrong place at the wrong time."

"That's for danged sure. You're dressed too fancy to have been prospeckin'. So how come you to be out here in the wild back of nowhere?"

"I was sent at a very young age to a boarding school," James Snow explained, "established for Paiute-Shoshones in Utah, where I was educated, and where I later taught English to children of both Northern and Southern Paiute tribes. When the missionaries sent me to school, I was... ah... I was separated from my family. Not having seen my mother and father for many years, I decided to make the trip back home." Snow teased out a rueful smile. "Which has not gone as expected, as you can see."

"Amen to that," Billy said. "Hey, you talk some pretty good American. For an Injun, that is."

"As do you. For a misanthrope, that is."

Billy thought about that for a couple of ticks. "Well... okay. Thank'ee kindly."

A blue jay settled on a low limb of Billy's tree and ki-ay'ed at him a few times before flying off. The sun had climbed high in the sky, but only spots of light reached the ground through the trees above, and a fresh breeze kept the temperature mild. All in all, it was a peaceful and comfortable place to have a sit and palaver with his new pal, James Snow. He liked to talk, not getting much chance to speak to human people or Injuns, what with traipsing all over the devil's backside in search of a bit of yellow metal. James Snow was a friendly enough guy, for an Injun. Were it not for the scent of Dorothy or Junior roasting over an open fire and his bladder full as a tick tapping a vein, Billy might have found this a nice way to pass an afternoon.

Two more little boys joined the one by the fire and belched something in their own tongue, which sounded to Billy like they were puking fur balls. He squinted at the newcomers, and his perspective shifted.

"Well, I'll be danged and sent to H-E-double-toothpicks. They's ain't boys a tall. They's fully-growed men, only they's stunted, little-bitty nubbins. Like 'em Lepre-corns the micks go on about."

"Worse than that, my friend," said Snow. "I believe these to be the manifest spirit of the Inyo, known by legend as the Nimerigar."

Billy scrunched his face in confusion. Where had he heard that word before? "The Nimme-what-i-gar?"

"The Nimerigar," Snow repeated. "A race of vicious little cannibals who live deep in the mountains. They shoot poison-tipped arrows and use stone axes to bash in the heads of anyone unlucky enough to trespass on their domain."

Billy picked one word out that sent a wash of cold down his back. "Wait. You said cannibals. Don't that mean—"

"Yes, they eat other humans, including their own. Translated, Nimerigar means 'people eater.' You and I"—Snow inclined his head toward where Junior or Dorothy rotated on a spit—"are bound for the same fate as your unfortunate mule."

Well, dadgummit. Maybe they won't eat me if I'm covered in piss.

Chapter Twenty-One: Kat-napped

Kat followed Reverend Weeks as the preacher strode along the road parallel to the river as if he had but one goal, to reach his destination in the shortest possible time and by the most direct route. They were half a mile past the last dwelling before she remembered the preacher's tent camp lay not far ahead, on the east bank of the Owens River. With his Bible in one hand and no other gear, his destination appeared obvious.

So not going to burn down a church, kill anybody, or rob a bank. Merely headed to work, like any other somewhat normal person in the real world. Following him would net her nothing but blistered feet—*haven't these people heard of decent socks?* What Geyser Falls needed was an Eddie Bauer outlet. Maybe an REI.

Kat clumped to a full stop, her round-toed boots kicking up puffs of dust. The trail veered close to the river, where willows clung to the crumbling banks and overhung chuckling shallows. The hot, dry air convection roasted Kat's skin and baked her like a potato inside her oversized clothes. The river begged to be jumped in, its cool water ready to flush away the heat and sweat and grime coating her body.

"Oh my God," she whispered, "what I wouldn't give for a king-size bottle of Head & Shoulders and a curved block of Dove soap right now."

Still... water washing was better than no washing at all.

Kat turned in a slow circle, studying her surroundings. Weeks had disappeared far ahead, and no one else shared the road with her. In fact, she had passed no one since the north edge of town, where two deputies snoozed under the brown tree by the rickety house. They had kept their heads down and paid no attention to her as she passed. For all intents and purposes, she was alone. She wasn't ashamed or afraid of nudity, and in ordinary circumstances would have loved to go skinny-dipping. Even so, stripping and jumping in the river seemed unwise. *We've seen that movie before, right? Naked girl in river. Unseen eyes watching. Bad things happen.*

But... water. Cool water.

"What the fuck?" With a final shrug, Kat walked to the river's edge, paused for a second, then stripped off her boots and kept walking, splashing into the deliciously cool water until it flowed up past the knees of her heavy britches. Her pants and shirt could stand washing, just as much as her body. She sat down and moaned. "Sweet Mother Earth."

Kat dipped her head back and scrubbed her fingers through her hair. "Die, mutant vermin." Then she just floated for a while, her butt anchored against the sandy river bottom and the sun warming her face. The river's low, deep voice lulled her into a near-trance. *A Katatonic state.* She smiled with her eyes closed.

When the heat on her forehead warned her of imminent sunburn, Kat submerged for one last dip then climbed from the river. Water streamed off her soggy clothes and splattered the riverbank. She tugged on her boots, slogged to a grassy patch under the willows, and plopped down, shivering a little in the mild breeze.

"Huh!" She jumped when a pair of quail burst from the undergrowth upstream and curved away. Kat eyed the spot from which they sprang, but nothing else moved. She stretched out with her eyes shaded by an elbow and let the sun pour its energy into her body. She dozed to the lullaby of the flowing water and the mild breeze.

The first indication she was under attack arrived by way of a tiny arrow zinging past her chin. The whiff of it passing startled her awake. The second arrow smacked into her right triceps, punching her the same way her brother did when they were kids and Mom wasn't looking. Kat blinked at the feathered shaft, no bigger than a crossbow bolt, stuck in her arm.

Rustling from the bushes. A half dozen or more of the pygmy people appeared as though magically conjured. Eyes glowered. Nostrils flared. Some had arrows notched to bows, and the tips of the arrows, Kat observed from a great distance, glistened with brownish liquor.

Fuck. Poisoned.

She could feel it now, working up through her shoulder and into her neck. A spreading heat stole through her muscles and robbed her of movement and of willpower.

Kat focused on her magic and forced the muscles around the arrowhead to loosen. In slow motion, her left hand traveled up, clasped the shaft, and pulled. Funny, she felt no pain. The poison must have been numbing the flesh as well as seeping through her veins to attack her nervous system. Had it soaked in too far? Only one way to know.

Kat channeled a thick band of power that contracted around the wound in her arm, squeezing it like a blood pressure cuff. She watched with detached interest as thick, gummy blood spurted, soaking the sleeve of her plaid shirt. Tighter. More blood pulsed. A weak fountain this time. Kat willed her magic to push from the inside, and she felt the hole in her arm tear wider, though the pain was muted. More bloody gunk came out. It trickled down her arm, leaving warm, sticky trails. It smelled bad.

Fuzziness crept into her vision. Sounds arrived in her brain long after the cause of the noise. Kat's world zeroed to a tunnel of light. At one end, her conscious mind slowly grew dim. At the other end, the bullseye of the arrow wound pulsed with crimson. She was able to give it one last, good squeeze before the tunnel dimmed, diminished...

Winked out.

Blackie had done his best. His frustration all but vibrated through our mental link, scraping on my nerves and adding dollops of anxiety to my cup full of jitters. It wasn't that the dog couldn't find the trail but a case of too many trails, all crisscrossing and meandering throughout the bracken and bristly trees between Geyser Falls and the western foothills of the Inyos. The exhausted pooch dropped to his belly under the meager shade of a scrubby greasewood and panted, sending me the dog equivalent of *I give up, dude. This shit is way too hard.*

I dismounted and poured water into my cupped palm for the dog. "That's all right, buddy. I've had about enough of this too." I eyeballed the sun's position and estimated the time at somewhere around four p.m. "Let's head back to town. By the time we get in, it'll be suppertime."

Yes, yes, yes. Blackie jumped up and lapped at my face. Food translated well in any language.

"Glad you agree." I palmed water for Misery, slung the canteen over my shoulder, then reached for the stirrup to get my foot seated prior to mounting.

A bullet *whapped* into the leather of his saddle, followed closely by the dull boom of a rifle fired from a distance. A bright streak in the leather seat marked the spot where the bullet had struck a glancing blow across the saddle. Misery's fatalism and near-catatonic depression apparently didn't cover getting shot. The horse bolted like a three-year-old at the starting gate of the Preakness, spinning me to the dirt in his passing. I ate sand and wriggled blindly into the dubious cover of the low-hanging greasewood bush. I pawed grit out of my eyes while Blackie danced in a circle, barking.

"Get down, dog," I growled. "And be quiet."

Blackie bellied down next to me, tongue flopped to one side and panting happily at the new game we played. The desert air soaked up sound. The sweat dried on my face as quickly as it formed. High above, a buzzard glided in slow circles, joined moments later by another. Low brush limited my view, and raising my head for a look-see seemed unwise. I estimated the time from bullet strike to gunshot and came up with a distance of three hundred yards, which required considerable skill using iron sights and nineteenth-century black powder. The bullet had nearly taken my head off on the first shot, and giving him a second chance at my noggin was not a plan I favored.

"I think we'll wait here awhile," I told Blackie. "See what happens next."

Blackie thought that was a fine idea and commenced chomping at a flea under his foreleg.

I limped into Geyser Falls well after dark with Blackie. Spending a hot, sweaty afternoon under a greasewood bush had done nothing to improve my outlook or disposition. I had given up the vigil for the sniper as purple dusk filled the valley, with no signs of the shooter appearing after that first bullet. As the light faded, I had crawled for a distance away from my original spot then clambered off the ground and set off at a walk toward the distant lights of the town.

Misery remained AWOL. I couldn't decide if I was annoyed by the betrayal or proud that the horse had enough sense to stay away from a hidden sniper.

I passed some folks out and about on the lamplit streets. A few called greetings, and I responded with a raised hand. For the most part, I stayed in the shadows and close to the buildings wherever possible, scanning for threats, though nothing triggered my threat sensors, such as guys skulking along with scoped rifles and guilty expressions. Business as usual in Geyser Falls. *Nothing to see here, folks, move along.*

Yellow light spilled from the Bannerworth's windows. Along with it came the mouthwatering smell of grilled beef and baked bread. The sound of voices and cutlery carried out to the porch, and Blackie whined a query that needed no special power to understand.

"Yeah, me too," I assured him. "Let's get some chow."

I pushed through the front doors with the dog following close behind. The lobby had been cleaned of dead pygmies, and raw wood slats patched the banister and stair treads. The burned rugs had been removed, and the place smelled of strong soap and fresh-cut lumber.

Merilee Soames looked up from the front desk, where she conferred with a clerk I had never seen before. She had regained her poise somewhere in the past few hours and appeared as coolly disengaged as a maestro in front of her orchestra. She had her hair pinned up and wore a starched white blouse with a high collar and an arch to her brow that suggested I had trodden raw shit on her mopped floors.

"What have you done with her, sirrah?" was her greeting. Along with her bearing, she had also recovered her drawing room diction. All traces of Cockney had disappeared.

I tromped up to the desk and stopped. "With whom, madam?"

"You know quite well with whom."

I sighed and scratched my bristly chin. "Pretend I don't."

"Miss Krawczyk."

"Miss Krawczyk? I haven't seen Kat since breakfast."

Merilee stood erect and fairly vibrated. "Are you saying you have nothing to do with her disappearance?"

"Disappearance? She's missing? Since when?"

"Since this morning. You were the last one seen with her."

A trill of irritation tightened my jaw. *Now what? Another setback to getting out of Geyser Falls and back to where I belonged.* I clamped down on the feeling, recognizing it as selfish and unworthy. Krawczyk wouldn't have disappeared without good cause. Blackie whined and butted his head into my thigh.

"She was going to..."

"She was going to what?" Merilee asked after I stopped speaking.

I had started to say she was going to keep an eye on Weeks then remembered that Merilee and the reverend were close, perhaps even intimate. Suggesting we had cause to surveil Weeks might not be the most diplomatic thing to tell the woman.

"She was going for a walk, last I heard." I patted the dog's head. "Blackie and I were backtracking the little people all day, then... then my horse ran off, and we had to walk back."

"Your horse?" Merilee blinked. "The one who looks like last month's chopped beef? He *ran* off?"

"It's a long story." I lifted my hat and scratched my fingers through tangles of damp, greasy hair. "Can you find something of Miss Krawczyk's? Something she wore, maybe? Blackie here's a pretty good tracker. I need to eat and fill my canteen, and we can get after her."

Some of the stiffness went out of Merilee. "James, show Mr. Shivers to the dining room. The dog may stay on the porch, sir, as he smells... quite strongly. But we will bring him a bowl of water and some table scraps. I will retrieve some of Miss Krawczyk's clothing while you eat. Is that agreeable?"

"Yeah, sure." I cupped the dog by the jowls. "You good with that, buddy?"

Blackie woofed, and his tail thumped the floor.

"Don't get too happy," I warned him. "We're going right back out as soon as we eat. I don't have a good feeling about this."

Chapter Twenty-Two: Invited to Dinner

I stuffed my face in the Bannerworth dining room, feeling the aches and pains of a long hike settle through my legs and back. The last thing I wanted to do was go back out on another snipe hunt, though I owed it to Krawczyk to make sure nothing bad had happened to her. It was my fault she was in harm's way to begin with. The first place I would check would be Weeks's camp to the north of town. If that prick had hurt her, he would be nothing but a scorch mark on the earth once I was done with him.

I hoped it wouldn't come to that. With luck, Krawczyk had gone haring off on her own somewhere, seeking peace and quiet, and was merely temporarily AWOL, perhaps hunting some incense to burn or a crystal to rub for luck. The uneasy feeling spreading under my skin said otherwise. She knew her situation remained tenuous, what with the townspeople suspicious and prone to using violence to calm their nerves. She had no friends beyond me and Merilee, so it was unlikely she would be just hanging out, having a cup of tea and chatting with random citizens.

I looked up and spotted Sheriff Bridger standing at the entrance to the dining room, scanning the smattering of diners. Our eyes met. Bridger hitched his chin and crossed the room. The sheriff walked with a bit of a list, stepping with the careful deliberation of a man who'd had a few or more shots of rye. When he arrived at the table, the aroma of stale whiskey confirmed my assessment.

Bridger sat without waiting for an invitation. "Any luck?"

"I haven't even started looking for her yet." His blank look caused me to shift mental gears. "Oh, you mean the little people? No. Nothing. Though somebody took a shot at me." I explained the bullet fired from ambush that hit my saddle and my subsequent walk back to town.

Bridger pursed his lips and contracted his brow. "That's odd."

"Odd. Yep. Have you seen Kat? Ms. Krawczyk?"

"Ahh, yes. Yes, I did." Bridger picked at a fingernail. "She was, ah, following along behind Reverend Weeks. Headed north, out of town, last I saw."

"Damn."

"Do you think... Should we be concerned? Why would she be following Weeks?" Bridger's blue-eyed expression seemed as open as a barn door but held a hint of mischief that tickled my nerves. The expression said he knew something I didn't.

"No," I said. "Not yet."

Merilee Soames appeared at the table with a piece of white cloth folded into a small square. She held herself as though wrapped in tight rubber bands from head to toe, and a blush colored her cheeks. "This... this is all I could find that... that Miss Krawczyk has worn. It's her... it's her..."

Panties, I finished in my head. "No problem." I took the cloth then tucked it in my pants pocket. The three of us stood around the table, contemplating the remains of the meal for a silent moment, like people on an elevator. Conversational gambits scattered and ran from my mind, and the harder I chased them, the faster they ran. I had never been good at small talk. I looked at Bridger, who glanced at Merilee, who studied her fingertips and cleared her throat. I wanted to ask Merilee about her Cockney-talking, dagger-wielding inner self and whether her starched-shirt-headmistress persona was some kind of superhero disguise. But the woman's outer shell was so hard,

I imagined her skin would ring like ceramic if I tapped it with a penny.

"Okay, then," I said.

"Yes," Merilee said.

"That's a curious stone, Judge." Bridger's eyes were fixed on my chest. I glanced down and discovered that my magic amulet had fallen out of my shirt.

"Oh this?" I tucked the stone away and stood. "Just a trinket. Anybody seen my dog?"

Intermission
Kat's up a tree

I'm in trouble was Kat's first conscious thought when the darkness receded and she could think again.

No shit was her second.

She reached for magic, and of course, it was tapped out. Dry as a mummy's tits.

Suspended from a jouncing pole by wrists and ankles, being carried by the Ewoks' ugly cousins over and along desert trails, Kat's head lolled back. She viewed the world from an inverted position. Ahead of her, she got a good look at a pygmy's tiny little butt cheeks. *Was it racist to call them pygmies?* It felt racist. *Maybe Short American would be better.* When she raised her head and chinned forward in the mother of all crunches, she could make out the trailing pole bearer, who resembled a cross between a troll and a Native American. *Height-challenged Native American.*

The trollish-looking thing grinned at her with a mouth of rotten teeth. Pointed, rotten teeth.

What time was it? Well after noon, she judged, given the shadows forming through the underbrush. Adding to her list of complaints, her stomach sent up a telegram saying, *empty. Please fill.*

By twisting up in a pretzel, Kat examined her aching left arm. It dripped sluggish red drops, thick as paint. That was bad. Worse, she couldn't feel her hands or feet, as the ropes binding her to the pole had clamped the circulation off like a pneumatic tourniquet. Whatever poison they had hit her with had left her woozy, too, and coupled with the swaying and bouncing, she wanted to hurl chunks, which would be really bad in this position. Kat gritted her teeth and held on to what was left in her stomach with a strong will and a rediscovered aptitude for prayer. She let her head drop back, which cramped her neck like a sonofabitch and dragged her hair through the dirt on the low spots. These people were seriously testing her peaceful and nonviolent nature.

"You just wait," she growled at the pygmy's upside-down ass. "I get my magic back, I'm going to give you a boil on your testicle the size of a walnut."

Kat passed out again somewhere along the way and only came back to awareness when the pygmies dropped her in a stand of trees after full darkness had swept the sun from the sky. Light and smoke filtered through the trees, the first allowing her to make out dim shapes of tall conifers surrounding a living-room-sized clearing and the smoke bringing her the scent of roasting meat, which set off her stomach rumbles. Her hands might as well have been lopped off and sewn back on, for all the feeling left in them. They dangled, useless as puppet hands. Ditto both legs below the knees. Kat concentrated a trickle of magic on getting her blood flowing and hissed when circulation fired the angry buzzing of a thousand bees through her extremities.

Two of the pygmies dragged her by the shirt collar and shoved her back against a tree. A third little bastard looped a rope around her midsection, cinching her tight and pinning her arms against her sides. A few others stood around and supervised. Having to smell creatures up close should have been labeled a hate crime. A combination of vinegary sweat and unwashed ass invaded her sinuses and forced her to sip air through her mouth. It was culturally insensitive of her to apply her own hygiene standards to a different race of people, but Great Maia, please...

"Please," she gasped aloud. "Take a fucking bath."

"They do carry a tang, don't they?" wheezed a voice from the darkness to her right.

Kat squinted, and the form of another full-sized human materialized from the gloom, outlined by the orange glow of a distant campfire. She got the impression of thick whiskers on one end and heavy boots on the other, not unlike the gear she wore on her own feet. "Who're you?" she demanded.

"Billy Minor," the shape said in a scratchy, old-man voice. "Pleased to meetcha."

The pygmies finished their tying. The group of small people wandered away, chattering in their guttural language. One paused long enough to lift his breechclout and urinate on the tree against which Kat was tied. Some spattered on her neck.

"Goddess, damn you to hell," Kat growled. Her cultural sensitivity was growing thin as latex, and she found herself unable to control an impulse at revenge. Kat tapped her amulet's puny charge and sent a bolt of fiery heat upstream and into the pygmy's penis. The little man yelped and hopped away, clutching his privates and squawking.

"Serves you right!" Kat shouted after him. "And you have a tiny prick, you ignorant little weasel!"

Billy Minor chuckled. "What was all the commotion?"

"I don't know," Kat said. "Wasp stung his pecker, looks like."

"Ouch," chimed in a new voice from her left. A younger man, based on the tone and timbre. "That sounds excruciating."

"I hope it rots and falls off," Kat said. "And who're you?"

"James Snow, ma'am."

"Jimmy there's a Injun," Billy chimed in. "His Paiute name is Little Owl. He talks like a white man, account-a he went to school for redskins where they eddicated him."

"Oh. My. God," Kat muttered, shaking her head.

"I know," Billy added. "But don't you worry none. Jimmy's a good egg. Ain't hardly Injun at all."

Kat controlled herself with an effort. *Escape first. Bring about social justice later.* "Where the fuck are we? Anybody know what's going on?" She worked her dry throat, attempting to swallow, but she was parched. Her hands and feet were on fire, but at least she could flex her fingers a little. The feeling seeped back in prickles of fire. Her amulet carried about a quarter charge, enough to get her loose from the ropes around her waist, but until she could trust her feet to support her weight, there was no sense getting loose. The effects of the poison left her sluggish and dopey. The ache in her neck from being pole-carried for miles was approaching migraine-level pain. Kat rolled her head around, but it did little to loosen the stiff muscles of her neck and shoulders.

The silence had grown long while she inventoried her personal situation. Kat realized after a moment that neither of the men had answered her question. "Umm... guys? What's the deal here?"

"It's... ah..." James Snow started and stopped. "I believe the Nimerigar... well, they... First, they'll prepare for a, ah, feast of sorts."

"Huh?" Kat said, "What the fuck? Just spit it out."

"What Jimmy's trying to say," Billy rasped. "He thinks these here Nim-riggers is gonna eat us."

Kat got the story from James Snow, aka Little Owl, in a series of starts and stops, interrupted by heapings of hick wisdom from Billy Minor along the way. The way Snow told the tale, with the three of them sitting in a circle near a campfire in a dark and sinister forest, made Kat feel like she was listening to a ghost story on a camping trip. However, instead of making s'mores, she was tied to a tree, and the campfire would likely be roasting her tender flesh instead of a marshmallow.

"I always believed the Nimerigar people to be a myth," Snow said, "a Paiute legend used to frighten children at night."

"They're doing a bang-up job of scarin' the willy-Jesus outta me," Minor added.

The Nimerigar, as Snow explained it, lived in hidden canyons deep in the mountains—the Inyos, the Sierra Nevadas, or the Sierra Madres, depending upon which tribe told the tale. They were often associated with the spirit of the mountains, either as a manifestation of the spirit made flesh or as agents of the spirit, sent to work its will in the material world. They were not a kind and benevolent people. According to legend, the Nimerigar were mean, vicious, and cannibalistic, eating their enemies' flesh to gain strength from the souls of their foes. These particular Nimerigar had been stirred up recently, and their rage was directed toward someone currently in or around Geyser Falls.

"I can only understand about one word in three," Snow said, "and I'm not entirely certain of the translation of the familiar words that mirror the Paiute language, so my interpretation may be off by quite a bit. In fact, I could be totally wrong..."

"Don't equivocate," Kat told him. "Just say it as best you know it."

"The tribe who attacked us," Snow said, "lived here in the Inyos. They owned or worshiped or were caretakers for—I'm not sure—a totem of some kind. That's the best translation I can come up with. It was something like a religious icon for them."

"What?" Kat asked. "Like the Holy Grail?"

"Yes, I suppose. Something like that..."

They kept the totem in a cavern, well protected and safe. But a few months ago, an earthquake—"An angry god shook the earth, so I'm assuming an earthquake," Snow said. The caverns flooded, and parts of it caved in. Many Nimerigar died recovering the totem from the chamber where it was kept, and many more were trapped in the labyrinth of collapsed caverns. The survivors frantically began digging their way through to rescue their loved ones, despite the frequent aftershocks. The chief ordered the totem to be carried to higher ground by an honor guard of six warriors. That was all he could spare, as everyone else was either trapped or digging.

"Uh-oh," Kat said.

"Hoppin-Johnny," Billy rasped. "I bet I know how this ends."

"Exactly," came Snow's voice from the dark. "When the chief ended the rescue effort and the earth stopped shaking, he sent for the honor guard to return with the totem. What they found was six dead Nimerigar, all killed by gunshot."

"And no Holy Grail," Kat concluded.

"And no Holy Grail. The tribe's trackers followed the trail as far as Geyser Falls but lost it before they reached town. They've been searching for it ever since, attacking travelers and settlers and even some Paiutes. Some, they merely kill. Others, they kill and butcher. And a lucky few—"

"They tie to trees and save for late-night snacks."

Snow cleared his throat. "Actually, I believe, if I understand them correctly, they plan to sacrifice us to appease the spirit of the mountain, whom they believe they've offended somehow. Then yes I, uh, I believe they plan to... to..."

"Eat us like fried chicken," Kat supplied.

"As you say."

Billy Minor cackled. "More like fried goat, come to me."

"Where's a vegan when you need one?" Kat muttered.

A gaggle of little people entered the clearing. The group approached Kat, who squinted and tilted her head to see by the dim starlight filtering through the trees. Her heart stuttered when she recognized the guy in the lead. It was the Big Kahuna, the nasty piece of work she'd seen in the Bannerworth the other night—*was it only last night? Jeez how time flies when you're being poisoned and dragged through the desert.* The vicious little man stopped and studied her as closely as she studied him. He had squinty eyes over a broad nose, dominant cheekbones, and a pointed chin. Curly hair capped his head. All in all, the Nimerigar were vaguely similar to Australian aborigines, she decided, with pointed teeth and a personal odor best described as rotten skunk overlaid with stale urine.

The chief's hand shot out and pinched her left boob. Hard.

"Hey! Stop that."

Chief Grab-a-tit turned to his cadre of yes men and said something guttural and obviously witty, for they all laughed on cue.

"He said," Snow chimed in from the darkness, "something about a woman hiding as a man."

"Har-fucking-har, Big Chief Peanut."

The leader of the Nimerigar considered her for a moment then spoke in passable English. "Moon come. Meet God."

"Oh, lucky me," Kat muttered past the sudden blockage in her throat. "And here I am, without a party dress."

The chief laughed, echoed closely by his lieutenants.

Chapter Twenty-Three: Missing Magic

I stepped out of the Bannerworth into full darkness. The lighted windows along the hotel's front cast yellow pools across the boardwalk and into the street. Night bugs circled and butted the glass in a futile attempt to reach the light. Blackie lifted his head when I appeared. His tail thumped against the boards, and the dog radiated the contentment of a full belly. In contrast, I belched a bubble of acid indigestion and wished I could share the dog's happiness.

Wrong time, wrong place. Strange environment. Casual bigotry. Strange pygmy people... a long time away from my sister. Each loose end represented another thread popping out of the weave, unraveling the bindings that kept me from losing my shit completely.

Anybody ever tell you you're a control freak?

And why is that a bad thing?

Striding out of the darkness and into the circle of light before me came one of the loose threads I needed to tie down. Preferably with heavy chains, at the bottom of the Owens River.

"Reverend Weeks," I called as the tall preacher mounted the steps. There was some irony in the reversal of positions from the previous night, when Weeks had cold-cocked me, if irony meant a strong temptation to beat the shit out of the preacher.

"Yes?" Weeks stopped and squinted. "Who—oh, it's you." The reverend altered his stance and bunched his shoulders. Evidently, he remembered our last encounter at the Bannerworth as clearly as I did. "What do you want?"

"Where's Kat Krawczyk?"

The reverend's dark eyebrows pulled together under the brim of his flat, black hat. "How should I know? And I resent your tone, *Your Honor*." Weeks laced the honorific with enough slimy contempt that I felt like taking a bath. He made "your honor" sound like "shit weasel."

I slid into a combat-ready stance and hammered out words like a blacksmith forging steel. "You're about to resent my boot so far up your ass, you can taste my toes. One last time. Where is she?"

"Judge Shivers!" Merilee's voice stabbed me between the shoulder blades. She rushed around in front of me in a swirl of skirts and got right in my face with a pointed finger. "What is wrong with you? How can you accuse the Reverend Weeks, a man of God, of having something to do with Miss Krawczyk's disappearance?"

"It's easy. I open my mouth, and the truth falls out." My eyes tracked Weeks as he mounted the steps and reached the porch. I turned to follow the movement, and Merilee shifted to stay in front of me. "Not hard to follow the smell to whatever stinks the worst."

Merilee stiffened, and her pale cheeks bloomed with color. Her hand twitched as if she wanted to slap me. By all appearances, she was an intelligent woman, and yet somehow, she saw me as the bad guy. *How is that fair?* Her voice dropped to a freezing whisper. "How dare you."

"Think nothing of it, my dear." Weeks's black eyes glittered. "Shivers is a mongrel, and like all mongrels, he has neither manners nor breeding. One cannot wash a Blackamoor white, no matter how much soap you use."

The moment hung suspended within me in the same way gasoline thrown on hot charcoals paused a split second before bursting into flames. Bridger stood in the doorway of the Bannerworth, hands on his hips. Merilee Soames stood in front of me. I noticed droplets of sweat dampening her brow and strands of hair loose from their pins trailing down her neck. An expression of distaste crossed her face—caused by Weeks's comment or in agreement with it, I couldn't say.

Weeks, a big man, confident of his strength, with blocky fists and lumberjack shoulders, watched me with the hooded eyes of a cobra. He carried no visible sidearm, though his black coat might have hidden any number of weapons. Shadows outlined the hard planes of his face, as strong and handsome a face as any comic book superhero's.

I burned through a full magazine of thoughts, each as distinct as a bullet, in the space between one heartbeat and the next. If I engaged Weeks, I would kill him. Simple as popping a soap bubble. I was a killer. It's what I did. Plus, I was very, very angry. There would be no stopping, once I got started. No mercy. No quarter.

If I killed the preacher in front of the sheriff, Bridger would be forced to try and arrest me. I could not afford to waste time under arrest, so to stay on mission, I would have to kill the sheriff as well. I did not want to kill the sheriff just for doing his job. Merilee Soames would be a witness. Maybe others as well. To avoid frontier justice, I would have to run for it with no ready horse, no plan, and no idea what happened to Krawczyk. I would have to leave the only other person from my time here, alone and potentially in danger.

Logic dictated that I back down.

I breathed out in one long exhale. Same on the inhale.

"Another time," I said, eyes locked on Weeks's. "Another place."

Weeks offered an oily smile. "I look forward to that day. Come, Merilee. Let's leave the... judge... to his hound." He guided Merilee toward the hotel door with a hand on her waist. Merilee looked back at me over her shoulder, her expression hard to discern—sympathy? Disgust? Pity? Something else?

Unlike earlier, she did not shrug off the preacher's touch.

The stable owner, George Bethlehem, had taken one look at my rigid jaw and left his supper without complaint. I waited by the stable door, as ramrod stiff as a rusted robot but with fewer emotions, while the man saddled and bridled a rental horse to go with my rental dog. My insides felt like a kettle on the boil with no spout, pressurized and ready to explode.

Blackie lay prone, chin on paws, and followed me with his eyes, as nervous as a virgin on her first night in a brothel.

I had backed down from Weeks.

You had to. No other choice.

Backed down and slunk away.

You had good reasons. Mission objectives.

Sure, there were good reasons to avoid a fight. There always were. As dear old dad always said, "Cowards always rationalize running away." Call it a tactical retreat, call it a strategic withdrawal, or hell, call it the better part of valor. It all amounted to the same thing: defeat. Failure.

"God*dammit*!" I spat the curse quietly, under my breath. I restrained the impulse to kick a feed bucket and checked another impulse to punch the wall, focusing instead on breathing, ratcheting off the pressure, one notch at a time. A song would be good, something about payback or hanging tough, but for the first time I could recall, my entire mental playlist was blank.

So yeah, maybe a tad more emotions than a robot. I stood corrected.

Bethlehem appeared with my new horse, a roan mare with a white blaze on her forehead. She seemed a little hostile at being rousted out of her comfy stall and forced to be transportation for an angry human. The horse tossed her head and danced sideways as the stable owner led her forward. I walled off my emotions so as not to spook the horse any further then counted out the deposit and rental fee with the exaggerated care of the recently injured. I suspected any sudden movement would tear open the wound in my pride, and any remaining dignity would bleed out and soak into the muck of the stable.

Bethlehem held out the reins. "I call this one Blaze."

I withheld comment and accepted the reins. I led the horse into the street and mounted stiffly.

"C'mon, Blackie. Let's go find Krawczyk so I can get out of this fucking nightmare."

Where, where, where? The dog bounded to his feet, tail wagging. It was good to be a dog.

Excellent question. Bridger claimed Kat had been headed north when he saw her, and Weeks's camp lay in that direction, so I aimed Blaze at the North Star and clicked the mare into a canter. It was supper time in Geyser Falls, and all the businesses—aside from the saloons—were closed. Cooking smells laced the air, along with the acrid bite of woodsmoke. I belched and slowed the horse to a walk. Bouncing up and down at a canter agitated the acid boiling in my stomach like a soda bottle.

When we reached the outskirts of town, I dismounted and presented Blackie with Kat's garment. I found it faintly embarrassing to hold a woman's panties up for a dog to sniff.

"Find her," I commanded. "Seek."

Yes, yes, yes!

Blackie bounded away, lost in the darkness in a matter of seconds. I paused for a moment and breathed in the night. Above, a few clouds, limned by the silver light of a crescent moon, scrolled across a sequined velvet sky. A shooting star crossed the heavens in an instant, and I stood, head tilted back, hoping for another. The heat of the day seeped away, and the breeze channeling through the valley from the north brought the scent of sage and creosote. Frogs croaked, and fireflies danced.

When Blackie bayed in excitement, it caught me by surprise. Well, well, well. The dog had hit the scent within minutes.

"Whatdya know," I said aloud. "Bridger was telling the truth about her heading north."

Not that I suspected the sheriff of lying about it, but having independent corroboration added to my confidence. I stabbed a toe in a stirrup and hoisted myself into the saddle. Leather creaked and groaned.

"Okay, Blaze," I said. "Follow that dog."

Before my horse took a step, an iron rope circled my neck and clamped my windpipe shut. I arched my back and clawed at... at... nothing. There was nothing there. No rope. But something clamped my throat like a vise. Chest heaving, I twisted off Blaze's back and dropped to the ground in a drunken stumble. The invisible ligature around my neck held tight. My face heated, and already, blackness framed my vision. My knees hit the dirt.

Magic. Somebody was choking me with magic.

I couldn't breathe.

The power hummed, now that I focused on it. Clumsy control, as though the person wielding the magic had little or no experience using it, like a baby's chubby fingers wrapped around a candy bar. A really, really strong baby who had enough control to keep me locked in a magical choke hold. Baby or not, the Magical would render me unconscious in under a minute and kill me soon after.

Couldn't breathe.

I reached for my own power, puny in comparison to the force holding my throat closed. A candle next to a bonfire. I pushed back, flailing, firing lightning into the surrounding trees, spraying and praying with magical energy.

Could. Not. Breathe.

I had one shot of magic left. Firing blind... it wasn't working. Accomplishing... nothing. I needed a target. Darkness all around. *Where? Where is...*

Breathe!

Nothing. No air. I raked my throat, desperate to open the airway. It felt like I'd swallowed a tennis ball. My vision tunneled to pinpoints.

Went black.

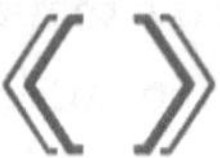

I snapped awake with a choking gasp.

I was breathing. *Had been* breathing, even while unconscious. That was important, as it meant I was still among the living. There at the end, right before everything went black, I had been convinced I would wake up dead.

No sign of the assailant. But there had been no sign until magic fingers cinched my throat tighter than a knot on a water balloon.

Not much time had passed. The stars looked the same. I was in the middle of the same road as before the attack, in the exact spot where I had fallen. A crescent moon hung low, near the tops of the eastern mountains, right where I remembered it. Blaze cropped greenery along the edge of the trail, reins dangling. Luckily, I hadn't burned the poor horse with a bolt of lightning. Blackie's occasional bark sounded from up ahead. My throat hurt, and a monster headache pounded behind my eyeballs.

But I could breathe. Nothing felt as good as breathing. Odd how one could take that for granted. I filled my lungs, over and over again, despite the coughing that followed. What was a little coughing compared to the wonderful sensation of full lungs? When I was certain of the process again, I gathered my concentration and addressed Blaze.

"What happened?" It hurt to speak.

Man came.

I interpreted this from the horse's remembered image of a human form wearing a duster and hat. Blaze recalled no details about the man's features. It could have been anyone. The fellow carried a bulky, cylindrical rock—no, more like a statue, for the stone appeared carved—under his arm, cradled against his body like a football. In the mental picture sent by Blaze, the man stooped over me, reached down with his free hand, and jerked something loose. Something—

My amulet.

I clutched my chest. No amulet. I patted at my shirt like a man trying to put out a dozen fires, checked my shirt pockets, stood and checked my pants pockets and the ground around me. Reached for magic... and found nothing.

My magical battery, the source of the power I had come to rely on almost as much as the air with which I filled my hungry lungs, was gone.

"Which way"—I rasped at the horse then swallowed—"did he go?"

No memory. Blaze had looked away, spooked still by nearby lightning strikes and having lost interest in the doings of humans. She was now happy with a patch of wildflowers and couldn't be bothered. It was not the first time I had been frustrated by communication with animals. Their attention span rivaled a teenager's, and as with a teenager, trying to get an answer would involve a battery of questions without intelligible responses, which would lead to yelling, tantrums, and living with a beast who would sulk for hours. Unless a human was threatening them, bringing food, or doing something interesting, nothing the two-legged folks did would stick in their memory for long.

Clamping down on the impulse to badger the horse with questions, I pushed myself to standing and retrieved the canteen hanging off the saddle horn. Several swallows of brackish water failed to cure the ache in my throat. Standing on watery legs, I leaned into the horse and tried to organize my thoughts, which scampered in random directions. A fluttery, anxious sensation capered under my rib cage, and cold sweat coated my skin. I teetered on the edge of a mental cliff, where falling over meant a headfirst drop into Panic Canyon. How long had it been since I had been totally without magic? Six years? At least six years.

"Face it, Shivers," I said to myself. "You're scared shitless."

For the first time in six years, my access to magical power had been severed. Even when my amulet was discharged, I felt the dregs of power and the potential for recharge in the same way I could feel my legs while lying in bed. They might be tired, or sore, or worn out, but they were there, connected to my body, and I could use them as soon as they were well rested.

But now? Nothing.

Was this how it felt? Before? I could barely remember the man I had been for the twenty-one years prior to finding the polished bit of agate that changed my life forever. Mundane. Limited. Weak. Nothing more than... than...

Human.

Which was the crux of it. Magic conveyed power. Power equaled strength—godlike strength. On a full charge, before this little time-travel adventure, I could call lightning from the heavens, like a modern Zeus hurling bolts to smite Titans. I could transmute energy at the atomic level, melting steel, liquefying helium, or slinging a Cadillac into low-Earth orbit, all without breaking a sweat.

And now, someone had stolen my power and my hope of power. Without magic, I was merely mortal, Superman in a Kryptonite overcoat. Green Lantern with no ring. Kent Allard instead of the Shadow. The person who had choked me was a Magical, too, wielding an ass load of power. Where did that much power come from?

Was it from the statue he carried? I had never heard of a Magical amulet the size of a table lamp, but the power radiating from it was undeniable. If the Magical had that much power, why did he need my amulet?

And why didn't he kill you?

Yeah, good question.

According to Blaze's memory, it was almost certain the man had come from the south, from Geyser Falls. I would need to return to town and hunt down a man carrying a three-foot statue under his arm, shoot him before he could reach for magic, recover my amulet, then take a long, solid look at the carved stone statue the man carried and figure out what it did. And I would have to avoid getting caught having murdered a man with no reasonable explanation.

Blackie's barking resumed, reminding me why we were out there in the first place. He sounded excited, as if the trail had heated up. I strained my eyes northward in a vain attempt to see the dog then turned southward, in the direction the Magical had gone, then back north again.

"Shit."

Krawczyk was still out there somewhere. And with the addition of this new Magical, her disappearance seemed even more ominous. If she had been attacked the same way I had, she could be injured or, well, dead. Not that I should have cared one damn bit. The woman was a grown-up. She knew the risks, same as anyone, and she had magic to boot. Not much, maybe, but more than I did at the moment. In the harsh calculation of life, her fate had no bearing on the mission's objectives, and in truth, she was more of a hindrance than a help. Continuing the mission was my prime directive, and sidetracking to locate one missing Magical in a land with little magic was a waste of time and resources.

I slugged back another gulp from the canteen and cursed when my sore throat took the impact. I mounted Blaze and clicked to get the mare moving north, toward the sound of Blackie's barking.

"Superman and Green Lantern," I sang hoarsely, "ain't got a-nothin' on me."

Chapter Twenty-Four: Icon of the Little People

"We're getting out of here," Kat told the others.

The night sky—what little of it she could glimpse through the forest canopy—flickered with bright pinpoints of light, more stars than Kat had seen in her life. She shivered, as the temperature had fallen steadily after sunset. Though not yet at foggy-breath stage, the air was colder than she liked. Her girlfriend, Carrin, who ran hot in more ways than one, liked to set the thermostat at sixty-eight degrees, winter and summer. Damn near froze Kat's nipples off. That was how cold she felt now.

"How'd'ya figger we're doing that?" Billy asked. "I been tryin' all day, but I can't get loose."

"However we do it," Snow added, "we'd better do it soon. Something is happening with the Nimerigar."

Indeed, the pygmies had gathered around a blazing campfire by the shore of the small lake. Barely visible through the trees, the tribe bulked into a dark mass of people. One voice rose and fell in rhythmic oration, while background vocalists accompanied him in chanting counterpoint and drummers pounded out a thumping beat: *tum-*

tum-tumppa-TUM. At irregular intervals, the audience roared their agreement with whatever the speaker said. Kat hadn't been to any human sacrifice preparties, but if she had to guess, this was what one looked like.

They needed to escape, and escape now.

At least her magic had recharged. A little bit. Not nearly as much as back home—or back to the future, or whatever—but it was enough to do what she needed.

Kat focused and applied superheat to a small section of the rope around her waist. The rope parted with a gasp of smoke, and she threw off the bindings. "I worked loose a knot," she said. "Wait a sec, and I'll come get you loose." Moving like a mouse under the whiskers of a sleeping cat, she scuttled between the two men and cut their ropes in a similar manner.

"Now," Kat whispered, "anybody know the way out of here?"

"Not me," said Billy. "What about you, Little Owl?"

"Um. Maybe."

Snow started off through the darkness, followed by Kat, with Billy bringing up the rear. Kat glued her eyes to the Paiute's white shirt and crept along behind him, wincing at every rustled leaf and snapped twig. The three of them sounded as loud to her ears as a crowd of Black Friday shoppers hitting the Walmart Door Buster sale at 6:01 a.m. on the day after Thanksgiving.

The night insects whined and buzzed. Sweat dripped from Kat's chin, branches swished and slapped her in the face, and roots reached out to trip her. Billy stumbled and hissed a curse, but Kat didn't dare turn and glare at him for fear of losing sight of Snow's dim form, weaving and bobbing through the midnight forest. The drumming of the Nimerigar pounded like the thumping of the Devil's heart, a deep *tum-tum-tumppa-TUM* as hypnotic as it was frightening. The drumming and chantIng rose and receded, waves of sound building, one upon another, climbing toward an inevitable crescendo the way lovers ground their hips together with increasing frenzy, except the conclusion wouldn't be the joy of orgasm but an explosion of blood and viscera and the primal scream of violence.

Tum-tum-tumppa-TUM. Tum-tum-tumppa-TUM.

Kat shivered at the chill in her blood. She wiggled forward and pressed up close to Snow, nudging him in the back.

"Let's move it, Little Owl," she whispered. "The natives are getting damned restless."

"Would you like to lead the way?" Snow sounded a little peevish, his tone losing some of its finishing school shine.

"No." Kat couldn't see six feet in any direction—finding a path under such circumstances would be like threading a needle blindfolded. She patted Snow's back. "No, you're doing fine."

Using a little magic to light the way might make things faster, but she might as well send up a flare to the Nimerigar. Plus, depleting her tiny store of magic would leave her defenseless in the event that the pygmies caught them again. She couldn't do much if that happened, anyway, not with her puny little charge, but something was better than nothing. What was that they always said in the Westerns? Save the last bullet for yourself? *In this case, save the last aneurysm for me.*

"No, fuck that," Kat told herself. "I'm not going out like that."

Snow stumbled through a gap in the trees, and Kat caught herself an instant before plowing into his back. Billy Minor crowded up behind her. The sweat-stink of the three of them piled close together made Kat's eyes water. She edged around Snow to get a better look and to give her nose some relief. They had come to the entrance to a canyon. Sheer walls rose to either side, capped with a blanket of starry night. The canopy of stars provided enough illumination that Kat could make out a narrow trail leading deeper into the canyon.

"Hey," Billy said. "I know this place. This is where they conked my noggin."

Kat thought the terrain at least looked familiar, though her view had been inverted at the time. If she was right, the pygmies had carried her through this canyon on the way to their camp. She snagged Billy by the elbow.

"Do you remember where it goes?"

"Mostly. It meanders around some but comes out somewhere in the western foothills of the Inyos."

"How far to Geyser Falls?"

"Ehh…" Billy's face scrunched up. Now that Kat could see him, she was unsettled by the old man's resemblance to Gabby Hayes, John Wayne's sidekick in a dozen or so old Westerns. "Mebbe fifteen, twenty miles?"

Snow held up a hand. "Listen!"

Kat pitched her ear to the sounds of the night—buzzes… chirps… hoots…

"The drumming has stopped," she said.

"Not only that…"

"What?"

"I don't hear a dang thing," Billy said.

"Voices," Snow said. "Anger. Shouting."

Now that he mentioned it, Kat picked out the vague sounds of excited jabbering mixed with the natural sounds of the night.

"They figured out we escaped," she said. "They sound pissed."

"I'm the one that's pissed… couldn't hold it all day." Billy scrunched his face like a wadded dishrag. "Sorry about that."

Kat shoved Billy toward the canyon and tugged at Snow's sleeve. "C'mon, boys. Run."

Mournful song after mournful song clicked through the jukebox in my head. Bob Seger's "Against the Wind," Johnny

Cash singing "Hurt," even goddamn "At Seventeen"—the Janis Ian version, of course, not the Celine Dion cover. What next, "Seasons in the Sun"? I shuddered. *No misery is worth that.*

A death spiral of depression swirled me down the toilet bowl of despair. Terry Jacks in my head meant things were bad. Really bad. I kept reaching for magic, but it was gone. Finding my source of power missing hit me right in the gut, every time, and felt worse than poking at a hole in my gum from a missing tooth.

My horse, Blaze, plodded along, guided by starlight and the distant barking of an excited dog. After my command of "follow that dog," I let the horse find the path, the reins slack in my hand, nodding with the horse's movement. Floating along in my sewer of self-pity, I was walled off from the world. I noticed neither the glittering swath of stars nor the plaintive song of a distant coyote. I ignored the smell of leather, horse sweat, and night-blooming sage. The horse kept her thoughts to herself, and I rarely took note of anything coming from her equine mind.

Black moments like those were rare and came upon me like a migraine. When the depression hit in full force, not much could stop me from sinking to the bottom of a very deep pit and staying there for a long time. A strong urge to drop to the ground and curl up for a short nap pulled at me as though gravity had intensified. The rhythmic clopping of hooves lulled me into a stupor. My eyelids drooped, and time disappeared.

Until I nearly fell off the horse and had to claw at the saddle horn to stay upright.

Once I tuned in to the dog's thoughts, I realized Blackie had been having trouble following the scent for some time. He was catching only whiffs here and there, more from brush hanging near the trail than the ground itself, almost as if Krawczyk had levitated along the trail instead of walking it. Was she being carried? If so, by whom?

We approached the entrance to a narrow canyon, and nearby brush all but disappeared. So did the scent trail. Blackie cast about in widening circles, looking like a very confused dog. Dawn's early light peeked over the mountaintops, and the first birds of the day flittered about, searching for illusive morning worms and generally being annoying with their happy Disney songs. I dismounted, poured water into my hat for the horse, then whistled the dog back to my side and repeated the hat trick. When I clamped the soggy Stetson back on my head, water dribbled down my temples. That was not something they showed in the old Western movies either. Clint Eastwood never had water dripping down his face.

Blackie's ears perked up, and his nose swiveled to point into the canyon.

People. People.

"What kind of people?"

The dog shot me a how-the-hell-should-I-know look and refocused on the deep gloom between the V-shaped cliffs. Backlit by the rising sun, the middle of the canyon resembled a developing Polaroid print, slowly gaining definition but too dark to make out details.

I eased my Colt out and held it by my leg then led Blaze in a circle so the horse's nose faced in the opposite direction.

"Be ready," I told her. "If we need to run for it, don't wait for me to say giddyap."

I heard them before I saw them. Scuffing and cursing echoed from the canyon. Didn't sound like pygmies, so that was a plus. I squinted and waited, one hand on the saddle horn, the other dangling loose with the Colt. Three figures materialized from the gap. Three sizes, all too big for pygmies. Staggering and gasping, though. One cursed, and I recognized the voice.

"Krawczyk? That you?"

The trio stumbled to a halt and stared in my direction. The smallest one detached from the group and stepped forward. "Shivers?"

"Yeah. Who're your friends?"

"Former dinner companions."

"Huh?"

"Look, I'd love to chat and catch up and all." Krawczyk bent over, hands on her knees like someone about to puke, just having finished a marathon, or both. "But we have a whole tribe of pissed off pygmies—"

"Nimerigar," said the taller of the two men following the small woman.

"Right on our fucking ass," Krawczyk continued. "And if we don't get moving, we'll all be pygmy shit, in no time flat."

"Pygmy shit? That's low. Really low," I said. "Okay, come on. We'll take turns on the horse. Kat, you first. You can tell me the story on the way back to Geyser Falls."

The morning sun climbed at our backs, and elongated shadows wobbled in front of us as we trudged across the scrub plain east of Geyser Falls. The distant buildings appeared as small blocks set along the glittering ribbon of the Owens River, overshadowed by the jagged purple range of the Sierra Nevadas. Ten miles, at least, I estimated, before we would reach the town. Two hours, maybe three, until I could find Weeks, beat the man to a finely pureed glob, and get my amulet back.

Somewhere along the way, I had decided Weeks was the Magical running amok, killing off the competition and helping himself to things that didn't belong to him. All my instincts said he was the guy, and it would be a distinct pleasure to backspace him off the page.

I picked up my pace.

"This icon the Nimerigar lost," I said to the Paiute scholar, James Snow, who hurried to catch up. It was Billy's turn on the horse, and Krawczyk lagged behind, keeping her eyes peeled for pursuit. "Would it hold a lot of magic?"

"To them, perhaps. Since there is no *real* magic, the totem's value would be purely symbolic, of course."

"Of course."

The object Weeks carried when he choked me unconsciousness and stole my amulet fit the bill for the totem Snow described. Was it the one stolen from the height-challenged cannibals of the Inyos? How many carved totems in and around these mountains could there be? I suspected the statue was some kind of super amulet, able to hold a tremendous charge of magical energy. Anyone with the talent for magic who possessed such a device would have a godlike ability to wield that power. Enough energy to, say, burn down a few churches and strangle rival preachers or open a bank vault and carry off all the cash. What was Weeks's goal, though? Money and power? Converts? If he set himself up as the only church in town, his congregation would grow enormously, of course, and he could preach to a wider audience. The burglary of the bank vault seemed at odds with a man who lusted after ecclesiastic power, though no one was immune to a little earthly wealth to go along with the adulation of a congregation.

Whatever his motivation, the most likely explanation was that somehow, Weeks had gotten his hands on the Nimerigars' idol, which had kicked over the little people like a mound of fire ants. Now, they were running around stinging everybody in the yard while hunting for their totem. During the attack on the Bannerworth, I had the impression that the pygmies were sniffing at doors in the hotel. Now I knew why. I would have bet anything that they could sense the totem's presence, at least generally, or they could track the scent of the person who killed their honor guard and stole the statue, which was why they were drawn to Geyser Falls and to the Bannerworth in particular. Weeks stayed on the third floor of the hotel.

Had the Nimerigar not been interrupted by yours truly before they reached his room, they likely would have carted off Old Dishonest Abe and eaten him for communion.

"Hey, Daddy Longlegs!" Krawczyk's voice rattled me out of my thoughts. "You want to slow up, there?"

I checked and found I'd outdistanced my companions by quite a bit. I paused in the sparse shade of a scruffy piñon tree and waited for the others to catch up. Blackie sat by my feet and panted. Snow and Billy traded places on the horse, the old miner grousing about missing his mules.

Of all the people I had met since jumping back to the Old West, James Snow seemed the most out of character. The Paiute wore a much-abused wool suit in light gray with the remains of a silk tie dangling around his neck. Small, round spectacles perched on his broad-blade nose. His Native American heritage stood out in his cheekbones and dark eyes, but his mannerisms and diction were more refined than any I had seen thus far... with the possible exception of Merilee Soames, who wore a veneer of manners the way other women wore makeup.

"Anything following?" I asked Krawczyk.

"Nothing I can see." She mopped her forehead with a sleeve. "But the people are little, y'know? Could be hiding behind a cow patty, and I'd never see them."

"How many of them were there? Back in the mountains?"

"I don't know," she admitted. "A big bloody bunch."

"I second that," Billy wheezed. "Never did get a good look, but they's all over the dang place."

We looked at James Snow sitting atop the horse. As the only knowledgeable source on the Nimerigar, he had been elected as the final authority on everything related to the little people. His expression had turned grim.

"Hundreds," he said. "Maybe over a thousand warriors."

"Great," I said. "And they're all pissed off and coming to town."

"No doubt," Krawczyk agreed.

"Sure as shootin'." Billy nodded along.

Snow merely looked inscrutable and stoic.

Another roadblock in my path, the Nimerigar, would have to wait their turn in my lineup of future violence, slotting right after my new objective one: find Weeks, kill Weeks, recover magical amulet and the magic-filled totem. The damn thing harnessed the power of a hundred amulets. With that kind of energy, it might be possible to do a whole bunch of things. Level a mountain. Throw Weeks into Pluto's orbit. Turn night into day.

And maybe... just maybe... do a little time traveling along the way.

Worth thinking about.

Chapter Twenty-Five: Good Luck Getting Laid Now

On the outskirts of town, I dug into my pocket and counted out five dollars in loose bills and coins to James Snow and to Billy Minor. That left me with almost the exact amount—six dollars and change—with which I first entered Geyser Falls three days before. Or was it four? I'd lost count somewhere.

Billy looked at the cash in his hand and moaned. "I'm gonna have to get a real job so I can buy more mules and supplies. Dangit, I miss them mules. Thankee for this though," he added. "I'm good for it."

Snow echoed his thanks. "Do you know where... someone like me can get a meal?"

"Try Gerda's," I said. "Although the sign says Maylene's. Stick with us. Krawczyk and I need to eat too. After that, I would advise both of you to pack some food and water and head west, out of town." I glanced up at Krawczyk, who sat atop the horse, throwing her a question with my expression. She shook her head and returned to scanning our back trail.

The late lunch crowd at Maylene's stirred when our motley band trooped through the open door. Conversation died in a wave from front to back as forty white faces turned to the newcomers. I cleared a place to sit at the nearest bench by approaching an empty spot between two farmers. Space appeared around me as though I carried a dead skunk in my pocket. Given how ripe I smelled, that supposition wasn't too far-fetched.

Food was laid out family style—people passed platters of meat, bowls of vegetables, and baskets of dinner rolls. I ate without speaking, only grunting whenever Krawczyk made words, although nothing of what she said penetrated my thoughts. I passed dishes when asked, loaded my plate as things came by, and ate as systematically as an assembly line.

The only way to win a stand-up fight with a wizard was to not have one. Second punch was first dead. To stop Weeks from employing his power, I would have to ambush him and kill him in cold blood or knock him out, which was easier in the movies than in real life. A gnat's-ass too much force would easily cause brain damage or a subdural hematoma of the fatal variety. And since Weeks had my amulet, the preacher didn't need to be in physical contact with the Nimerigar idol to touch magical energy.

You have to murder him.

No shit. Thanks for the update.

All I had to do was wall off my emotions, brick off all my quaint notions learned in the first twenty years of my life—honor and fair play and being a good sport. Change from the human Calico John Shivers to Judge Shivers, BattleMech. I fancied I could feel the shift in mindset manifest through my body, as though I'd swallowed a magic potion that hardened my skin, sharpened my eyesight, blocked out extraneous noise, and infused my muscles with strength.

You're a Transformer. More than meets the eye.

"Shivers? Calico? Hey, you here?"

I heard Krawczyk's voice and rotated my head ninety degrees to look at her. She had been speaking to me for some time.

The blue-haired woman flinched when she met my gaze. Sweat had ringed the grime on her face to muddy circles under her eyes and left chocolate tracks down her cheeks. She blinked. "Shivers?"

"What?"

"We need to warn the sheriff. About the Nimerigar? Remember them? Little ugly fuckers with poisoned arrows."

"'Poison Arrow.' ABC Band." I named the song reflexively. Heard myself say it and wondered at the impulse.

"Huh?"

"Nothing." I stood and high-stepped off the bench. "You go see the sheriff. I have a wizard to kill."

I dropped enough money on the table to pay for our lunch then marched outside on a beeline course for the hotel. Krawczyk worried at my heels—a terrier to my Doberman—as I strode toward the Bannerworth. I had a vague notion of the blue-haired woman saying something to Billy Minor and James Snow, but the words did not register.

Afternoon sun baked the street dry. Dust puffed around my ankles and fogged the air with every gust of wind. The town appeared to be drowsing in the heat. Few people occupied the streets, and those who did moved with deliberation and kept to themselves. That was fine with me. I had no time and less patience to deal with interference.

"You can't just kill him," Krawczyk said for the third time.

Speaking of interference...

"I can." I touched my chest with a thumb. "Me, Judge. Remember?"

"Hell-*low*? Evidence, anyone?"

"Follow the money. Who stands to benefit from all the church attacks? Weeks. Who were you following when the pygmies caught you? Weeks. Who lives in the Bannerworth, where they were obviously searching for their statue? Weeks."

"And who's dipping his butter knife in a bit of English crumpet? Weeks."

I whipped around and glared. "What's that got to do with anything?"

"You're not as stoic as you think, Judge Shivers. I've seen your eyes follow her around." Krawczyk stood her ground, hands on hips. "It's the same look Carrin gets when she sees the free sample ladies at Costco. *Oooh*," she crooned in sarcastic falsetto. "Look, little sausages in cheese dip. I'll just have a tiny nibble. Yum-yum."

"Soames has nothing to do with this." I spun on my heel and stalked away, forcing Krawczyk to skip-run to catch up.

"All I'm sayin' is—"

"Enough," I growled, and miracle of miracles, something in my tone must have registered with the woman, as she stopped talking. Unfortunately, she continued her dust-churning speed-walk to remain glued to my side.

The lobby doors of the Bannerworth stood open in a vain attempt to stir the air inside. The sounds of a few lingering diners clattered from the adjoining restaurant. I angled right and approached the desk, behind which a clerk mopped his brow with a soggy handkerchief and looked up from scratching a ledger with a blocky pencil.

"Reverend Weeks," I rapped out. "What room?"

"Uh. Three-oh-two, sir."

"Is he in?"

"Ahh." The man patted his sweating bald forehead and checked the keys hanging above mail slots behind the desk. "No, sir. No, he is not."

"Key." I stuck out a hand.

"Excuse me, sir?"

I leaned forward and laced menace through my words as though stirring poison through my coffee. "Give me the key to Weeks's room."

"I'd do it, Charlie," Krawczyk said from my side. "The man's riding the red cotton pony."

Key in hand, I thundered up the stairs two at a time, noting in passing that the repaired section had not been carpeted yet. I turned left, crossed to the second flight of stairs, and jogged up the narrow switchback tunnel to the third floor. At the landing, I found a hallway with rooms lining each side. The first door on my left was 302. I stabbed the keyhole as if I wanted to murder the lock, twisted the iron key, and jerked the door open.

In my singular focus, I hadn't realized Blackie had remained at my heels until I stumbled over the dog entering Weeks's room. I picked up a mental impression from the dog that suggested Blackie was having a great adventure with his new pack, and life was much better with me than hanging around the stable with his previous alpha. Some of the dog's happiness leached into my awareness and helped me dial back the intensity of my anger.

Weeks's room was more of a suite, with a sitting area out front and a separate bedroom. The sitting room featured a writing desk against the right wall, a settee and chairs arranged around a coffee table in the center of the room, and a buffet used as a bookshelf on the left side. Next to the desk, the door to the bedroom hung open. Tall French doors on the far wall opened onto a balcony facing the street.

I searched the front room while Krawczyk took the bedroom. It didn't take long to scour the place from top to bottom. We found dust bunnies and dead spiders but no amulets, magical or otherwise.

Krawczyk appeared at the bedroom door. "Nothing. You?"

"Not a damn thing." I sighed and absently scratched Blackie behind the ears. "He must not keep it here."

"Maybe he's not the guy."

"Maybe they don't want ice water in hell, but I'm not betting on it."

A new voice cut in. "Just what do you think you're doing? What's going on here?"

I turned to find a thunderous Merilee Soames framed in the doorway, arms crossed and eyes narrowed. Heat bloomed up from my neck, and I stiffened. Blackie whined.

"Looking," I said, "for something."

"By intimidating my clerk? By invading my guest's privacy?" Merilee pronounced *privacy* in the English manner, like privy instead of pry. Her fiery eyes fixed on Krawczyk. "I expected this type of heavy-handed behavior from the, the *judge*, but not you, Miss Kraw-czyk."

"There are bigger issues at play here—"

"I'm not interested in your issues, Mr. Shivers." Merilee fired words at me like bullets. "In fact, I've had about all of you I can tol-erate. Pack your things and depart these premises immediately, or I shall fetch the sheriff and have you forcibly removed. As for you, Miss Krawczyk, you have a choice. Continue associating with this... this ruffian or leave him to himself and behave like a proper lady."

Without waiting for acknowledgment or argument, Merilee spun on a heel and vanished, leaving behind traces of rose-scented soap and indignation.

After a long pause, Krawczyk cackled a brittle laugh. "Well done, Romeo. Good luck getting laid now."

I stood on the top step of the Bannerworth porch, saddlebags draped over my shoulder, at a momentary loss regarding what to do next. Blackie flopped down in the shade and panted, and Kraw-czyk appeared at my elbow like some evil genie. She had taken the time to wash her face and put on a fresh shirt while I packed my lim-ited belongings.

"How, kemo sabe," Krawczyk said in an overdone Tonto imitation. "We fucked. What do now?"

"You sure you want to hang around with a ruffian like me?"

"What I'd like to do…" She sucked in a deep breath and let it out. Her tone turned low and serious. "I want to go home, Shivers. I don't like it here. No toilets, no medicine, no… no goddamn showers. People are so fucked up about… well, everything."

"Not so woke, are they?"

"True. But you know, here's the thing. I can't see leaving these folks to deal with a rogue Magical and swarm of vicious cannibal pygmies. That doesn't feel right. I don't know."

I pinched the bridge of my nose then rubbed my face. "Mm-hmm."

Tell her about Alizandra! Tell her there are more important things than saving this little Podunk town.

Shut up.

We stood together and watched the street. A freight wagon rattled past, stirring up a cloud of fine white dust. The teamster on the bench seat appeared ghostly, coated as though rolled in flour. The four-horse team reminded me…

"I should probably take my horse back to the stables. I left her parked in front of Maylene's."

"I asked Billy to take care of her."

"That old man'll probably steal her," I grumped. "Sell her for a mule."

"I doubt it. Despite how backward these people are about most things, they're mostly trustworthy. I have to give them that. Very few locked doors. My-word-is-my-bond kind of thing. Not like back home."

I grunted, not convinced but too tired to argue. "All right, then. I guess we better go see Bridger and tell him about the Nimerigar.

Maybe the little people will back off if they see the town is ready for them."

"You saw the chief, right?" Krawczyk squinted at me. "Hell-*low*? Did he look like the giving-up type?"

"Hmm."

"Oh fuck no, he's not. That dude acts like somebody stuck a hornet's nest up his butt. And that rave they were having last night? That wasn't a going-away party, trust me. No, no way. I'm telling you, man, they were getting revved up for some old-fashioned pillaging. They may be small, but I got a feeling they're going to blow this town apart, looking for their magical statue-thingy."

"Then I guess we better find it first, huh?"

"Oh yeah, sure. That's working out real well so far."

Chapter Twenty-Six: The Biggest Hombre in the Valley

I followed Kat through the open doorway and into the dim interior of the sheriff's office, blinking away the bright sun until I could see again. I spotted Bridger seated at his desk in the right corner. Deputy Barton dozed in a straight-back chair tilted against the wall to my left. The homely deputy started awake at the sound of footsteps and scrambled to stay upright. The room smelled faintly of burnt coffee and old toenails.

Bridger's hawkish gaze raked me from head-to-toe in a practiced sweep. "I see you got your saddlebags, Your Honor. Going somewhere?"

"I wish."

"The Judge got kicked out of the hotel," Krawczyk said. "He's a ruffian and a scoundrel."

"No doubt," Bridger said. "No doubt at all."

I resisted the urge to roll my eyes. Mostly. "We have a problem, Bridger. Actually, the town has a problem. The little people who attacked the hotel, remember them? Well, there's several hundred more up in the mountains back east. Fifteen, twenty miles as the crow flies. They're, ah, on the warpath. We—Krawczyk and I and a couple of others—believe they're headed for Geyser Falls as fast as their tiny legs will carry them."

"I expect we can handle a bunch o' damn midgets," Bridger drawled. He leaned back, a twinkle in his eye. A man without a care in the world.

"No, Howdy Doody," Krawczyk said with her normal diplomacy, "you can't."

Bridger's face turned ugly. He recognized the tone if not the reference. I put up a hand to stop her, but Krawczyk was on a roll. She ducked under my arm and planted her small fists on Bridger's desk.

"Did you not hear the man? There are hundreds and hundreds of them, and they all have teeny bows that shoot poison arrows. See this?" She unbuttoned the top two buttons of the man's shirt she wore and peeled one shoulder down. Barton let out an alarmed squawk and clamped hands over his eyes at the exposed female flesh, but Bridger never flinched. Krawczyk pointed to the ugly scab in her upper left arm. "See that? I had a poison arrow in there that I got out in time to keep from killing me. Even the little bit of poison I got nearly put me under forever." She pulled her shirt back up, and Barton relaxed. "They hit this town with everything they got, a lot of people are going to die. Men, women, and kids."

Bridger ignored the harpy, looking instead at me. "Why do you think they're headed for Geyser Falls? Why attack the town at all? Why at all?"

"Because they're looking for something," I said. "A statue or a totem pole–looking thing. It was stolen from them, and they want it back."

"What's that?" Barton asked. "What's it look like?"

I held my hands out like measuring an eight-pound trout. "It's about yay tall and about as big around as a coffee can."

"Hey!" Barton snapped his fingers and pointed at the sheriff. "Didn't we take something like that off that dead drifter awhile back? That fellow we found keeled over in the street. Never did know why he died, but he had a hole in him, just like hers. Maybe it was a poison arrow!"

"I don't know what you're yappin' about," Bridger said.

"Sure you do!" Barton pointed to the gun cabinet. "You put it right in there."

Bridger sighed and sagged in his chair. "Well... hell, Ermal." The sheriff rose from behind his desk, holding a long-barreled Colt. The muzzle jumped, and white powder smoke bloomed. The shot struck Barton on the bridge of his nose. The deputy's head snapped back, and gunk spattered the wall.

I saw it coming, but my instincts betrayed me. Instead of the weapon at my side, I reached for magic and found a big, gaping bunch of nothing. Bridger swung the barrel toward me, already thumbing back the hammer. Over the whine in my ears from the first shot, I distinctly heard the *click-cli-click* of the cylinder rotating and the hammer locking on the sear. My palm slapped the grips of my .45 and pulled. I was way too far behind the curve to ever catch up. *Second punch is first dead in a gunfight too.*

I braced for impact.

Krawczyk screamed, and a solid blow of invisible force struck Bridger in the face. His gun discharged, and a line of burning fire branded me across the neck. The sheriff crashed back, hit his desk chair, and tumbled ass over elbow. His head hit the floor like a dropped bowling ball.

"That's all I got!" Krawczyk yelled, followed by a smaller "Is he dead?"

"He's moving," I said. "Just dazed."

Thunderous pounding came from the back stairs, and Deputy Potts appeared. His hair was tousled from sleep, and he wore nothing but long johns. He carried a repeating rifle. The deputy's eyes popped when he saw both Ermal Barton and Sheriff Bridger prone on the floor and me holding a weapon. The dots visibly connected, drawing a picture without all the crayons, and Potts concluded I was the bad guy before I could say otherwise.

"You killed them!" He jacked the Henry's lever.

"No, wait—"

But Potts wasn't listening. The rifle bucked, and the heat of another bullet plucked at my sleeve. That made two too many close calls with angry bits of hot lead. I snapped off a return shot, splintering the doorframe over the deputy's head. Potts ducked back into the stairwell.

"C'mon." Krawczyk tugged at my sleeve. "Don't kill him. Let's go!"

I cranked off two more rounds at the lintel over the stairwell door to keep Potts under cover. I backed away with the tiny sprite pulling at my shirt and guiding me to the open front door. When I felt the boardwalk under my heels, I pivoted and ran, following Krawczyk, who was already sprinting for the corner. My heels hammered the boardwalk, then I careened into the nearest alley. I kept Krawczyk's blue hair in sight as she whipped a quick left-right-left down nearly deserted streets and alleys.

Blackie had wisely departed the scene at the first gunshot. The dog was nowhere in sight, and I caught only a vague sense of direction from the dog's mind, which registered as *far away and fuck this.*

We skidded to a stop at the mouth of an alley between an empty building and yet another mining supply store. I had no idea which street we faced until I heard piano music and spotted the Broken Wheel halfway along the line of buildings to my left.

A train of thought built up steam and clanked into motion. I snagged Krawczyk's shirt sleeve and stopped her from running out into the street. Paradigms shifted in my worldview with the impact of tectonic plates, and I needed a second to let the new reality settle in my mind.

Bridger had something resembling the stolen idol.

Bridger killed his deputy when Barton blabbed about it, meaning he wanted to keep it secret.

My attacker had carried a carved statue that had to have been the same one stolen from the little people. The Nimerigar idol was some kind of super-charged amulet that conveyed a whopping load of power to the user. It was probably Bridger who had choked me out and stolen my amulet, not the reverend.

Oops, my bad.

With that kind of power, Bridger could do just about anything his mind conceived. Bridger was a Magical.

"But why all the churches?" I said aloud.

"Because he hates Weeks and wants him to go away." Krawczyk had obviously been on the same logic train, following the same tracks but on a faster locomotive. "He pins the church attacks on Weeks, probably plants some evidence that somebody quote-unquote *discovers*, and hell-*low*, Weeks is strung up or killed trying to escape."

"Why? What does Bridger—oh. A clear shot at Merilee Soames."

"Duh."

"No, that's too weak. If he wanted that, all he had to do is kill Weeks in his sleep or drown him in the river."

"It's not enough to kill the guy," Krawczyk said. "He has to make him look like a bad guy—otherwise, he's a martyr. Or fuck, I don't know, maybe Bridger's just an asshole. Not like there's not precedent for people doing dumb shit when they have magic dropped in their laps. With great power comes great party."

I shook off the reconstruction of what-ifs and maybes to focus on the right now. "The stables are close by. We should grab some horses and get out of Dodge before they string us up for killing the deputy. Or before Bridger comes after us with his magic totem."

We hugged the wall as a pair of miners drove past in a wagon. Pots and pans hung from the sides and clanked as the vehicle rumbled by, dust fogging the air.

"What about your amulet?" Krawczyk asked.

"It'll have to wait until things quiet down." I scratched my unshaven chin. "Going after Bridger now, when he's aware and armed, would be suicide."

Shouts echoed from somewhere behind us, still one or two streets away. "Bridger and Potts are rousing the town to come after us," I said. "At least everybody will be armed and ready if the Nimerigar come to town."

In her bad Tonto voice, Krawczyk said, "Time for us to run, kemo sabe. Make like jackrabbit and hop."

I nodded and set a course for the Bethlehem Stables.

Intermission
Bridger says "Aw, fuck it."

Archie Bridger picked himself off the floor and muttered a few choice curses. It had been a nasty surprise to find out that the blue-haired, bush-licking, cunt-bumper had the Power. He always suspected she had magic but had never found the woman's amulet, despite numerous searches. Obviously, he had been too much of a gentleman to peel her naked and look everywhere.

I won't make that mistake again.

When he took the so-called Judge's stone, he believed the man dead. The damn darkie had nine lives. The first try, with a rifle at long range, Bridger had missed. One too many whiskies had thrown off his aim. But then he miscalculated the amount of choke required to kill the coon. Another nasty surprise, him showing up after Bridger believed he had neutralized one of the three magic users in Geyser Falls The second was himself, and the third wouldn't hurt a fly, let alone try anything with Bridger. Evidence had proven him wrong. A fourth person had power, and it had come as quite a shock when the little bitch hit him with an invisible fist and knocked him on his ass. What was that she had yelled? "I'm out," or something like that? She had blown through her charge, then, and would be out of the fight for a time.

Clay Potts ran into the room in his red undergarments and a sweat-stained hat. "Are you all right, Sheriff?"

"The darkie killed Ermal," Bridger said. "Him and that little bitch. Go get some pants on and gather up some men with guns."

Bridger holstered his sidearm and cast a long look at the gun cabinet. The statue locked in the cabinet's base tempted him with the lust for Power, lighting him up with an urge to grab the ugly thing and shred the town like a tornado, wrecking and burning until Geyser Falls lay as flat as the valley surrounding it. Then he would grab Merilee Soames by the throat and shake her until she understood her place. He didn't expect much sense from a woman, but with the right... incentive, Merilee would get the picture soon enough. He could take her to San Francisco or Sacramento—or hell, even back East—and they could live like a king and queen. With the statue, no one could stop him.

It was about time to show these dirt-grubbing miners and shit-stinking cowboys who was the biggest hombre in the valley. With the statue, anything was possible, and anything could be his.

Why have I waited so long? It's time.

Bridger touched the tiny stone in his pocket. The smooth bit of agate had been his first taste of the Power. He had found it as a boy, fishing the creek out back of his parents' house in Virginia. As soon as he picked it up, he felt the Power. Not much. Just a smidge. Enough to lift a pencil, light a match, or blow air up a girl's skirt to see her ankles. One time, even Mrs. Pringles's gartered thighs—and hadn't that been the talk of all the boys in her class for weeks on end. But it was puny, that little dribble of power, so weak that Bridger pretty much forgot about it, leaving the pebble on his nightstand for months at a time.

Then a few short weeks ago, a rider on a lathered pony had sagged off his saddle in front of the barbershop, black blood crusted around a wound in his shoulder, asking for a doctor. He died before the doctor arrived, but in his saddlebags lay a treasure beyond the wildest dreams of a mortal man. Bridger had almost fainted the first time he touched the carved cylinder of shiny black rock. The Power had surged through him like a lightning strike that never stopped. Shutting it off before it burned him to a charcoal lump had taken every last ounce of strength he possessed. He had passed off the episode as "too much sun" to Ermal and Clay then confiscated the stone as "evidence."

Practicing in secret, Bridger began to learn what he could do with all the Power in the artifact. Creating fire, lightning, air pressure and temperature changes, and even some small successes with defeating gravity were well within his abilities. Some lessons had been more instructive than others—the first church fire, for instance, had been a misjudgment while experimenting in the alley behind the building. He'd felt bad for the damage, but then he'd seen Merilee and Weeks together at dinner in the Bannerworth, and an idea had been born: destroy Weeks by reputation first then put him on trial and hang him. Show Merilee what sort of man she'd taken up with.

Then the scrawny bitch with the colored hair appeared on the scene and threw things off-kilter. People said she was a witch, but Bridger searched her when he arrested her and found no stones of Power on her person. He was ready to get back to his plan when the goddamn coon—*excuse me, quarter coon*—had shown up and started acting all uppity. And lo and behold, he had a power stone too.

Which is now in my other pocket.

Bridger chuckled silently. Had he been too tentative? Too cautious? Too stuck in his role as sheriff and model citizen? He'd been dancing instead of calling the tune.

Potts's feet pounded the stairs, and Bridger tore his eyes away from the cabinet. The temptation was strong, but he put it aside.

Not yet. But soon.

"You ready?" he asked Potts when the fully dressed deputy barged into the room. At the younger man's nod, Bridger said, "Okay, then. Let's go kill a judge."

Chapter Twenty-Seven: It's Not the Size of the Arrow...

Bridger led Potts through the office door onto the boardwalk and nearly caught an arrow in the knee from a pint-sized Injun sneaking around the corner of the building. Bridger palmed his six-gun and fired from the hip. His shot splintered wood where the critter's head had been, a near miss, as the Injun spun away and disappeared around the corner. Two more dashed out from the alley and volleyed tiny arrows in his direction. Bridger fanned shots from his Colt and drove them back. He spotted dozens more of the little fuckers dashing and darting along the street, appearing and vanishing before he could draw a clear bead. Screams and panicked cries for help echoed from distant quarters of the town. Gunfire pocked the air.

"Damn it!" Bridger stepped back into the office to reload. "Potts, we're under attack. That black bastard brought his little pals with him, I guess. They'll kill everyone in town if we don't get organized."

"What do we do?" Potts's eyes were a little too wide, a little too crazy. Ermal's death and the attack of the dwarf Injuns had him spooked. Bridger needed to get him focused.

"Start getting folks together. Pass the word. Evacuate everyone across the River Bridge. The men that can shoot, form 'em up into a rear guard to protect the women and kids. We get everyone across. We can hold the bridge until hell freezes. Watch your ass. Them arrows are poison."

Potts nodded and bolted from the room. The deputy commenced yelling and shouting at people to do this and that. Bridger tuned it out and beelined straight for the gun cabinet, digging for the key to unlock the base. In seconds, the statue was in his hands. It felt like the sun breaking through the clouds on a rainy day, filling him with warmth and hope. And power. Lots and lots of power.

Okay, I was wrong. I guess it's time after all.

"You're sure an ugly thing," he told the carved face on the stone object. Made from a solid chunk of what he guessed was black granite as long as his thigh, the engraved face of the thing would give a blind man nightmares. Mashed-together lips, a broad nose, and bug-a-boo eyes made up the face, along with some markings that could have been elongated ears or something else entirely. More carvings of either letters or pictures decorated the shaft. Centuries of wear and handling had left chips missing, and abrasion had worn the artwork almost smooth. "But who gives a shit? You can be as ugly as you want, as long as you stay charged up with the Power, my friend."

A thickening stream of panicked citizens hurried past the open door to his office. Women with babes in arms and older children clutching at their skirts. Paiute and white, it made no difference. In their rush to escape the cannibals, everyone was equal. Men with rifles, shotguns, pistols, as well as the occasional farm tool, chivvied the women along, occasionally stopping to take pot shots at the attackers. Bridger crouched in the dark corner of his office, wrapped in a blanket of power, and watched them pass.

"What now, Archie Bridger?" he asked himself.

What now, indeed. Power filled him from toes to hair, enough that he could lay waste to the pygmies, flatten the entire town, burn it to cinders, and flush the ashes down the river, all without breaking a sweat. There would be nothing quiet or subtle about it. He could see no way to remove the Nimerigar without raising a huge magical ruckus. The Power wasn't, ah, discreet, no sir. He couldn't direct it to target only the pygmies and leave everything else intact. No, any counterattack would be big, splashy, and obvious. He could do it, but...

But why? What was the point of ruling a Podunk town that would have to be rebuilt anyway? Weren't there better options for a man with unlimited power? It was only the limits of his dreams holding him back. He'd been thinking too small. It was time to make a play for the brass ring.

A pair of tiny warriors rushed past the door. One skidded to a stop and stuck his head inside, blinking from the sunlight. Bridger burned him to a crisp with a jolt of power. The blackened husk fell with a brittle clatter and lay there, smoking. His buddy ran on, either oblivious to his companion's death or unwilling to suffer the same fate.

Bridger scratched his chin. He needed to get word to Esmeralda to meet him at the shack, but his horse was at the Bannerworth Hotel's stables. Ezzie had a talent he needed to learn in order to become entirely self-sufficient with the Power. Also at the Bannerworth, in his third-floor room, a couple of bags of cash were hidden in the bottom of his wardrobe. He had more stashed in an abandoned shack south of town, buried under the porch. And there was another reason to go to the Bannerworth, wasn't there? A big-bosomed brunette reason. Esmeralda had her uses, and he would definitely keep her around, but Merilee... oh, man, she was the stuff of dreams. The stuff of dreams.

"Come on, tall, black, and ugly," Bridger told the statue. "Let's go get what's ours."

Krawczyk and I ducked into the dark, stuffy interior of the stables and followed the sounds of scratching and shuffling to the last stall on the left. Inside the stall, an old man worked down a pile of hay, spreading it into an even layer. In his ragged clothes and shapeless hat, he looked familiar...

"Billy!" Krawczyk cried.

Billy Minor spun on his heel then clutched his chest and staggered back. "Land-a-Goshen, woman. You like to scared a week of my life right outta me."

"I'm sorry, Billy." She hugged the old man then stepped back to hold him by the arms. "I was surprised to see you. What're you doing here?"

I relaxed my clenched jaw with an effort. Why did people enjoy chitchat so much? It was as if everyone else on the planet had nothing better to do than catch up on each other's life stories, disregarding that they had seen each other ten minutes before. The sheriff and his boys would be hot on our trail, and every second not spent putting miles behind our asses was time wasted.

Billy leaned on his pitchfork, and I groaned, sensing it would be a long story. "Bethlehem said I could work here for two bits a day and double that in credit. I get forty dollars credit, I can buy one o' his mules. I figgered it out, and if I work six days a week, I orta have enough by Christmas." He grinned a three-gap smile. "Then it'll be back to minin'."

"Look," I said, "this is nice and all, but—"

Huh. Is that you? A familiar, mournful voice sounded in my head.

I whirled around to find a tired-looking brown horse poking his nose over the stall door. "Misery! You're alive!"

Who cares?

"Useless nag." I crossed the stable then patted the brown horse's neck.

"Bethlehem said your horse came back yestiddee," Billy supplied. "Gave him a rubdown and some oats, so he's as good as new."

"That wasn't a high bar." I scratched under the horse's chin. "But I'm glad to see him, anyway. Can you get him saddled up for me? And we'll need to... to borrow Blaze again."

"That horse is tuckered out," Billy said, "but I can let you have Old Roan."

"Old Roan, huh. Let me guess, he's a roan-colored horse."

"Nah, he's more reddish colored."

"Fine." I paused when a screaming man ran across the front of the stable. His scream pitched higher when a tiny arrow appeared in his back. Two more sprouted from next to the first, and he collapsed.

Shots popped in the distance.

"Ah, hell," Krawczyk said. "Time's up."

I clamped a hand on Billy's shoulder. "Saddle up Roan and Misery then pick one for yourself. We'll guard the door."

Billy gaped at the man in the street then scooted off toward the tack room.

"Then what?" Krawczyk propped her hands on her hips and stuck her chin out. "We're going to just run away?"

"Krawczyk..." I sagged against the stall. The weight of this extended song of doom dragged at my willpower. It was as if *American Pie* had been looped so it never ended. "I have one antique six-gun and thirty-some-odd extra rounds. I have no magic, and you're almost tapped out... Once that runs dry, we're down to snide remarks and dirt clods."

Krawczyk snatched Billy's pitchfork. "We can fight with this if we have to. We need to get the statue back from Bridger and give it to the rightful owners."

"The cannibals."

"They're people, and they're the ones who've been wronged here."

"Twelve hours ago, they were going to eat you!"

"Which they would not have, had not somebody *stolen* their *property.*"

I squeezed my eyes shut and marshaled my arguments for retreating and regrouping. No words came to mind. Deep down, I knew she was right. I just didn't want to admit it. I wanted to get back to my time and line up my rematch with the Wonderful Wizard of Ohio so badly, it was eating a hole in my stomach. I needed his tech to cure Alizandra. With the DNA cloning technology, growing my sister a new liver would be a cinch. But every time I thought I could get back to her, something came along and tripped me up. The distractions were clouding my judgment.

I shuffled to the open stable door, holding the Colt by my leg. The man with three arrows in his back lay facing the stables, and his glazed eyes seemed to bore right into my conscience. The man's tongue stuck out, touching the dirt. People raced to and fro, kicking up dust and yelling about an Indian attack, though none of the pygmy warriors showed themselves. More than a few townsmen made a beeline for the Broken Wheel.

You could fort up there. At least there's beer.

In other words, give up on Birnbaum.

Birnbaum hasn't even been born yet! Stop being a jackass.

"Look." Krawczyk appeared at my shoulder. I showed her how tough I was by not looking at her. Me macho. "The Nimerigar are after the statue that Bridger has. They want it back, right?"

"Mm."

A miniature warrior peeked around the corner of a building across the street. I aimed, but the warrior withdrew before I had a good sight picture. I let the Colt fall to my side.

"All we have to do, then," Krawczyk was saying, "is sneak up on Bridger, knock him out, and take back the statue. Then we can give it back to the little people, and all is right. Right?"

I barked a short laugh. "Easy-peasy, lemon-squeezy."

The gunfire picked up in intensity, from sporadic pops to a ragged crackle. Bethlehem Stables was on the southeastern side of town, and most of the shots seemed to be coming from the north, not far from the Bannerworth. I shied away from that thought. No good thinking about... anyone who might be under siege at the hotel. I had more than enough shit sandwiches on my plate.

The Nimerigar were probably infiltrating from the northeast and expanding through town, seeking targets of opportunity or sniffing for their idol. It was impossible to know without looking whether the entire horde had attacked at once or if the townspeople engaged only a probing force.

Lack of intel meant no battle plan. No battle plan equaled dead soldiers.

An old man and a younger woman popped out of the alley from the other side of the street, followed by two Nimerigar. I again was struck by how childlike and silly the pygmies looked, though there was nothing silly about the poisoned-tipped arrows they leveled at the people they chased from the alley. I triggered off a round that tumbled one warrior into a bloody heap and spoiled the aim of the other. His arrow arced into the sky and fell to the dust. I delivered a second bullet that shattered the warrior's pelvis and spun him to the ground, screaming. A third bullet ended his screams. At this rate, I could kill all the Nimerigar by the time they invented plastic dishware.

I loaded the Colt's spent chambers. "Getting involved in this fight means Bridger catches up to us on his ground. He catches us, we're never getting back to our time. It would be suicide to go sneaking around a town full of cannibal pixies looking for a Magical with enough power to blow up the sun, carrying nothing but a Colt .45 and good intentions. It's time to pull back, regroup, and set a trap for the sheriff."

"But we have to tell people!"

"Tell them what? Their sheriff has a magic totem pole and the cannibal pygmies want it back? Tell them to ignore their trusted lawman when he says the witch and the colored man killed Barton? Who do you think they're going to believe, Krawczyk?"

She stepped back, her brown eyes rounded into saucers. "Wow. Just... wow."

"The tactically sound course of action is to live to fight another day. Wait—where're you going?"

The small woman marched away, the pitchfork over one shoulder. She wasn't much taller than the tool she carried. She stomped along in her too-big shirt and too-big pants, workman's boots engulfing her feet. She crossed the street, went down the block, and entered the Broken Wheel without a word or a glance back.

I ground my teeth and holstered the revolver. The sound of shots had drawn closer, as had the raised voices. More people spilled from the streets and alleyways, evacuating southward, away from the commotion—women and children, by and large, though a few men scampered away from the fighting. Emotions ranged from wild-eyed fear to tightly controlled panic. One woman led a group of four youngsters, ranging in size from medium to small, along the cross street at the end of the block. They all held hands in a chain and sang a nursery rhyme. Except for the woman's repeated looks over her shoulder, I would have guessed they were on the way to a church social. They passed the intersection and disappeared.

Billy walked up, leading three horses by the reins. "We gettin' outta here?"

"The town is outnumbered," I said, "by a factor of at least ten-to-one. The people here all hate me or want me dead, and the sheriff's a Magical with unlimited power who is set on nailing my dick to the barn door. It's a hopeless situation with no chance of a favorable outcome."

Misery nudged me in the back with his blunt nose.

"Yeah, I know," I told the horse. "Who cares, right?"

Billy's face scrunched. "Huh?"

"Let's get a drink, Billy."

The old prospector smacked his gums. "Best idea I heard all day!"

Chapter Twenty-Eight: Who Cares?

The uproar inside the Broken Wheel approached pandemonium. Amos McKenzie slapped down foamy mugs of beer as fast as he could fill them from the keg, slaking the thirst of a throng of stalwart town defenders. The barman's bald head glowed bright crimson from heat and sweat. The gathered men checked loads, cranked lever actions, and otherwise fiddled with firearms, each one competing to tell everyone else his personal story of the marauding, child-sized "Injuns." Even the faro dealer was in on the action—from somewhere, he had acquired a monster of a double-barreled shotgun with bores the size of freight tunnels.

I stepped around Krawczyk, who had sort of frozen just inside the entry, and yelled, "Hey!" A few of the closer individuals looked up, but the majority of the men in the saloon kept right on jabbering. "Hey, listen up!"

Nothing.

Krawczyk stuck two fingers in her mouth and shrilled a piercing whistle that cut through the chatter and brought a moment's respite.

"Thanks," I muttered side-mouth. "I never learned that trick." I pitched my voice to carry and said, "Listen up, men! The Nimerigar are after something your sheriff stole. A statue, about yay high." I demonstrated my trout measurement again. "They get the statue back, they might leave us alone."

"Who the fuck are you?" This from a man I didn't recognize, a miner with bib overalls and a pinched face covered in black hair.

More comments boiled from the crowd, mean and hot, seasoned with fear and stirred by bigotry. "Why're you running down the sheriff?" and "Who let the smoked Irish in?" were two that cracked out, loud and clear. Faces stared back at me, not so much with hatred as disgust, as though I had dropped a bucket of dog shit on the floor and tap-danced in it.

I glared at the tidal wash of white faces, not letting the sinking feeling in my gut show through. I knew very few of the gathered men, and those I did know seemed disinclined to leap to my side. McKenzie acted like Switzerland, keeping his attention fixed on serving drinks, carefully not looking in my direction. Another man I recognized from the hotel met my eyes for an instant before his gaze slid away.

I slathered Krawczyk with a look as if to ask, "This is who you want to save?"

"He's telling the truth!" She stood by my elbow. Her shrill voice drilled into a wall of distrust. "The sheriff—"

Ugly laughter rolled over her words. Shouts lashed her into silence. Krawczyk flinched with every slur hurled her way, and the white heat of unstoppable anger crackled at the edges of my control. Tendons in my arms stood out like over-tightened guitar strings. Calling me names was one thing, but now...

"Let's go." I took Krawczyk by the elbow. "I'm done here."

"Yeah, get out!" someone yelled.

"And take the perverted bitch with you!"

"Lookit the coon and his cock-lady!"

I dragged Krawczyk from the Broken Wheel, the peals of mocking laughter lashing my back. I gritted my teeth against the powerful urge to turn and fight, to stand my ground, to smash through the crowd with a hammer forged of righteousness to beat the ignorance out of those racist, misogynist bastards. The fucking assholes may have been a product of their time, but I had run out of patience. The next son of a bitch who threw a racial slur in my direction would be eating it, raw, unsalted, and crammed sideways.

Billy Minor stood at the hitch rail, looping the reins of three horses around the pole. He squinted at me. "I thought we was going to the saloon."

"Stay or go"—I jabbed a thumb over my shoulder—"or ride south with me. You too, Krawczyk. Choose now."

I wrapped Misery's reins around my hand and climbed into the saddle. I tugged his head around and kicked the buckskin in the ribs. I didn't look back to see if Krawczyk or Billy followed me, just rode to the first cross street that would take me out of Geyser Falls by the shortest possible route. Fighting a horde of pissed off savages was not an option anymore. I had a job to do back in my time, and I'd be damned if I would get my ass in a crack before I had a chance to get it done. The whole fucking town could burn to a crisp, and it would be just fine by me—probably an improvement, truth be told.

From behind me carried the sounds of Krawczyk cursing her horse while climbing into the saddle. Billy said something about getting a beer and maybe coming later. Kat said something back that I didn't catch.

The crackle of gunfire popped from the north, along with faint screams of terrified people. I ignored it.

Who cares, right? I said to Misery.

The horse tossed his head and snorted.

A staccato rattle of hooves pounded from the cross street ahead. Two or more horses, running hard, were coming from the north, probably carrying people intent on escaping the hordes of Nimerigar. I pulled up and waited for the racing mounts to cross in front of me, and a moment later, two horses thundered past. My jaw dropped. My prayers had been answered.

On the first mount rode none other than Archie Bridger, hat brim tugged low, a canvas tote tied over one shoulder. He led the reins of a second horse carrying the unmistakable figure of Merilee Soames, hands tied to the saddle horn and a bandanna wrapping her mouth as a gag. Merilee's print dress suffered from riding astride the saddle, hiking up to expose her legs all the way to her knees. Wind whipped her hair into chestnut streamers, and her eyes burned red daggers into Bridger's back.

The pair left behind a cloud of dust and the receding drumming of hoofbeats.

I snorted and shook my head in disbelief. "Well, well. Santa came early this year."

At first, Bridger and Merilee were not hard to follow, as the dust from their passing hung in the air for a long time, and the road paralleled the river without forks or crossings to deviate from the main trail. But Misery's top speed was no match for Bridger's mounts. The dust thinned minute by minute and soon evaporated completely. Trails that split into the eastern desert began appearing. I was forced to inspect every intersection for fresh tracks pounded into the dry roadbed, lest I ride past the point where my quarry left the road.

Your quarry? Unless you catch him asleep, Bridger will fry your guts to a blackened crisp the second he sees you.

No problem. I'll send the horse in as a distraction.

Misery snorted.

Krawczyk caught up the first time I stopped to check a side road. She remained silent, but her expression could have microwaved a frozen dinner. She sat atop a roan, her feet barely reaching the stirrups, and waited in stony silence as I scouted around. She maintained her silent outrage as I remounted and kicked Misery into motion. *Jeez, the way some people can hold a grudge...*

The sun seemed determined to stay overhead and follow us with scorching heat, which reflected off the powdery dust and threatened to broil us alive. I was tempted to divert to the Owens River and do a full-body dunk to cool off. We needed water, sooner or later, as Misery had already sent me mental images of watering troughs, rivers, waterfalls, lakes, and ponds.

Krawczyk jounced along beside me. When she wasn't freezing me with her cold shoulder, she was cursing Blaze in a low, steady murmur of creative obscenity. I felt an odd creeping sensation that I couldn't immediately identify. I picked at the feeling until I could bring it out into the open and examine it. Riding off and leaving the townspeople to the Nimerigar had left me vaguely unsettled and less than satisfied with my conduct.

You feel guilty for running away, dummy.

I'm not running away.

Of course. Traveling in the opposite direction from the attack in town is a clever ruse to lure the enemy to their doom.

"You don't like riding?" I said to Krawczyk.

"Fuck no," she snapped. "I fucking hate it. I never want to see another horse forever and ever amen. I want my Camaro." She sighed and fanned herself with her floppy hat. Her eyes took on a dreamy look. "Back home, I have a 1968 Camaro SS with a bored and polished 350 coupled to a Muncie four-speed and a ten-bolt Posi rear end. Cherry red with white striping around the nose. Oh man... she flies."

"A flower child like you? I figured you for a Prius."

"Fuck you, Shivers." Krawczyk glared at me and straightened in the saddle, obviously having temporarily forgotten that I was an asshole and she hated me. She kicked her horse into a canter and bobbled away, riding with the grace of a potato sack on a pogo stick. If both hands hadn't been occupied by holding the saddle horn, I suspected at least one would be upright with an extended middle finger.

Note to self: Don't try talking to people. It never ends well.

Misery's tail flicked and swatted my leg. *That's how I feel.*

I twisted in the saddle to look behind me. Geyser Falls had disappeared long ago, and the sound of shooting had faded. I knew very few people in town and liked only a small subset of those. The bartender. Billy Minor and James Snow. Gerda from the diner. And Esmeralda was back there. She was cute but tough—a survivor. Even with one foot, she would have been a match for any pygmy.

"They'll be fine," I told Misery. "Right?"

Another slap from the horse's tail stung my leg.

The sun dipped behind a line of thunderclouds over the Sierra Nevada. Rain slanted from the distant clouds, a slate gray banner hanging from the sky, far across the Owens River, moving north. I wished it would move toward us. I needed some rain to go with the cloud of gloom hanging over me. Maybe whatever hopeless melancholy had infected my horse was contagious. Maybe my long-forgotten conscience was twisting its panties over having abandoned Geyser Falls. Or maybe my mission directives were in a giant muddle, with only one clear task that made sense: find Bridger and kill Bridger.

And then what? I still had no clue how to manipulate time and get back home to snuff Birnbaum and learn to use his equipment to save Alizandra.

And this is important because?

Because she's my sister! You don't abandon your kin—especially the only kin you have left in the world. Plus, Birnbaum makes nightmare creatures in his secret lab. Bad wizard.

You're not thinking this through. You could take ten or twenty years here and now and still get back in time to zap little Dusty and save Al-

izandra. Alternately, bring Krawczyk with you. She's a healer. Fuck the Admins. Use the gifts she has and save your sister.

"Winners never quit, and quitters never win." My father once jerked me out of a baseball game and delivered that little gem after I failed to run out an infield hit. All the other parents in the stands, the coaches, and my teammates pretended to go on with the game, but I felt their sidelong looks and frowns of pity. My father's breath had smelled of wintergreen gum, which he bought by the case and chewed like he hated it.

Back then, my face had burned under my oversized batting helmet, and I still remembered the shame and guilt and preteen humiliation, which was like no other embarrassment. I snapped back, "Is that right, Dad? Then who's the genius who said, 'Quit while you're ahead?'"

My father's eyes would have melted stone, and the grip on my bicep had tightened like a tourniquet. His voice was ice-cold when he said, "No one in this family."

I could quit following Bridger, and who would care? Krawczyk? She would dance for joy if we reined around and headed back to Geyser Falls. Defend the town, win the day, and then I could retire to a nice corner of the world and forget all my problems. Maybe find a spot in the Los Angeles foothills, somewhere near where Hollywood would arise. Or in the San Fernando Valley. Buy some property, sit back on my rocking chair—

Taking the time to do the right thing will not hurt Alizandra one bit. She won't even be born for another hundred-plus years.

Then why does it feel like giving up?

"Hssst!" Krawczyk had pulled up at the top of a rise and raised her hand. She sawed at the reins and dragged Blaze around more by brute force than skill. She bounced her way back to me and dragged the poor horse to a stop. I sensed long-suffering annoyance from

Blaze and something along the lines of *let me buck, just once...* "Come take a look," Krawczyk said. "Just over the hill."

I dismounted and handed her my reins. My legs felt rubbery after so long on horseback, so I stretched them back to life before proceeding up the hill. I crouched and duckwalked into the sparse cover offered by a clump of sedge grass at the top of a slight rise. Its weedy smell tickled my sinuses.

Before me, a gentle slope dropped to a wide plain. A U-bend in the river curled in, bringing the water close to the trail. Between the trail and the river's bend, an abandoned homestead was busy being reclaimed by time and weather. A small wood-frame house, no bigger than two rooms max, was the middle of three structures. Fifty yards beyond the house stood a decrepit barn, its roof collapsed inward, studs poking up like broken ribs. An outhouse completed the trio, leaning sideways in a drunken cant, sufficient for nothing more than the residence of endless hordes of spiders and scorpions and snakes.

Our vantage point made it feel like looking down from the nosebleed seats in a football stadium to the field below. Two horses, tied to the porch rail of the decrepit house, drowsed in the late afternoon sun. I identified them as the same two horses last seen passing me in the streets of Geyser Falls, bearing Bridger and Merilee away from town.

Krawczyk slid up next to me and whispered, "This looks too easy."

"Hmm."

"What are you going to do?"

"Hmm."

"I have maybe one decent shot of magic. But I won't kill him for you, if that's what you want."

"Pop a tendon in his knee? Punch him in the face? Shrivel his testicles?"

"Ew." Krawczyk rested her forehead on the ground. "No. I won't. Can't you just knock him out and take the statue?"

"Why didn't I think of that?"

The cabin door banged open, and Archie Bridger stepped out. One hand was fisted in Merilee Soames's hair, and the other was buried inside a burlap bag looped over his shoulder with a piece of rope. "Hey!" Bridger's voice boomed, magically amplified to sound like the voice of God. "I saw y'all coming a mile away. A mile away. Whyn't y'all come on down and join the party instead of creeping around like a pair of Injuns. Which you ain't good at." He jerked at his bound and gagged captive, who stumbled and nearly fell. "Or maybe I start taking pieces off my future wife here."

I sagged and blew out a sigh. Dust puffed under my face.

Krawczyk groaned.

"I'm open to suggestions," I said.

Chapter Twenty-Nine: Try Not to Die

"Any ideas?" Krawczyk asked on the long trudge down the slope. Fingers of her blue hair poked out from under her floppy hat, and sunburn flushed her cheeks. She resembled a small child who'd been rolling in the dirt all day being called in to face her mother's wrath.

"Try not to die." I felt as baked as an overdone potato, salty with old sweat, my skin leathery and chapped, and trapped in a sauna of my own sour smell.

Shadows like elongated alien bodies stretched to our left, one tall and one short. An amalgamated blob followed those skinny shadows, eight spidery legs topped by two horse bodies. Misery and Blaze kept pace without being led, coming along at my mental command. The underside of the western clouds burned orange, painted by the dying sun.

In the packed earth at my feet, footprints had been impressed in the soil and hardened there. I frowned at an odd-looking set of prints, which seemed to be one shoe and one round hole. A peg leg? Had Esmeralda been there, or was this from another single-legged person walking around the cabin? Seemed a coincidence, but I had seen more than one amputee stumping around town—veterans of the Civil War.

We stopped well within pistol range of the sheriff. If I could get off a shot, I could nail Bridger through the forehead at that distance.

With the man touching a bottomless well of magic, that would be stupider than your normal.

True. Quicker than a speeding bullet, Bridger could convert energy to defeat or deflect the shot as soon as it left the barrel. Unless I could pull a miracle out of my ass, Bridger had won the battle and the war, all without breaking a sweat.

I hawked and spat to the side with tough-guy bravado. "What now?"

"Well," Bridger said, "as much as it would amuse me to pull your dick off and nail it to the door, I'm pretty well done tired of your uppity coon ass."

With a look of narrow-eyed concentration, Bridger crushed me with a fist of magical energy from shoulders to hips. I had a moment to think, *Well, that was fast,* before the wind exploded from my lungs. As easily as crumpling a beer can, the invisible force squeezed me like a hydraulic press. I strained against the force, but I might as well have tried holding back a dump truck.

Bones snapped. I screamed without sound. Organs ruptured. Gore pulsed up from my guts and spilled past my lips. Blood and worse warmed my pants, stained my crotch. It happened so quickly that I barely felt any pain, just enormous pressure.

I dropped when released. I didn't feel the impact with the ground.

My cheek lay in the dirt.

A pool of red soaked into my vision.

Pain would come. Soon. I knew it would hit with a vengeance, once my nerves recognized and reacted to the damage. I experienced a moment of clarity in that calm before the outrage. I couldn't breathe. My lungs were crushed, shredded by broken ribs. Somehow my heart still pounded as blood pulsed through torn veins. Wetness showered the dirt and clogged my throat. My guts felt liquefied, pureed and somehow poured back into my skin sack, leaking from places best left unexplored.

So this is how it ends.

That I would die in the dirt at the hands of a Magical, I had never once doubted. I just hadn't expected it *today*. It was too soon. Would any day *not* be too soon? Probably not, but I had always pictured it happening at some point far in the future, after I was worn out, tired, and ready to quit. Now, with my blood and guts dribbling through my teeth, I had to face facts. I was dying, and there wasn't a thing I could do to stop it.

Krawczyk was shrieking something in cursive. Something so blisteringly foul that birds should have been falling dead from the sky. I felt her hand on my shoulder. I wanted to say something, warn her that her knee was in a puddle of blood. She would never get the stain out, if she wasn't careful. My mouth moved, and a shudder wracked me. More gunk puddled out. I tried to breathe and remembered I couldn't.

"Now," came Bridger's voice, smarmy and full of false cheer, "what should I do with you? Are you good for anything, you little blue-haired bitch? Or do you want to join the coon there? Stop your squawking, darlin', and talk to me sweet, else I might be inclined to think you're not worth a flying fuck."

Bridger's boots entered my line of vision. He'd left Merilee somewhere, probably on the porch, as he approached. Daylight was going—or maybe it was me going. I couldn't be sure. It was getting dark, whatever the cause. Hooves thudded nearby, and Misery snuffled my ear.

The pain was coming on strong, but pain was nothing new. Pain was pain, and this was no different—except in intensity, depth, volume, and scope. A grin threatened to lift the corners of my lips. *Okay, so maybe it is something new.*

"Go to hell, Bridger!" Krawczyk screamed. She was really quite pretty when she was incensed. I felt the tingle of magic flowing through her touch into my shoulder. Bless her, the woman was trying to heal a broken water main with a sponge. The best she could do with her meager shot of magic was fix a few broken blood vessels, maybe hold off the worst of the pain. Even as I recognized the magic trickle for what it was, the flow tapered off and died.

Bridger took another step closer. "I think I'll—"

Fuck that.

The words rang in my head, clear as if spoken in my ear. A flickering shadow passed over me, and I heard a double thud. Bridger landed on the ground a few feet away. The sheriff's mouth hung open, and there was a half-moon horseshoe print etched on his forehead.

What. The. Hell. I had trouble connecting thoughts in a logical sequence. I tried piecing together events from my limited viewpoint and found the needed concentration slipping from my mind. Thoughts seeped into dark corners and faded away.

Horse lips tickled my ear.

One thought finally solidified enough to have meaning. *Misery? Did you...*

Who cares?

My miserable excuse for a horse had kicked the evil supervillain in the head. My horse. Had kicked. A Magical. To death.

If I had any air in my lungs, I would have died laughing.

Instead, I died with a smile on my face.

A persistent, irritating voice wouldn't go away and leave me alone.

"Come on, Shivers, stay with me. Come on, you stupid bastard."

Things were happening inside my body. Hideously painful things. I found out I could breathe because I realized I was screaming. Warmth radiated from a palm on my shoulder—no, not warmth, cast-iron-skillet heat. Krawczyk's voice chanted the refrain, "Stay with me, stay with me."

Why do people always say that when you're dying? And then agony ratcheted up the scale from unbearable to fucking incredible.

No, I howled inside my head. *I don't want to stay with you, because you're fucking killing me worse than Bridger did!*

Misery snorted, and I heard Krawczyk say, "Hold that horse before he tries to kick me too."

Kick her! Kick her!

The horse ignored my order. What else was new?

Merilee cooed at Misery, and the traitor let himself be led away. *Stupid horse!*

"Owww, fuck, that hurts!" My eyes snapped open, and I found Krawczyk crouched over me, one hand on my shoulder, one hand touching an ugly statue the size of a working man's thermos.

The Nimerigar magic totem.

Magic energy flowed through healer and into my body, repairing, rearranging, and redressing the heinous damage done by Bridger's bear hug. I could... *feel* things inside my skin moving around. Ribs snapped back into place. Guts twisted into their original shape and placement. Organs popped back out like flat tires being filled with air. And every bit of it was accompanied by wall-scraping, rug-chewing pain.

Something crackled in my backbone, and feeling rushed back into my legs and feet, arriving with the sensation of having stepped into live voltage.

"Jesus Christ, Krawczyk!"

"Shut up, you big baby," she said. "This is hard enough without your bitching and whining. You want to live or not?"

Not really, no.

Shut up, you're not helping.

Minutes dragged their way over hot coals, and time stretched itself on a rack. Things inside my body popped and crackled and aligned, and the pain receded as though riding the overlapping waves of an outgoing tide. At some point after a million years or so, Krawczyk slumped, and her hand fell away. The burning spot on my shoulder where she had touched me cooled. I breathed normally, without pain. My body felt wrung out—a thought that made me laugh silently.

Wrung out. Hah. You're hysterical.

"Hey," my crusty voice croaked. I brushed Kat's knee with a knuckle. "I hate you so much right now."

"Don't mention it." She sounded as tired as I felt, shaking herself awake at my touch. With a lift of her chin, Krawczyk indicated the totem squatting beside her. "This thing. This thing is fucking awesome. I've never... I never knew there was this much magic in the whole world. I can't feel the end of it. It's like, uh, standing on the shore of an ocean and not being able to see the other side."

I rolled up on my side, bracing for pain and surprised not to feel any. Dried blood caked my lips and flaked off my cheek. Something best left unexplored had fouled my jeans. I ignored the mess, reached for the statue, and touched it.

My stomach, so recently healed, threatened to plummet through the center of the Earth. Krawczyk was wrong. This was no mere ocean of magic. This was a galaxy of magical energy. It felt like jumping off a cliff and into the deepest watering hole imaginable. By comparison, the magic of my amulet, at full power, was a swimming pool.

I looked at Krawczyk.

She looked back.

"This is a lot of fucking magic," I said.

"You got that right, Harry Potter." She scraped her splayed fingers through her choppy hair. "A Magical with that much power could change the world. End poverty. End hunger."

I forced my hand away from the stone. It felt like parting from a lover's embrace. Krawczyk was still speaking.

"I could cure everyone," she murmured, her eyes locked on the ugly little statue, "of every disease. Build dams to bring power and water to this backward-ass place."

"Level mountains," I added.

"Save the Native Americans from persecution."

"Destroy cities."

"End suffering."

"Yeah, sure," I said. "All that's great, but more importantly, maybe we could use it to get home."

Alizandra.

Merilee appeared, leading Misery and Blaze back from the river. Both horses dripped water from their muzzles. She stopped and goggled at me. "You're alive. That's bloody amazing." Her nose wrinkled. "But you smell awful. Wait a sec." She handed the reins to Krawczyk and detoured around us to enter the shack.

I groaned, staggered to my feet, and took Misery's reins. "Nice kick."

Who cares?

"Not you, of course." I tucked Misery's head against my shoulder and scratched the buckskin's chin. "You're just a big sack of meanness wrapped in horsehair. Whoa..." My legs wobbled, and I clung to the horse's bridle to stay upright. I shook my head to dispel the cobwebs.

"Take it easy, Your Honorness," Krawczyk said. "I could knit together the broken veins, but I couldn't put the blood back inside.

Best I could do was drain the internal bleeding out of you, along with all the other waste inside your abdomen. Otherwise, we'd risk peritonitis."

What I heard sounded a lot more like Charlie Brown's teacher than real words. I rattled my head again, clearing more of the blackness around the edge of my vision. "Peritonitis? That's bad, right?"

"Very bad."

Merilee appeared on the porch from inside and crossed the yard to lay a bundle across Misery's saddle. Jeans, shirt, and long johns. "Archie—ah, that is, Sheriff Bridger—had apparently stashed clothes and... other items under the floorboards."

I noted the pause and wondered if the "other items" happened to be banded stacks of bills stolen from a certain Geyser Falls bank.

Merilee stepped back onto the porch and continued, "He had just finished pulling this out of his hidey-hole when you lot arrived. There are dresses and a woman's things in there, as well, but they are all too small for me. I have no idea for whom he intended them." She gestured to the men's clothes. "You may have to roll up the edges a bit, but I believe they'll fit. Might I suggest you hie yourself off to the river and clean up, Mr. Shivers?"

"Yeah, dude," Krawczyk said. "Some things, all the magic in the world can't fix."

I slid a hand along the buckskin's neck until I had hold of the saddle horn. "C'mon, horse. Show me the way to the river." I took a second to cast a glower at the two women. "Hate for my smell of recent deadness to offend anyone."

Misery snorted and tossed his head. *You stink.*

"Shut up and drive."

Clean though damp, I walked back from the river while gnawing on a piece of jerky from a sack in my saddlebags. My legs, feeling as rubbery as boneless chicken wings, threatened to let go. Some of the dizziness had cleared, although if my willpower had been a battery, it would have been sorely in need of charging. The only thing stopping me from curling up on the ground and sleeping for a week was the promise offered by the Nimerigar totem. The memory—the power flowing through my fingertips and electrifying my mind with possibilities—kept driving me up the riverbank to the cabin, one staggering step at a time. I had, for a moment, touched the sun, and I wanted to do it again.

Krawczyk met me with fists on hips the moment I wobbled up. "So what'dya mean, maybe go back home? Have you figured out how?" She and Merilee had found some rickety chairs and dragged them to the porch. They sat together in the slanted evening light, nearly invisible in the shadows of the cabin's front wall.

I opened my mouth then closed it, glancing at Merilee.

"Oh, don't worry," Krawczyk said. "I told her everything."

"Everything?"

"Every detail."

"I must say, it's all a bit much, isn't it?" Merilee said.

The statue sat between their chairs. Squat and crudely carved, the stone could have been anything from onyx to granite for all I knew—I also slept through geology. As far as I was concerned, rock was something to play at very loud volume. I stared at the smug little face atop the totem and wondered who'd carved it, where they found it, and most importantly, how it had come to contain such vast quantities of latent magic.

"What's the tune you're humming?" Merilee asked.

"Hmm?" I broke off my staring contest with the statue. "Oh... ah, 'I Am, I Said.' Neil Diamond."

"I keep thinking about making my way back," Krawczyk sang.

I chuckled silently. "And we're sure as hell lost between two shores."

"So back to my original question."

"I don't know," I admitted. "Bits and pieces are coming back. Something about pinching off a bubble of mass and moving it sideways through a huge application of energy. I'll need time and a metric ton of magic to figure out how Birnbaum converted that much energy and how he... did whatever he did." I paused. "The good news is, we now have a ton of magic. We'll just need to hole up somewhere until we can figure it out. We know it can be done, so we just have to recreate the wheel."

Krawczyk, who had grown more agitated throughout my speech, jumped off her chair, sending the fragile contraption into a death rattle. "Are you kidding me? We have to give it back!"

"Back? To the pygmy cannibals?"

"Yes! Don't you see? Look what happened after Bridger stole it. The Nimerigar came out of the mountains and started slaughtering right and left, trying to get it back. They're killing people right now for this thing. We have to let them have it so they'll leave everybody alone."

I blinked. *Never give in. Never surrender,* my father had said once when I came home, beaten and bloody from a schoolyard fight. *You don't stop a bully by giving him what he wants.*

"No," I said to Krawczyk. "That's ridiculous. We can't hand this much power to a tribe of cannibal savages."

"They held onto the thing for years, and nobody noticed. I don't think they can even access the magical energy. I doubt they know it's there."

"How do you know that? You can't know that."

"I know that people are dying!" Krawczyk stabbed a finger at me. "And I know you're being a jerk. If we leave without helping those people, we're as good as killing them, and what does that make us? We'll have the blood of an entire town on our hands."

Merilee rose from her chair much more elegantly than the smaller woman had. She swished off the porch and approached me. By the early starlight, her beauty shone through the dust and weariness and fatigue, and I was reminded of the toughness that underlay her remarkable appearance. She placed her fingers lightly on my forearm. "Please, Mr. Shivers. Miss Krawczyk says you're kind of a battle wizard in your own time and that you can fight with magic." Merilee looked at the ground and shook her head before meeting my eyes again. "I still can't wrap my mind around saying that. 'Magic.' But please, if you can save my town, I would be most grateful."

I frowned and straightened. It was hard to read Merilee's expression in the dark, so I played back her last words in my head, listening between the lines, as it were. After a few replays, I realized I could uncover no hidden meaning behind the hotel owner's words, no double entendres or offers implied by her statement. No quid pro quo sex. She would be grateful, and that was it.

"At the very least," Krawczyk added, "we need to go back and see if we can help the town. No matter what we do with the statue." It looked like it cost her a lot to add that final sentence.

I picked at a loose thread on my saddle. A dozen and one reasons to say no played in my mind, but what came out, as if torn from my chest, was "Fine. Let's go take care of the Nimerigar." I kept my expression neutral in case my poker face slipped at the wrong moment. "Take care of" could have been interpreted any number of ways, and I did not want either Kat or Merilee to force me into being more specific.

Keep your options open.

Exactly.

"Oh," Krawczyk said. "I almost forgot. Bridger had this on him." She handed me a small round stone. My amulet. Fully charged. The knot of anxiety around my chest unwound a turn. I put the stone in my pocket and nodded my thanks without speaking. I led my horse away from the others and occupied my hands by adjusting bits of tack.

"Let's go," I said when I could trust myself to speak.

I mounted Misery and kicked him into plodding motion.

Chapter Thirty: Bring the Lightning

We met the first refugees within minutes of taking the road back to Geyser Falls. A bedraggled column of townspeople marched southward on foot, in wagons, and on horseback. Some carried lanterns, and the yellow globes marked their progress like headlights on a single-lane highway. The line of glowing dots indicated that at least half the town was headed south.

I held up a hand to stop a grizzled man on a paint horse. "What's happening back there? Why the exodus?"

The old man's face scrunched up, and he leaned over to squirt a stream of tobacco to splatter the dust near Misery's hooves. He jerked in surprise when he saw Merilee ride up next to me then belatedly tipped his hat. "Sorry, Mizz Soames. Didn't see you there."

"Quite all right, Jenkins," she said. "But please answer the man's question. What's happening back in town?"

"A bunch of fuc—ah, dadblamed little men, no bigger'n a corn cob, done invaded. They's like ants, biting and stinging, except these stings kill ya dead. They's ever'where. Whole town's overrun with them. Some of us got out and headed south, toward Independence."

"Why there?" I asked.

"I don't know 'bout the others, but I plan to catch the train there and get my aaa—behind outta this here valley."

"You think the little people will keep coming this way?" Merilee asked. "Down the valley?"

"Can't say." The old-timer shrugged. He seemed to be having a hard time not staring at Merilee's exposed calves, which set my teeth on edge for some reason. "Deppitty Potts and some men are holding this side of the River Bridge, last I saw. The little critters don't seem to want to cross the water. Can't swim, or they's afraid of water."

I kicked Misery into a reluctant canter then a gallop. Merilee and Krawczyk—who had been uncharacteristically silent for a long time—thundered along behind me. Not having to look for tracks meant making better time, but Geyser Falls was miles away. As I rode, I crafted and discarded plans for how to settle the Nimerigar uprising. With the magic at my disposal, I could easily burn, crush, suffocate, freeze, or do anything, up to and including a nuclear blast, to eradicate every living thing in a dozen square miles or more. If I was willing to commit genocide, I could eliminate the Nimerigar as a people.

You're a cold-blooded assassin for the Administrators. What's the difference between one murder and a thousand, except in scale and statistics?

There's a difference.

I could target the chief, the butt-ugly leader of the Nimerigar, and vaporize the pygmy in a flash. Would that solve the problem, or would Ugly's second-in-command just take over and resume the tribe's search-and-destroy mission? I grinned without humor. *More of a destroy-and-search mission, so far.* Was the entire tribe prepared to die for their relic? More likely, the leadership would simply stop presenting themselves as targets for the crazy chief-killing wizard. I would have to keep burning leaders until someone down the command ladder brought some common sense to the table, which might take months or years, and end up with the same result as nuking the valley. Genocide by attrition.

I pulled my horse from a gallop to a walk to let the buckskin recover. "More work than you've done in a while, huh?"

Misery snorted and tossed his head, apparently too winded to think up a good comeback.

Merilee and Krawczyk reined up as well, mercifully keeping their distance. I had too many questions and not enough answers rolling around in my skull, and being nagged by Kat Krawczyk was high on my list of Don't Wants. I heard their voices as they spoke with each other and promptly tuned out their conversation.

I scratched my sandpaper chin. My genetics meant I didn't have to shave often, and my beard grew in sparse and patchy, made up of tiny, curly black hairs. It itched like crazy when I let it go more than a few days. A thought hit me, and I paused midscratch.

The Nimerigar were after the statue. They could sense it like bees to nectar, by scent or some other sixth sense. They had demonstrated that by following the trail of the statue to Geyser Falls then specifically the Bannerworth, where Sheriff Bridger had taken it at least once, and now, they seemed to be on the trail again, pushing down to the south. Could I raise the siege on Geyser Falls by showing the Nimerigar I had their totem then bolting west, away from the town? Wouldn't they abandon their invasion and pursue me instead? I had a horse and enough magic to fly both me and Misery to the moon, so we could definitely outrun the little people. Avoid towns, live off the land. With magic, anything was possible.

All I needed was time to figure out the smattering of clues I remembered about time travel. With enough time and unlimited magic, I could solve the riddle of *how* and start planning the *when*—as in, when to reenter the twenty-first century for maximum impact.

How far did the Nimerigar attachment to the stone extend? The Pacific Northwest? Russia? Tibet? Would they lose the scent if I jumped on a ship bound for Hawaii? Anywhere was possible. All I had to do was lead the pygmies away from the town then just disappear. The Nimerigar would either have to cross an ocean to find me or give up and go back to their caves in the mountains, diminished but still alive.

The bark of distant gunfire woke me from my speculation.

"Uh-oh," I said. "Come on, horse. Time's wasting."

I hate you. Misery snorted again but broke into a canter then a gallop. He complained bitterly about slave-drivers and horse torturers. I ignored him, formulating a new plan along the way.

I rode into a scene from Exodus. Women. children, wagons, carts, horses, mules, donkeys, goats, dogs, and hens spilled along the trail in a tide of dust and racket. Torches and lanterns threw light around in splotchy patches, enough to confuse everyone and illuminate nothing. Some folks moved themselves and their animals away from town, making for the Independence rail station, while others milled in a stew of shouting and crying humanity, either searching for their loved ones or reluctant to abandon their town completely. They hung on in clusters and groups, holding hands, praying, or comforting those wrought with tears.

A canvas tarp had been tied to the branches of scraggly trees, and under this dubious cover, a doctor moved among two rows of injured people, some with blankets, some without. I turned in the saddle to Krawczyk and made sure she noticed the medical tent. She flicked her chin in acknowledgment and climbed off her horse. Merilee started to follow, but I stopped her with a raised palm.

"Stay with me, please," I said. "Potts is likely to shoot me on sight. I might need a character witness."

I swung wide of the press and circled around to the bridge. About halfway there, I spotted a lone figure seated on a rock, wearing a tattered suit and look of utter abandonment.

"James Snow."

Snow raised a hand in weak greeting. Smoke had blackened his face, and his eyebrows appeared a little singed.

"Glad you're here." I slid off Misery and lent Snow a hand up to his feet. "I need a translator."

"Translator?" The man looked bewildered.

"Yeah, translator. We're going to parlay with the Nimerigar."

"Parlay?"

"It means talk nice."

"I know—I mean, yes, of course."

I stood by to help the Paiute into the saddle, as Snow moved like a man nursing sore ribs. "Mr. Snow, meet Mrs. Soames. She owns the Bannerworth."

"Assuming it still exists." Merilee studied the orange glow on the horizon. Fires burned somewhere in Geyser Falls. It wouldn't have taken much for the entire town to burn to the ground, should the Nimerigar decide to help things along with a few well-placed torches.

At the bridge, a cluster of men with rifles stood behind a buckboard turned sideways across the road. Other men lined the creek in either direction, spaced at irregular intervals and hunkered down behind whatever cover they could find. In the middle of the group behind the wagon, the Broken Wheel bartender, McKenzie, stood a head taller than the others. When he spotted me, he waved me over. The men surrounding McKenzie parted with dark looks and cold shoulders. When they saw Merilee, those looks changed to surprise.

"Ah'm certain glad to see ya," the Scotsman drawled as I approached. "Deputy Potts is dead, and both Bridger and Barton have buggered off. Some say Bridger ran—"

"You didn't seem so glad this afternoon." I bleached the words with enough scorn that the big man shifted his feet and looked away.

"Aye, yer right. I'm no' proud of meself for that." McKenzie cleared his throat and straightened. He stuck out a hand. "I do sincerely apologize for leavin' ya to the wolves, laddie."

I considered for a moment then took the outstretched hand. "Fuck it. Drive on. What's the situation?"

"We're here, and they're there. So far, the little people won't cross the creek, though the water's nary ankle deep. Won't take them long, though, before they go far enough upstream to just step across, and they'll come back down on our flank."

"And the town? Any people still there?"

"Aye, plenty. Many what's still holed up in their houses, behind locked doors."

"So nuking the town is out of the question."

McKenzie's face twisted into confusion. "Huh?"

"Nothing. Never mind." I grimaced. "Time for negotiations, then. Not my strength, but any new skill needs practice." James Snow and Merilee Soames stood a little apart. I gathered them close with a gesture. "Come with me. I'll need you to translate, Snow. I need you, too, Mrs. Soames."

"What do you need me for?" she asked.

"Your conscience," I told her. "I need someone with a conscience."

I stopped in the middle of the bridge and held the totem high overhead. The instant I stopped moving, a dozen tiny arrows flew from the brush on the far bank of the arroyo. The missiles arced in short parabolas and converged on me with amazing accuracy. I channeled a tiny stream of magic, and the arrows flashed alight, burned to black twigs, and turned to ash in an instant. Their remains blew away on the breeze, while the stone points pattered to the ground like thrown gravel.

Controlling the impulse to overuse the totem's magic was a lot like learning trigger control on an M240. The temptation to cut loose and hose the area with destruction was overwhelming. Using the totem sparingly was a bit like filling a thimble from a waterfall without spilling a drop. But at that point, maybe a little overkill was appropriate.

I reached into the pool of energy and exerted my will. Clouds boiled up from a clear sky, and the temperature dropped into a bitter chill. My breath fogged, and I magically amplified my voice to that of a stadium announcer. "Hear me, oh people of the Nimerigar! I am Calico John Shivers, and I'm here to render judgment upon ye!" I ignored the open-mouthed gapes from the defending townsmen and quieted the maniacal evil-villain laugh that wanted to bubble up from my belly. "Show thyself or face my wrath!" On the last word, I triggered a massive bolt of lightning that ripped from the sky and detonated on a bare patch of ground at the far end of the bridge. The light was strong enough to show through bodies like an X-ray. People screamed, and thunder boomed hard enough to vibrate my teeth.

In the back of my mind, AC/DC's "Thunderstruck" played at full volume.

"Come before me, chief of the Nimerigar!"

I felt the nearly unlimited energy of the totem's magic as though standing on a beach with my toes in the water of a vast ocean. So much power. So much potential. How could I give this up? Why should I? What possible benefit would it be to allow a tribe of cannibal savages to hoard this bounty for themselves, never using it, never exploiting it? Such a waste was unthinkable.

I felt my lip curl into a smirk.

No, the solution was obvious: blast the Nimerigar into eternity. Burn them to ash and blow them away with a powerful, cleansing wind. Wherever they hid, I would root them out like stubborn weeds, ripping them from the earth and exterminating them for good. My soul was so tarnished that a few extra deaths wouldn't matter.

And then?

My choice. Stay on mission, on task, and get back to the business of killing Birnbaum and saving Alizandra, or...

Many things about this world needed fixing. Injustice. Oppression. Starvation. All it would take to set the world on the right path was a man of vision, somebody who knew the pitfalls the next century would offer and who could help humanity avoid the catastrophic mistakes they were destined to make. Somebody who would get the job done, not shirk the responsibility. Somebody who could make the hard choices, do the right thing, and guide the world to a better place. *Forget getting back to my own time—what if my time is now?*

I could be the man my father wanted me to be. Successful. Powerful.

Wind-whipped dust swirled around my legs. I drew a breath, and light blazed from the totem as though I held the sun between my upraised hands, as though a miniature star had been born on the desert floor. Stark faces, bleached white by the incandescence, fixed on me with open-mouthed shock. Townspeople shrank back, hiding their eyes from the intense light. I glanced to my side and saw Merilee Soames backing away from me, eyes wide, her face etched with horror. James Snow crouched beside her as though ready to kneel. Sickness squeezed my gut.

Feel special now, do you?

Not so much, no.

Alizandra regarded me from a corner of my mind where I kept my memories of her. I could see her clearly, sitting up in bed. The viral Hep C eating her liver and yellowing her skin. A chessboard was laid out on the bed next to her. She had cocked her head and looked at me with speculative eyes.

"If you were God, what would you do?"

"Give you a new liver."

"Besides that, dummy." Alizandra rolled her eyes in a way that only teenage girls can manage.

I remembered thinking about it, my mind blank beyond the one thing I wanted most in the world. "I don't know. The right thing, I hope."

The chief of the Nimerigar appeared at the far side of the bridge. The squat, toad-faced pygmy waddled into the light as boldly as a superhero on a sunny day. Decorative scars peppered the chief's face in swirls and twists of dark dots, and two malevolent eyes burned beneath bushy brows. He strode forward as calmly as if on parade, stopping a dozen feet away from me and crossing his arms in the pose of an angry parent confronting a wayward child. The chief spoke in a series of guttural barks and glottal stops.

"I gotta give it to you," I said. "You've got giant balls."

A mule kick slammed me in the back.

The totem flew from my hands, shutting off the light pouring from within. The small statue whirled high in the air in a lazy somersault then dropped onto the middle of the bridge, a foot from the chief's feet. It landed with a crack at the same moment I belly flopped onto the stone surface.

For the second time in one night, I found I couldn't breathe. A burning lance of coal-red heat transfixed my chest, taking my wind. I watched as the chief of the Nimerigar danced back, slapped and jabbed by invisible fists. The sound of gunfire came dimly to my ears. Blood jetted from the back of the pygmy leader's skull, and the small figure toppled backward. The chief flopped down in a comical butt-plant, a tiny red hole decorating the look of surprise on his face.

A pair of boots stopped next to my nose. I tracked upward until I recognized the man standing over me, calmly reloading his Colt revolver and grinning.

"Hello, Judge," said Archie Bridger. "Good to see you again."

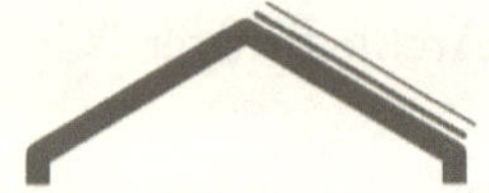

Chapter Thirty-One: Treachery and Tricks

Next to Archie Bridger stood the slender shape of—

"Esmeralda?" I croaked.

Bridger laughed. "You're not the only one with a witch who knows how to heal people."

"I waited for you to take me away, but you didn't come, Señor Shivers." Esmeralda pouted then followed my eyes as I checked out the peg leg she used in place of a foot. "Not everything can be healed." She seemed sad for a moment then took Bridger by the arm and leaned into him. "But is good I got to the sheriff in time, as he has promised to take me to San Francisco."

"Yeah, peachy." Blood bubbled from my lips, and I fought off the urge to cough. The pain in my chest flared at the thought, causing me to grimace and bite my lip. Magic... I needed to do something with magic.

The thought scattered into a jumble of broken pieces and refused to reform.

Bridger laughed over the sights of his reloaded pistol. He fired once, and a bullet slugged me in the chest, matching the wound in my back with one in the front. I bounced at the impact, eyes gritted shut against the pain, then blacked out...

...and waded to a semiconsciousness with the world shrouded in fog...

...or as though viewed through a camera lens covered in tissue paper.

Bridger approached the totem, appearing twelve feet tall from my worm's-eye perspective.

Esmeralda drifted out of my field of view, her expression one of sadness.

Sounds echoed through muffled cotton. I couldn't feel my fingers or toes. Icy coldness spread through my body.

Dying twice in one day sucked.

I focused my attention on the totem, the moment frozen in time. Bridger's fingers were almost in contact with the magical storage battery. The stone of the totem was grainy and pitted since its carving with centuries of wear. A narrow crack in the middle appeared new, as though the stone had broken when it flew from my fingers and landed on the bridge. I sensed the power trickling through that tiny fissure, even from this distance. I couldn't reach it, feeling like a desert wanderer too exhausted to crawl the last few feet for a life-giving sip of water.

Who originally crafted the statue? How had they managed to imbue it with enough magic, so much it was like all the magic in the world? How had—

Wait. All the magic in the world.

Blood dribbled from my lips when I smiled. My eyes narrowed. I focused on the crack then tapped the amulet in my pocket, which had been refilled with magic. Electricity. I was good with electricity. Control was something else, and I needed every scrap of focus I had ever managed to develop if I was to hit the target.

I gathered electrons by the billions, holding them against me like a basket full of blackberries. I sucked in negatively charged particles in a storm-swollen lake of seething potential. The effort sent heated spikes of agony driving through my skull, and my vision tunneled out to a narrow point. Still, I gathered more.

Time ground to a halt.

Bridger's fingertips paused a gnat's whisker away from the rough surface of the totem. As if viewed through a telescope, I zeroed my focus on the crack, falling into it the way a stunt pilot flew into the Grand Canyon. I had time to see and feel every bump, every grain, every pit and scratch of the ragged split...

Now.

I blasted every ounce and joule and erg at my disposal, driving a knife of electrical energy into the split, forcing it to cleave the rock as though chopped by a lumberjack wielding an ax—or perhaps more accurately, like a propane tank struck by a howitzer. Magical energy flared, bloomed, discharged, and exploded in the way a transformer struck by lightning would rupture. The sound of a dozen cannon shells split the night open, and a new star was born in the middle of a narrow bridge in the valley between the Sierra Nevada and the Inyo Mountains. The radiation was undetectable by the average, nonmagically attuned human, though for those so talented, the force swatted them like the open hand of an angry god.

I had anticipated the blast. In the space between one nanosecond and the next, I seized enough power from the ambient magic to create a cylindrical wall of super-hardened air around the totem, open at the top and bottom. The blast flowered upward as it pounded the earth in equal measure. It lasted as long as the fission of a single atom, the upward force mushrooming into a glowing blue cloud of mystical power, invisible to all but the few Magicals able to view it.

Although invisible to the mundane eye, the power was very real. The downward explosion blew through the bridge as if it were paper, slamming the ground below with the force of a meteor. In the instant before the world blew up and sent me and the remaining bits of the bridge flying, I saw Bridger disintegrate from the waist up. His hips and legs stood propped by inertia for the millisecond between the explosion and the reaction.

My lips peeled back in a snarl.

Heal that, you sunuvabitch.

I came back to life for the second time. *Reborn again. Hallelujah.*

I lay between cool sheets, my head pillowed on down-filled cotton. A breeze stirred lace curtains, and daylight streamed through an open window. A pitcher sat atop a dresser on the far wall, and under the window stood a writing desk with a chair tucked into the knee hole. In a wingback chair at the foot of the bed, Kat Krawczyk lay curled, snoring lightly.

Déjà vu. I've been here before.

The Bannerworth. The name of the hotel came back to me, telegraphed as if from a distant country. Every part of my body ached, from scalp to heels. I tested my fingers and toes and was pleased to feel them wriggling. When I tried to move my leg to stand—and hopefully find the chamber pot before I wet the bed—a bolt of pain shot up my back. I groaned, and Krawczyk snapped awake.

"Don't move," she groused. "I only just finished the latest round of sticking your innards back together."

"Have to," I croaked. "Get up."

"What for? Oh."

Krawczyk helped me take care of business then eased me back to bed. She held a glass of water to my lips, and I drained it in a few seconds. Once I was situated and the aches were under control, I tried speaking again. "What happened?"

"What happened? Is that what you asked?" At my nod, she continued. "Well, after you set off the magic nuke, the bridge blew up. You tried flying without a plane then fell down and went boom. A big chunk of rock fell on your legs right after. I swear, it was like a

Road Runner cartoon, and you were the coyote. That plus two bullet holes left you damn near dead. Again. I burned through a shit-ton of magic to keep you alive. Again. Good thing you blew up the totem—my amulet never ran dry, not even for a second."

I blinked and drew a cautious breath. "Who else?"

"Merilee's okay, if that's who you're worried about. Bridger's dead. All we buried was his bottom half." Krawczyk shrugged. "A few other people were hit by debris, but no one died. The Nimerigar packed up and left, quiet as you please."

"Esmer—ah, Esmeralda?"

"Missing, presumed dead."

Damn. I gritted my teeth and looked to the window. "Guess I'll never know."

"What?"

"How she lost her foot."

"Yeah, that was big on my list of mysteries too." Kat's tone indicated that she couldn't have given a shit. She sat up straight and grinned. "On the other hand, looks like you solved the mystery of the missing magic. The statue thingy is still pouring magical energy into the ground like crazy. Three days, and no signs of slowing down. I can't say for certain, but it feels like it's powering the whole world."

I let that thought soak in for a minute. "So if I hadn't come back in time..."

"That's right, Mr. Paradox. No magic. I need to snort some mushrooms to get my mind around that one."

"C'mon." I tried to throw the covers off. The sheets tangled my feet, and I gasped at the effort of kicking them off. "We need to go."

"Lie back down! You're not going anywhere."

"Have to." I slid my legs to the floor with effort. The world tilted, and I held the bed to stay upright. "While there's still enough magic. So I can figure out. How to get us... back."

The next thing I knew, I was facedown on the floor. Many pairs of hands were lifting me into bed. After that, the lights went out for a long time.

A week later, I stood by the blackened spot where the River Bridge had once spanned the Owens's tributary south of Geyser Falls. That tributary was now a trickle of water meandering along a flattened clearing blown out of an arroyo. At the center of the blast zone, on the north side of the creek, a small pile of black powder gradually dissipated in the breeze, a few grains at a time. The grainy dust was the only remains of the Nimerigar totem, and soon, even that would be gone.

Krawczyk had been right about the magic. The energy infused the surrounding area in the way I remembered from my time in the twenty-first century. My amulet refilled at the same rate it always had, back in my future, maybe even faster. I refused to think about causality and time paradox and all the flavors of predestination versus free will that the situation demanded I resolve. At some point, I needed to come to terms with my near miss at megalomania. During the time I channeled the magic from the totem, a whole new Calico John Shivers had appeared, and not one my mom or Alizandra would have been proud to see. The memories left me somewhat sickened, and I shied away from touching them too hard, lest the pain flare up anew.

It was enough that I was alive, whole, and magically charged again. My sister's illness was in the future, not the past. I would get back before things went bad for her. I would find Birnbaum and use his tech to make her well or get Krawczyk to cure her. I had to stay fixated on that goal, no matter what. I had nothing else to my name but stubbornness and a will to succeed. It had to be enough.

I stirred at a snuffle behind me. "Yeah, yeah, I know. I have a horse too. How lucky can a man be?"

Misery stepped up and laid his chin on my shoulder, asking for a scratch. I obliged the buckskin and watched as the last of the black sand flickered away on the wind.

"I guess we ought to mosey back to town," I said. "Gerda promised to make an *apfel* pie for dessert tonight, and I don't want to miss it."

Misery snorted. *Who cares?*

But by the blissful look from being scratched under the chin, it was apparent that Misery's heart wasn't in it.

"From now on," I said, "I'm calling you Happy."

The horse bit me on the shoulder.

About the Author

Scott Bell has over 25 years of experience protecting the assets of retail companies. He holds a degree in Criminal Justice from North Texas State University.

With the kids grown and time on his hands, Scott turned back to his first love—writing. His short stories have been published in *The Western Online*, *Cast of Wonders*, and in the anthology, *Desolation*.

When he's not writing, Scott is on the eternal quest to answer the question: What would John Wayne do?

Read more at www.scottbellwriter.com.

About the Publisher

Dear Reader,

We hope you enjoyed this book. Please consider leaving a review on your favorite book site.

Visit https://RedAdeptPublishing.com to see our entire catalogue.

Check out our app for short stories, articles, and interviews. You'll also be notified of future releases and special sales.